# When Dreamers Wake

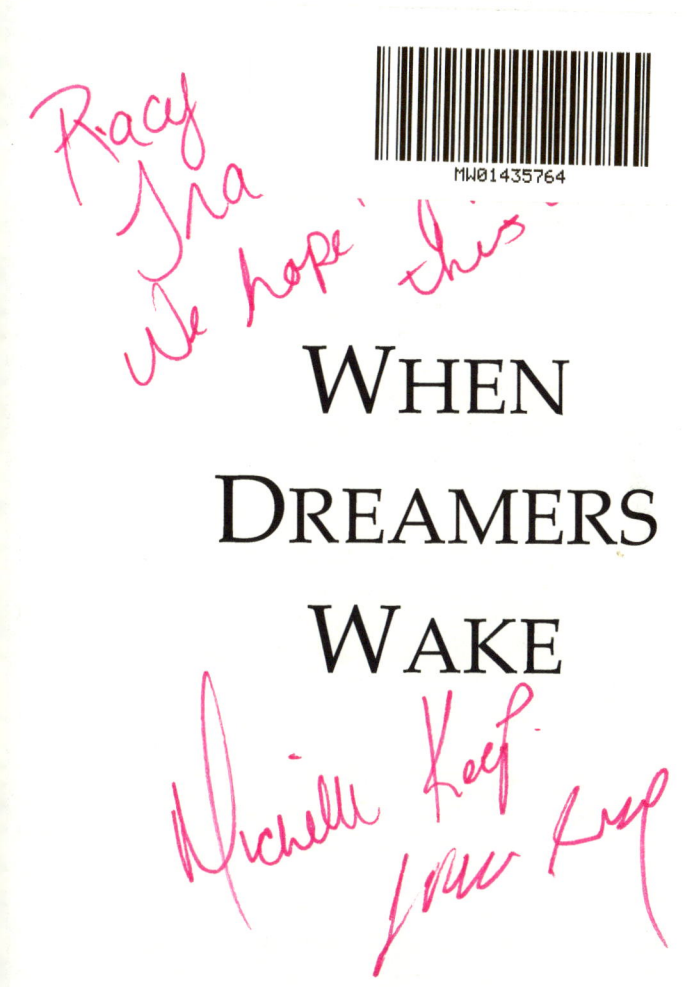

J.E. & M. Keep

This book is intended for sale to Adult Audiences only. It contains sexually explicit scenes and graphic language. All sexually active characters in this work are of legal age.

Copyright © 2013 J.E. & M. Keep

All rights reserved.

ISBN: 1492902217
ISBN-13: 978-1492902218

# DEDICATION

To our friends who didn't judge, readers of The Keep back when we were first starting out, and Darknest Fantasy Erotica who encouraged us to keep going.

# CONTENTS

| | |
|---|---|
| Acknowledgments | i |
| Chapter 1 | Pg 1 |
| Chapter 2 | Pg 24 |
| Chapter 3 | Pg 33 |
| Chapter 4 | Pg 37 |
| Chapter 5 | Pg 53 |
| Chapter 6 | Pg 57 |
| Chapter 7 | Pg 66 |
| Chapter 8 | Pg 77 |
| Chapter 9 | Pg 89 |
| Chapter 10 | Pg 94 |
| Chapter 11 | Pg 107 |
| Chapter 12 | Pg 119 |
| Chapter 13 | Pg 147 |
| Chapter 14 | Pg 157 |
| Chapter 15 | Pg 168 |

| | |
|---|---|
| Chapter 16 | Pg 170 |
| Chapter 17 | Pg 189 |
| Chapter 18 | Pg 192 |
| Chapter 19 | Pg 197 |
| Chapter 20 | Pg 200 |
| Chapter 21 | Pg 214 |
| Chapter 22 | Pg 223 |
| Chapter 23 | Pg 228 |
| Chapter 24 | Pg 239 |
| Chapter 25 | Pg 245 |
| Chapter 26 | Pg 250 |
| Chapter 27 | Pg 255 |
| Chapter 28 | Pg 265 |
| Chapter 29 | Pg 275 |
| Chapter 30 | Pg 280 |
| Chapter 31 | Pg 284 |

# ACKNOWLEDGMENTS

J.E. & M. Keep recognize that erotica can be very personal, and that everyone has their limits on what they wish to read. Because of this, we provide content warnings for all our erotica so that you can avoid any **triggering material** – or find the story you most want to read. If you want your book spoiler free, please skip this section!

This particular story contains polyamory, barely legal, harem, interracial, unprotected sex, male rape

# CHAPTER 1

The forest on the horizon was completely untouched, undestroyed by the mad gods and their baffling ways. They had left years ago, yet had left so much confusion and pain—and death—in their wake. The death of humans, the death of buildings, of natural wonders, of pristine forests and barren deserts. Everything had changed with their arrival, and changed once more on their departure.

It was as though they were simply passing through.

The lands surrounding Leon were a testament to the randomness of their destruction, with the beautiful trees in the horizon, and the strange dust of ruined buildings under his feet. There wasn't much in the way of civilization around these parts. Most of the population had died off, and winters were hard.

Many told him they were heading to warmer climates and he never heard from them again.

Still, there were a few pockets of civilization that remained. Small bands of traders and farmers, trying to rebuild in the mad gods' wake. Infrastructure of society had collapsed, leaving them mostly without power and running water. People had tried to drive for a while until gas became rarer and rarer. Bicycles rose in popularity, and most people used them or animals to get around.

There was no one on his path, however. Nothing stood in between him and that forest, and through that forest was a small farmhouse that he had traded with in the past.

Cautious as always, Leon scanned the area through a pair of binoculars before daring to rise up and gather his things. He was a large, dark man, and the heavy military trench coat and helmet he wore atop his thick layers of leather and clothing only added to his seeming bulk.

Beneath it all he was a broad, muscular man, with hardly any excess fat left on his body, even though he was able to eat better than most in the wastelands. With his military rifle in hand, he began to make his way forward, heavy boots thudding upon the ground.

Stones and debris crunched under him, leaving his footprints behind as he got to the tree line, the route much more unsteady. A dog howled in the far distance, and then the sound faded further into the woods. There was a path that he had followed, though it was a bit muddy in areas, and bandits were always on the lookout for someone.

Not such as he, he assured himself. With his training, his determined survival over the past three years, he'd make any attempt to jack him the most costly thing in that poor fool's life. Or so he reassured himself.

Pushing on ahead he kept his head low and gun at the ready, comforted by knowing that with the gear he'd looted from a police station and his old army base, he was a bit better equipped than most.

A crow cawed in the trees, staring down at him through beady eyes before taking off, the forested light dimming and growing bright as the bow swayed. As he walked deeper into the forest, he saw more and more small, skittering animals that somehow survived and prevailed after the descent of humanity.

In the distance he remembered there was a small pond at the end of a river. He often refilled supplies there, resting near the halfway point through the forest. There was always a threat that others might be using the pond as well, however, as there were fish and small mammals that called it home.

He felt no need to deviate from the norm, and took his time approaching the pond. If someone else were there, he'd make damn sure to see them before they saw him, or so he told himself.

There was, in fact, someone this day, though she certainly didn't look to be a threat. A young woman, clad in a simple dress that ended high along her thigh and low along her shoulders. She was fishing absently, seeming unaware of the man so near to her, despite the rifle at her side. Her pole was of good make, obviously not homemade, though the fishing line seemed a bit makeshift.

Her brown hair was swept back in a bun, leaving her shoulders and back exposed, her feet bare and digging into the dirt, a book propped up in her lap. As her fishing pole jostled, however, she tossed the book on top of her canvas bag, holding on tight and coaxing a rather large fish adeptly out of the water.

The happiness radiated on her kind face, her plush lips turning up, her blue eyes dancing with pleasure. She was fairly young, probably just into adulthood, and she put the fish in a bucket at her side before returning to the process.

A beautiful woman was always a welcome sight to Leon, and he caught himself smiling widely. Taking care not to appear too threatening, he pulled off his helmet and shook free his head of dreadlocked hair. When you got rid of the accoutrements of survival, Leon was a remarkably attractive man himself. With a wide but well-chiselled jaw, sparkling dark eyes, cocoa skin, and well shaven, thanks to his adeptness at scavenging.

With his helmet in one hand his rifle slung over his back, he approached from the clearing, his deep voice soft and nonthreatening. "That's one hell of a fish you caught there," he announced, hands held up as if he were under arrest.

She gasped and dropped her book into the mud, cursing lightly at her clumsiness and surprise, yet still grasping for her weapon. It was as though the old ways and the new were clamouring inside of her: the desire to salvage her book and her need to defend herself.

Her voice quaked. "D–don't hurt me!" she ordered, holding her gun like a hunter would, despite her hands shaking. It was obvious to his skilled eyes that even though she had used the rifle—and often— it was never against a human. She still had a look of fresh innocence to her—a look that too few still had.

With careful motions, his hands still held up uselessly, he lowered himself down to one knee, and then placed his helmet and gun on the grounds.

"No worries, miss," he said in his soothingly deep voice. "I don't hurt a soul who doesn't try to hurt me first," he explains. "Name's Leon. Leon Degaise." He gave a light smile, the look brightening up his already strikingly handsome face.

She was still quaking, but she did lower her rifle, suddenly becoming aware that, in her position, he could likely see right up her short skirt. Clenching her thighs together, she tried to fix her skirt and hide her white panties from his eyes.

"Why are you here?" she asked skeptically, her heart beating so fast that her skin prickled and flushed with the heat.

Seating himself on the grass he watched her with some quiet fascination, taking a moment to be thankful his eyes didn't lead him to put down his guard and get killed. "I always stop by on my way through here," he explained with a shrug of his heavy set shoulders. "Good place to fill up my canteen on the way to one of the cabins I trade at." Gesturing to her, making no sign he saw her panties, though he most certainly did, he asked, "What about you? Just fishin'?"

She nodded, her shoulders slowly unknitting and some of the panic leaving her wide, expressive eyes. She was one of those people who you could read so easily, their facial expressions telling all to any who cared enough to look.

"Yeah," she said tentatively, reaching for her book and trying to smudge the dirt off the paperback cover, "I don't like eating just vegetables."

Resting his elbows on his knees, he gave a toothy smile. "Farmer, huh? My type of gal," he said, chuckling lightly. It was amazing how, despite three years of hell, he still slipped back into flirting when a pretty face was before him. "Unless I trade all I have to eat is tinned this and that that I scavenge." Farming was an odd career choice in this new world. Scavenging was dangerous, but lucrative.

She nodded to him curiously, her nose crinkling a bit. She obviously didn't care for food in tins. "You should learn to hunt. Unless you trade for proper food?" she asked curiously, and a small hint of pretension slipped under her tongue.

Undeterred by her tone of voice, he nodded with a big smile. "Mmhmm. Fresh vegetables and meat. And sure, I can hunt if I want. But ain't many as good at scavenging as I am, and I like to stick to those things I have to offer the world that I'm best at. Know what I mean?" he asked, rubbing his hands together a moment, trying not to focus on what a pretty lass she was.

She nodded, pressing back some of her loose hair

from her smooth skin, her flesh slowly returning to its natural peachy hue as she became more comfortable with him. "I guess." She looked instinctively toward the path to the cabin, then at her smudged romance novel, fretting over its ruined cover.

"Well, they got lots of meat to trade 'cause of me and my brother," she breathed out. "So I guess you're in luck."

With a light chuckle he nodded. "Good! Though now I wish I had met you before. Could've traded directly, instead of giving them a cut," he said with a good-natured grin. "Because if you need something out there that ain't grown or hunted, then I'm the one to get it for you." He winked, playfully at the young woman.

"I couldn't have given it directly to you. We gotta contribute to the others. We won't be allowed to stay otherwise."

He points off in the direction of the cabin. "Ahh, you stay with them?" Rubbing his broad chin, he drew attention to his smooth, dark skin, and the appealing way his thick dreads framed his face. "And I've never run across you before. Damn shame. I live out on my own, got a big stead to myself." The large, former store depot he'd claimed as his own was home. "Gets lonely."

"Just got here," she confessed, her eyes dropping with a hint of sorrow to her tone. Something had happened to her to force her to move.

"What'cha readin' anyhow? I'm a big book guy."

Her nose crinkled again, and she clasped the book a bit tighter to her lap. "You wouldn't like this one," she explained, her eyes flicking away guiltily. Immediately her cheeks reddened and she willed her body not to give away her embarrassment—or interrupted arousal—to the man.

She pushed back some hair that was already stuck behind her ear. "How often you get out here, huh?"

With a shrug of his heavy shoulders he stated a bit sadly, "Only every couple of weeks or so." The disappointment that he wouldn't see her more often was a bit obvious.

Pointing back to her book, he brightened a bit. "But if you want some more books... or if ya just care to tell me what sort of thing you're into. I'm the man that can supply that stuff. And for you, nameless pretty"—he smiles cheerfully—"I'll consider it a gift, not a trade."

She flushed a bit, her heart palpitating. "Really?" she asked, hope eeking into her voice. It was obvious she had a passion. "I like a lot of things"—she paused, scrutinizing him—"mostly... Romance stuff. Stuff about people." She bit her lower lip, drawing it into her mouth and sucking on it for a moment before letting it pop out.

"And... Fiona. I'm Fiona," she rephrased her answer.

The large mountain of a man gave a pleasant smile and nodded. "I like those too, Fiona," he confessed, also truthfully, though he'd have lied for this beauty. "Keeps me warm on all the lonely time at my place. Imaginin' big romantic scenarios of takin' on everything the world has to offer as a pair. Always did it for me, especially now," he said, his deep voice honeyed and warm, some longing there.

Her eyes went soft and her shoulders slumped with that strange mixture of desire and sorrow as she nodded her agreement. Her head stooped a little, looking down at the simple fabric of her short dress. "Ain't fair all this stuff happened," she pouted.

Her lower lip protruded slightly as her eyes blinked away tears. Oh, she was too easy to read. Her heart was on her sleeve, without a doubt.

Seeing her pout and grow grim like that, he got up and moved over toward her. He was an intimidating man, but he had a way of radiating warmth and protectiveness, rather than danger. Well, to women anyhow.

Moving to sit beside her, he reached out with a large hand to touch her shoulder blade upon her back. Normally he had no time for such moping about the lost past, but for her? "Musta been rough for you. Only havin' your brother now..." It didn't need to be said. Everyone had lost family. To have any family made her one of the luckiest ones alive, to tell the truth. "It just ain't enough," he said soothingly in that deep, husky voice of his.

She nodded her agreement, letting out a wistful sigh. "I had to leave my stuff. All I have now is the stuff the new people can give me. Probably going to get killed for ruining their books now." She looked up at him, her big eyes so easily read. "I... I gotta finish fishing but... when you gotta be there by?" she asked curiously.

He rubbed her back gently. It was a subtle thing

at first, but he had a way with his hands and women, and he massaged her pleasantly. "I go where I want when I want," he said with a smile that was full of bravado and confidence, but still had that tinge of sympathy and comfort for her. "Perks of bein' an independent man, Fiona."

Her pulse quickened and she looked away from his gorgeous face, toward the water. Her breathing hitched before she forced the words out. "Will you stay 'til I get some more fish then go back with me?"

That invitation was music to his ears, and at it, he pushed that arm around her, resting it lightly at her side, above her hip, the other coming over to massage her shoulder. "Of course. Now that we've met, I wouldn't stand to let you be out here, and wanderin' back all by yourself. Ain't nothing safe anymore, Fiona," he said in a way that was more reassuring than troubling, his voice holding such masculine confidence and security.

Her skin perked up with his more enthusiastic touch, and she felt something clench between her thighs. She had managed to do a decent job hiding it until that point, but the little quirked smile and the alternating tension and release in her body quickly gave her away as she shifted closer to him, her hands shaking as she reached for the pole.

"It shouldn't take long," she murmured.

With a big, friendly smile, his arms about her, gently caressing and rubbing he too had felt a stirring in his loins, though he kept it out of his thoughts. He had to focus. Leaning so close to her, his fingers brushed along her hair, and he could smell her.

"Don't worry about time," he said huskily, "I enjoy just spendin' time with you." And that was true.

"I don't get opportunities to just... sit with someone very often. Certainly not like this," he said, his hand holding her a bit more firmly. "Though I think on it often."

Even though his words might be construed as false by someone more worldly, she ate it up, her heart leaping with excitement. Her hands trembled as she threaded the line, throwing it back in the water. She moved nearer to him, soft, pleasant sighs escaping her pink lips as his hands worked over her.

She craved him.

Her cheeks flushed at her inner thoughts, and she tried to push them away. Her thighs clamped shut again.

His hand rubbed along her bare shoulder, feeling that smooth skin of hers. Damn, he was nearly lost in that feel alone. It was nearly enough to make him lose control then and there, but he managed to keep his lusts in check.

Slowly he rubbed down from her shoulder to her arm. "You're real good at this," he said softly, "bein' able to catch such a big one in this lil' ol' pond. Gotta confess, fishin' ain't one of my strong suits," he chuckled lightly and his hand found her thigh. That large, powerful grasp of his gently stroking.

She nearly lost her grip on the fishing pole as her eyes fluttered back in her head, the sensation utterly divine. She choked back her moan, struggling to regain awareness of her surroundings, tightening her grip on the pole. His dark hand on her pale skin excited her further, and she studied it thoughtfully before she yanked the line out of the water, a large fish attached to it which she skilfully released in the bucket.

Seeing yet another big one on the end of her line he gave a surprised whistle. "Damn. I wanted to flatter you, but you are good." His hands never left her though, he, too, admiring the dark cocoa of his work-hardened hands upon her smooth, pale flesh.

His large fingers pried a little at the valley between her thighs. "It'd be somethin'," he muttered softly, as if to himself, "havin' a woman like you around." And he leaned in so close that his lips were nearly touching her ear, his breath a pleasant, warm wash on her skin.

Was it possible for her heart to stop and quicken all at once? The myriad of pleasant sensations: his breath, his scent, his flesh. Her breathing caught in her throat as her lips parted, exposing those straight teeth. She trembled, and her thighs tightened before releasing around him, her eyes rolling up slightly.

That little gesture made way for his hungry hand, and he delved between, stroking over the soft flesh of her inner thigh. Though noto leave it at that, his lips moved on down and he kissed beneath her earlobe so that his nose brushed against her. He kissed again softly, his lips big and soft against her pale skin, and he muttered in a low, pleasant husk, "You're beautiful."

She gasped, her eyes closing as she shimmied closer to him, letting the fishing pole slump into the dirt. Her knees fell away further, and her entire skin seemed to burn with desire. She wanted him. Oh yes, she did.

Her palm lay atop his, stroking him gingerly before she whimpered, "I can't get pregnant." She paused, her eyes finding his. "You can't finish in me."

Those words confirmed that she'd accept him, but at the same time, he couldn't help but feel a bit disappointed. He was a strong bull of a man, and he wanted her, wanted to claim her. Fully and completely.

Squeezing her thigh and hip firmly, warmly, he kissed her neck again, then her earlobe, suckling it briefly. "Even if I did," he began in his low, masculine voice, "I'd take ya back to my stead and take care of you there, forever more." His fingers trailed up between her thighs until they felt the soft cotton of her panties, his dark eyes meeting hers, strength and certainty in his gaze, but with a certain tenderness to his desire.

She gasped a bit, the risky thought still holding some taboo appeal to her. Childbirth was dangerous, one of the most certain dangers in a woman's life in this new, destroyed world. And yet his words caused her to squirm and moan, trying to fight the desire.

Her legs went lax, and she leaned into him, her eyes catching his for a moment before they moved away, suddenly shy.

His thick, dark finger stroked over that pure, white cotton, tracing along the outline of her slit. He stoked her fires in an expert manner, his nose nuzzling here and there as he kissed her neck, her cheek, her ear.

That other hand of his crept up from her thigh, to slide beneath her top and feel out her flesh, groping for her breast. He was straining within his pants, nearly bursting out with his excitement. It'd been so long since he'd lain with a woman, but then a day was too long by his old measure, and his lips and hands grew more excited as his passion built.

She hadn't managed to salvage a bra since her last one tore, and she was bare beneath the soft cotton of her dress. So deliciously bare.

Her nipples were already hard, aching for his touch, and her back arched just so to encourage him. Her head tilted back, exposing her throat as she moaned, biting down on her lower lip to keep herself as quiet as possible. It wouldn't do to have a bandit come across them. Not like this.

She murmured his name softly, the sound so erotic to his ears; the purity of her voice and the longing it contained as her clit throbbed under his fingers.

The delight of finding her breast bare was immense. He cupped it and squeezed, gently kneaded its supple flesh. She was an angel in the wastes, and he clung to her, pressed his hands against her harder in case she turned out to be a mirage.

Before he could do more, his lips found hers. He kissed her, head tilted to the side, deeply implanting his tongue in her mouth. All the while his fingers deftly lifted the fabric of her panties, pulling them aside so that he might stoke her fires directly, feel those delicate petals on his bare fingers. His cock responded, throbbing and straining against his pants, which could not afford it enough space in its swelling.

She was oblivious to all else as she felt the shock of his body touching hers, and she moaned into his mouth, her tongue lashing against his, sucking his lower lip and biting it teasingly. She was already so wet, so ready for the near stranger. The book at her side had likely started her off in the right strain for him, but his deep voice and his eager hands were really toppling her over the edge.

Her hands found his arm, then down his side, resting on his thigh. Her thumb pressed into the sensitive inner flesh, and then her fingers shifted toward his pelvis, down along the inner seam of his body, so teasingly close and distant all at once.

That set him off, a deep groan that reverberated up from his broad chest and nearly hummed into her mouth. He was a massive man compared to her, and it only became all the more apparent as their bodies intertwined. He eclipsed her with his size, and the old, thick military-style cargo pants he wore could not hide the nearly frighteningly large shaft he bore beneath.

With powerful arms, he lifted, shifted, and began to lower her back to the ground. He was eager, but he was a powerful, in-control man, of himself and her, and he was going to set her body out before him like a platter to be enjoyed.

She was so light and delicate, even with her toned legs and arms, and she was only too willing for him. Her eyes were partially lidded as they dropped over his impressive body, her pulse quickening and causing her to feel so warm.

Her hands reached to the strings along her back, tugging out the bow and desperately trying to free herself of the material.

Seeing her do that, he rose up onto his knees, towering over her. He watched her undress in his shadow as he shrugged off his own heavy trench coat, then, with a few deft flicks of his straps, shed the material of his heavy vest beneath. "However it goes," he began in his voice that emanated such a commanding, authoritative presence, "know I'd take care of you, so you'd never need worry again." His turtleneck sweater came off next, and its removal unveiled a series of chiselled muscles, peppered with scars, but absolutely gorgeous in their sheer masculinity.

Unbuckling his belt, he continued, "I'd scav the best medicines in the waste for you." It came undone, the bulge of his boxer briefs beneath, gray and straining against his size. "And see nothin' bad come to you." And when he lowered them, the broad ebon shaft that came into view could only be described as massive, wanting. Of her. The crown of it bejeweled with a gold ring that pierced his member.

She tossed the dress on top of her book, leaving herself so nearly bare. All that was still hidden was underneath those panties, her wetness leaving a discolouration between her slick petals. She was athletic, far more athletic than she seemed in her outfit. Smooth skin and taut muscles were present throughout her form, yet her breasts were glorious. Just smaller than his large palms, her nipples were erect, begging to be bit. They were a perfect shape, still so perky and firm.

Her eyes dropped over his body, and she crooned at the sight of his member. Eyes widening, she couldn't help but move closer, her hand reaching out to touch him.

In the time before the fall, Leon would've been an Adonis amongst men. Though these days it most often lay hidden beneath layers of protective clothing. His muscular, broad physique was glorious. Her hand reaching out and touching that member looked so tiny, so dainty in comparison. It felt so heavy against her palm as she went to touch and lift it.

With that, though, he was done waiting, and he descended upon her. His mouth moving to those breasts, needing to bite and sup upon them as they seemed to silently beg for him to do. His broad back arched, and he squeezed and massaged one mound of breast flesh, his mouth devouring the other, giving a light groan as he brought himself down upon her carefully, positioning himself near her quim.

She was so easily manipulated by him, her body moving to his tempo as though involved in a dance without music. With every reach of his body, hers closed the distance. She was a fair bit younger than him, but that didn't matter after the fall, and regardless... he was gorgeous. Her entire body excited at the fact, her muscles clenching in desire as she craved him to push her harder and harder into oblivion.

His free hand moved down as he continued to work her two breasts. With his strong grasp he tugged her panties to the side, for there was no time for anything more in the face of his lusts. The bulbous tip of his broad crown prodding her wet cunny lips, its size so enormous it made the penetration about to occur seem like it could be nothing but uncomfortable for the younger woman.

Leon's dark form descended about her, his tongue flicking her nipple between sucklings, and his muscles tensing with desire. He took his time so as not to hurt the girl, but when he pushed up into her, that dark ebon shaft pierced her pinkened cunny so deliciously he groaned aloud.

It was made easier by the fact that she certainly wasn't a virgin, and there was no barrier or resistance. Aided by her physical arousal, the pain seemed to be only pleasurable to the woman as her body lay back, her spine arching her breasts into the air, her groan louder than was wise.

She was caught up in the sensations, her smooth legs and dirty feet wrapping around his body as her pink pussy stretched over the massive, piercing cock.

His mouth finally broke its seal about her breast, as he groaned with her into the outdoor air. He sank his length into her, though nowhere near all of it would fit. The ring that capped his crown pressing against her inner most depths before he tugged back and pushed again, beginning to plough the sweet young woman full of his dick.

With hands upon her breast and hip, he held her in place as he began to fuck her, his powerful body all ripped, the muscles shifting as he moved, his heavy sac lightly slapping against her flesh with each push in. Gods damn, she was tight and tasty, it'd been so long, and he wanted this so bad.

Her body ached for him, her blood brightening her mons, the hair trimmed so short against her pale flesh as she pulsed around him. Her eyes rolled back in her head as her throat went dry from her heavy breathing. As he pressed in faster, though, she couldn't help but cry out, nearly drowning out the sound of footsteps. They were heavy and certainly not rushing, but they were still so distant.

Through the noise of her cries he heard it. A shock went through his spine and he bent over her, his hand covered her mouth as he peered about. Though through his caution he never ceased his motions entirely, continued to pump his hips as his body reacted of its own accord, so that her stretched pussy continued to take his shaft. He didn't want to stop, but he murmured softly in her ear, "Footsteps."

He reached for her gun with his free hand, as it was closest.

It startled her and she sucked in a breath through his hand, holding it and trying to keep from moaning, but his continued thrusting did little to help her. She bit down on her lower lip beneath his hand, her eyes searching the tree line.

There was little by way of cover but for the trees, and she somewhat struggled underneath him, finding that his weight pinning her down in such a frightening situation caused her blood to quicken and her cunny to clasp him tightly.

Something about this was thrilling her, even as she tried to resist it. Even as she heard the footsteps draw nearer.

He should've been focussed on whoever was approaching. He should've been up and out of her immediately, gun aimed, but this beauty beneath him—around him—kept his mind addled, and the clench of her pussy about him was too much. His world went a bit hazy for a moment as he came, his large cock pouring its thick seed into her with wild, spasming throbs. The torrent of his virile seed buried deep inside her.

With that, he pulled out of her and took her gun to the ready, trying to pinpoint the source of the footsteps and aim, still barely dressed.

A rush of emotions filled her as he left: confusion, fear, and an overbearing sense of loneliness. She felt the wetness slide from her, and immediately she touched herself, her hand coming away covered in his cum. "Fuck!" she cursed under her breath, anger blazing in her eyes as she reached for her dress, covering herself just as a twig cracked nearer still.

"Fiona!" a singsong voice cried out, male and pleasant.

"Fuck!" she cursed again, this time louder, "Go 'way!" she shouted.

There was a good-natured laugh, and she looked to Leon, panicked. She obviously didn't know what to do, so she ran forward, toward the voice, still clutching her dress to her chest, but she couldn't stop the mysterious man in time. He broached the tree line just in time for her to run into him, her hand nearly dropping her clasped dress.

The intruder laughed again, eyes twinkling in

good humour until he realized her dress was off, and there was a large man in the background with a gun pointed his way.

His brow knit, anger tinting his voice. "What's going on?" he hissed to her, grabbing her naked arm and jostling her. He looked so similar to her, with his dark hair and fair skin. His readable face and plush lips, downturned in anger.

She swatted Will's hand away. "Fuck off, Will, I told you. Not now."

Leon knew what was happening immediately, and the large muscled man, his cock still turgid and hanging out, lowered the gun, his muscles relaxing with some relief. Though it did little to make up for spoiling his first fuck in ages, at least he wasn't in danger of dying. Well, he hoped not.

He laid the gun down aside and began to close up his pants, hoping the pair finished their talk quickly.

"What the fuck, Fiona?" he snarled into her ear, standing a little too close to her. "Can't even leave you alone to fish now? I'm going to have to be with you every fucking minute?"

She pushed on his chest, anger still brewing within her at both of the men. "I'm an adult! I can do what I want!" she hissed.

Will looked over her body, at the dirty hair, her barely hidden breasts, and she tugged the dress up, almost exposing her slit. Instead, all that could be seen was cum dribbling down her inner thigh, and she tried to step away. He gawked at her, eyes turning dark.

"You let him cum in you?" he snarled, rage contorting his face as he pushed her toward the tree line, stomping in front of her and past the stranger, gathering the bucket of fish, her backpack, and her romance novel, sucking a breath past his teeth.

Not bothering to gather the rest of his things, Leon stood up, his height and size making him one imposing figure. He glowered at that shove of Fiona. "Hey, don't treat her like that," he commanded, his deep voice trembling with repressed rage, or at least the semblance of it as he tried to pick up for the poor girl, stepping between the two.

Will glared at the rebuff, and Fiona shrank behind him, though neither was on her good side at the moment.

"You're the one risking her damned life," he snarled, glaring toward Fiona. He didn't loft his gun again, not seeming to be threatened by the larger man, fuelled by his own emotions.

Fiona struggled into her dress, leaving herself oh, so bare for a few heartbeats before she pulled up the dress, her brother's eyes flicking to her angrily, and then back to Leon. "Look, I don't blame you." His words were a lot more calm, but regardless he tried to stalk by. "She has to be cleaned up."

Leon softened. He wasn't about to butt into their lives too much, but he just couldn't stand to see her pushed around. Turning his gaze toward her he gave an apologetic frown. "Sorry," he said lowly, seeming to mean it. "Things happened so fast." Staying where he was, however, he added, "I meant what I said though," and he did. For he trusted few people in these days, but a woman who relied on him because she carried his child? Well, he figured he could trust a woman like that.

She couldn't do up the back of her dress in such a hurry, and left it hanging tantalizingly low over her shoulders, and though she gave Leon one last, confused look, she took off into the forest, heading back toward the cabins with Will close in step.

# CHAPTER 2

It was beginning to get dark, but he was fairly close to the outpost, just a half hour walk or so.

It was a strange end to the tryst, he thought, certainly not as satisfying as he'd intended. Not with that damned interruption. But it had a certain sort of satisfaction to it, and he gathered up his things, redressing and preparing to venture on ahead once he was dressed again.

By the time he finally arrived, he could smell the roasting meat, the fire crackling high. It was just a small little cropping of cabins, likely summer homes for rich people in better days but now convenient hideaways for the Traditionalists, as they liked to be called.

After the mad gods had ravaged the lands, they became convinced that it was a dawn of a new era.

Not something bad, but a reset for humanity. A chance to right the wrongs. Mostly environmentalists, they had been joined by a few religious people who heeded the call for a more simple life. Their days revolved around farming, hunting, and telling each other stories, passing on their history through word of mouth.

This one only had a couple dozen people, but they were typically happy and friendly to all but those that dealt unfairly with them. His contact was the young woman that ran the "general store" as she called it, and he knew she could be found in the furthest cabin from the tree line.

He didn't see Fiona or her brother anywhere around, though there was a makeshift family of various genetics sat around the cooking fire, huddling into one another affectionately.

At times he felt a pang of longing for such closeness, and normally laying with a woman mitigated that somewhat. Though the rude interruption that prevented him from ending the affair in a pleasant manner left him a bit... off.

He turned from the sight of the families and made his way over to the general store. Doing business and seeing the familiar face would, he hoped, cheer him up some.

She brightened immediately as she heard the bell ring and saw his face. Walking around the counter, Tia reached up, embracing him in a familiar, loving manner. They had a past, back when they first met, but the distance had grown tough on her. The last time they'd spoken had not been pleasant, but it seemed all was forgiven.

Her smooth skin was a beautiful, light brown. Her cocoa eyes twinkled at him good-naturedly before she released him from her grips.

"Hey, stranger," Tia purred before backing away. The sudden removal of her large breasts from his rib cage was unpleasant, especially after seeing her in that simple white dress that delved so teasingly low. Her hands were hard from all the work she did out on the farm, and her arms were well muscled, but that did nothing to distract from her ample and quite visible cleavage.

Being lovers with someone led to a certain familiarity that persisted even after the lovemaking ended. He stared a bit openly at her breasts, giving a very obvious and dramatic shiver.

"Damn, Tia," he said in his gruff voice, a bit huskier thanks to the postcoital weariness and day's journey he was suffering from. "Seeing you again is enough to make me forget I just hiked through the damn countryside all day." With a broad, handsome smile he rested his gun, helmet and pack aside, "How've you been, gorgeous?"

"Busy." The backs of her fingers ran down his chest before she forced herself away. "You know how it is. Planting season. We're lucky we got a huge stock of seeds in from one of the communes in California." She smiled, obviously having had a large role to play in procuring that.

"What about yourself? Guessin' you got something for me?"

With a somewhat reluctant nod he hefted the

heavy bag he was carrying up, carrying it over to her countertop. "The usual sort of stuff," he said, brightening up a bit as he began to fish things out. "Some useful tools," he said, referring to the knives as well as other more traditional tools. "Some entertainment," he said, bringing forth some books. "The best, of course," he added handsomely, "for my favourite lady in all the wastes."

She rolled her eyes playfully, appraising the items before she walked back to him. "You know, you're always welcome to stay with us. It'd be so much easier," she tried gently. It was how the discussion always started, and it never ended well.

He was determined not to let it go that way though, and with a sweep of his powerful arm about her waist, he tugged her in against him firmly, as if they were performing some dance maneuver. Grinning down at her, he bent his head near her level, and he said, "Or you could come hold up with me in my castle. My queen, fat with child and more satisfied than you can imagine."

She laughed, the sound playful as she flicked at his chest. "Oh, just show me what you got me, you big lout."

She'd lost everyone in the disaster, watching her family dematerialize before her eyes. The dust, whatever it was, ate through their flesh, but it did nothing to her and she had no way of knowing what it meant. The religious among them said she must be blessed, but the memory burned into her skull and she felt the words lacked conviction.

He was sad to feel her peel away. He knew, of

course, she would refuse him again, but he hated it nonetheless. He finished pulling out the rest of the things for her, having truthfully saved some choice finds for her in the vain hope of winning her over. "I won't be staying for good, but you don't mind my staying the night, do ya?" he asked, the look he gave her hinting at how much it tortured him to stay away from her.

She bit down on her lip, her face tilting down as she inhaled.

"Leon," she murmured. Looking back up at him, her eyes were a little more watery, but she nodded. There was a lot of emotion welled up inside of her, but she was trying to be strong for him. She wanted to salvage what she could, and she simply couldn't resist the idea of spending a little more time with him.

She always wanted more from him, never less.

His broad face, so chiselled and strong, softened with his warm smile. He finished with the things and laid his pack aside before he moved to her, his strong hand rubbing from her shoulder blade to her spine. His voice was soft, losing a bit of that commanding authority it usually held. "And I'll try to keep myself from stealing you away to my fortress in the night." A light smirk teased his cheeks, and he wanted to lighten the mood for her.

She chuckled, but the sound was a bit hollow. She stayed next to him for another moment before walking to the new items he'd unveiled, suddenly all business. "Well, alright. I think we could set you up with enough food to last a month, but it might just be my kindness speaking. We got a pair of new hunters lately and they've been doing great to add to our supplies."

He gave a kindly smile to her remark, shedding his heavy protective vest and trench coat. "Your stuff beats the pants out of my canned goods," he confessed. "Though there's something to be said for the odd tin of pineapple, or a chocolate bar. Can't get that up here," he said, teasing her with that remark he knew she'd find goading.

She rolled her eyes before turning back to him, her arms folded under her chest as she pushed up her breasts teasingly, leaning slightly to expose her cleavage. "Yeah, well, you can't get these over there," she goaded him back, the line between a true fight and good-natured humour razor thin.

His nostrils flared, and his eyes widened a little as he gazed at her breasts. Damn, was she ever right. He stepped to her, reaching out with a hand upon her hip, the other reaching about her back, lightly tickling her spine. "Could never argue with that," he said lightly, his thick, dark thumbs stroking her flesh through that dress. "Wish at least one of us weren't so damn stubborn," he said and bent down, kissing her forehead tenderly as their bodies touched.

"You always try to argue, though," she whispered.

She was a lovely woman, but he was right. She was stubborn, and could be a terrible bitch at times, depending on her mood. Today, though, she just seemed lonely. She licked over her lips, and though her eye twitched. She confessed to him, "Marcia and Luke lost their baby."

They were another couple in the commune that Leon knew, though not well, but he had noticed she was practically bursting last time he saw her.

Leon frowned deeply down at her, for though he didn't know them well it troubled him deeply to hear of such things. "Is she alright?" he asked hopefully, his hands stroking her sides until finally he just took her in his arms fully and gave her a warm, tender embrace, resting his cheek to the top of her head, which his height made so easy.

"Don't know yet. Martin says they just have to wait and see." Her arms clutched about him tighter, and it was obvious that she was needy of him. Needy for his companionship, for his affection, and for the warmth of his body pressed against hers. She wanted to feel safe from the outside world, even this perfect slice of heaven she'd tried so hard to cultivate.

Squeezing her so firmly, tight almost to the point of discomfort but knowing the limits of his strength not to pass over it, he murmured to her in that strong voice of his that sounded as if it could do anything, could command any outcome no matter how silly or preposterous. "I'd never let anything happen to you," and it was silly, but it sounded so true the way he said it. "I'd keep you safe in my castle and stop anything bad from ever happening for as long as you were mine."

She hugged him back, and even on the brink of tears, she was strong, refusing the relief they'd award her. She tilted her head back and looked up at him so affectionately. "Look, Leon... I know this isn't ever really going to work but... just for tonight?" she asked quietly.

It wasn't the first time she'd asked, but it had been a while.

With a cheerful smile that was part teasing, part confident and cocky, but all loving and comforting, he brought a hand up to her face, stroked his thumb over her cheek, and said, "I'll never turn down the opportunity to spend some time with you. You'll always have a place in my heart, Tia. A prime, ladylike spot."

With another of his hearty, full squeezes, he lifted her up off the floor a good couple inches, bending down and tilting his head so his dark lips met hers.

She kissed him back, her lips moving against his so tenderly, her hands wrapping around his neck as she helped him hold her body aloft. When finally they parted, she jerked her head back toward the stairs, her brown eyes full of promise.

She didn't share the cabin with any others for the most part, except for in the winter when their numbers swelled, and there hadn't been a sound since he arrived.

They didn't walk to those stairs, however. He ran a hand down her spine to her ass, cupping that swell of flesh, and hefted her with a display of strength that made her look easier for him to carry than the satchel he brought in.

With her in his arm, he stroked his other hand over her leg, then along her arm, and back, placing a kiss on her lips. "I am going to savour this night," he said, his voice almost a growl as his fingers grazed her breast. "And I'm going to suck these sore."

She bit her lower lip, her nose nuzzling along his thick neck, her breath hitting against his collarbone. He could hear it quicken at his threat, and her hands clasped him more desperately. She'd always loved the things he could do to her, even before they got involved.

Even after they stopped, she found it hard to say no to him.

"Bedroom," she growled, biting his ear and tugging it.

# CHAPTER 3

The downstairs was laid out like a store, and there were several windows that could easily be spied into. She never cared for being spied on.

He carried her into that room, never showing any strain from her weight. By the time he was in there with her, it was like he was back to how he was this morning; ravenous for affection and sex as if he'd been without for months.

Bringing her to the bedroom, he didn't want to part from her. He just kissed her aggressively, shoving his tongue into her mouth, and felt her up as he pressed her back to the wall. The woman earlier today was delicious, but Tia, and her gorgeous breasts, were beyond compare. He revelled in that voluptuous flesh, delighting in the feel of it, groping, squeezing, and kneading it as their tongues intertwined.

Her room was simple, with a dresser and a bed, her curtains still open. It was darker up there, no candles or oil lamps to light their movements, but the silver moon cast a flattering glow on both of them. She was so lonely and afraid that her motions were more passionate, more needy, her thick lips pressing against his skin as she sucked.

She lusted for this man like no other.

Pressing against her, his engorged cock ground against her body. It'd had a taste of sweet release, but it didn't feel like it with the way he needfully rubbed himself against her body. Those groping hands moved up, pulling down her dress from her shoulder, trying to make those sumptuously large breasts bare to his touch.

It was all happening so fast, yet felt in slow motion. Or was it vice versa? He took her from the wall and moved to the bed, laying her out there before he moved to tug off his turtleneck sweater, revealing that mass of ripped and scarred muscle.

She squirmed out of her dress so eagerly, revealing her simple, white underthings. It contrasted against her light brown flesh, and made it look so enticing, even in its simplicity. She reached behind herself, unclasping the bra and tossing it away unceremoniously, her legs already parted for him.

She was a beautiful woman, with strong arms and a fine body, and there was an undercurrent within her. She wanted him.

In the same time he was stripped down to nothing more than his snugly fitted boxers that cupped and accentuated the shape of his more-than-generous organ. Even for his broad and tall frame, he bore a large package, and he tugged down that last stick of fabric to reveal it, the shaft veiny and thick for her, glistening at its dark tip with his precum, his heavy pair of balls swaying as he moved onto the bed with one knee, taking hold of her panties and sliding them down her legs.

There was a certain reverence in the way that he did that. This wasn't the random seduction in the woods. He cared for this woman deeper. And though he'd seen her nude so many times before, it was special to strip away that last piece of clothing yet again nonetheless, and everything about how he did it and gazed at her suggested as much.

She tried not to show how eager she was, but she had to focus quite hard on not just leaping into his arms. She wanted this to last, for him to be with her, comforting her, for quite some time. She trembled, her bare foot rubbing against his shoulder before she hooked her heel in against him, tugging him closer.

"I need you."

Leon was prepared to savour this moment, but that plea of hers, that tug of her heel; it was all he could take. He held himself up with one palm by her head, and gripped her leg as he lined up his member with her cunt. It was so thick and full it stood out on its own quite well, needing no guidance from his hand to push it against and into her wanting cunt. He let loose a loud, reverberating groan of satisfaction, no longer needing to be constrained for they were in the privacy of her home.

Her head tilted back, a wide smile playing on her lips. It was the look of a woman who had spent many nights thinking about this, and was finally getting just what she wanted. The look quickly faded, however, as an angry fist pounded her door downstairs before whoever it was let themselves in.

"Tia!" There was a feminine shout, frantic in its plea. "Are you home?"

Tia's eyes opened wide, and she hissed, "Fuck!"

# CHAPTER 4

Tia's face was full of apology, her lips kissing along his jaw gently. "She needs me." He'd recognized the voice as her adopted sister, a young woman who had lost her entire family to the strange aftermath of The Leaving, and was now devoted to Tia's cause. There was a sorrow and fear in her voice, and quickly the footsteps clamoured up the stairs, the door flying open, and a quick gasp followed.

Leon didn't rush things, even though he knew it was over. Instead he gave Tia a slow, loving kiss and began to rise up as he turned. Just in time to see the door fly open, he slid his impressive cock from its all too pleasant sheath in Tia's cunt, only to kneel on the bed, fully exposed, before the other woman. With a casual, warm smile that belied the situation and his nudity he said, "Hey, Faith."

The petite woman hid her smile behind her hand, looking equal parts apologetic and pleased. "Hey, Leon," she purred, her eyes not darting away from his body and face. "I didn't know you were back.

With his shoulders back, and his broad, well-muscled chest—and member—out, he gave a wry smile to the small woman. "Only just barely got in," he remarked, not entirely referring to his arrival. He was terribly shameless in general, and in front of her he had no qualms with his nudity, and rubbed a hand down over his abs as he gave a deep exhale.

Tia pushed herself up, her face contorted in frustration as she leaned forward. "What is it, Faith?" Despite her annoyance, her words came out only concerned.

Faith looked back to Tia, her eyes widening as if she had just remembered why she was here. "Oh! There's someone new! They're pretty beaten up, said they got chased by the dogs. Said they ain't eaten in a week or more, nothin' but berries anyways."

The woman looked quite exotic, her brown hair pulled back in a casual ponytail and showing off her olive skin with the high cheekbones and catlike eyes. She was quite thin, though not unhealthily so, and was constantly in her shorts and tank top. Even in winter she was the last one to reluctantly cover her skin.

Leon shifted to the edge of the bed, sitting there and reaching over, beginning to gather his things slowly. "She or he got a name yet?" he asked curiously, brow raised as he looked to the exotic beauty. He liked her, even if she did cheat him out of something he'd longed for.

"Naw, don't even know if they're a he or she. Kinda hard to tell," she admitted with some embarrassment. "Anyways, they passed out I think, or they're half in and out. The doctor's looking after them," she added on, trying to ease the situation, "but they wanted your help. And some food, of course. Doc's hoping they can stay with you 'till they're well."

Tia nodded, grabbing her dress and standing to slip it on over her head, rearranging her large breasts so that they sat more comfortably, albeit braless. "Right."

She was usually such a giving woman, and Leon could tell that their interruption was rankling her more than she was letting on, if only because she hadn't already rushed the door to help. There was something in her posture and tone that was unfamiliar to him.

She moved toward the door, her arm going around Faith's waist, walking with her down the stairs. Tia was a fair bit shorter than Faith, and looked a lot more curvaceous next to her, but they made a good-looking pair.

They were the stuff of his dreams together. If only it weren't for their stubborn insistence he could have the two of them together back at his place... or so he liked to think.

With the two of them going ahead, he gave a sigh then pulled on his turtleneck and clothes, getting dressed promptly before he followed them on down. No point in sitting around waiting.

Most of the town was gathered around, though his earlier tryst-partner and her brother were strangely absent. The doctor, a good-looking, silver-haired woman, was crouched next to a crumpled heap of a human. The new-comer's hair was long and blonde, though it was dirty and matted in places. Their skin was tanned on the verge of burning, and their eyes were clenched shut as they convulsed slightly into the dirt.

Tia had grabbed a bowl containing some bread and beans, the latter courtesy of Leon, and gave it to Doctor Benson. Bringing her hand to the person's head, Tia's brown eyes searched the doctor's. "Will they be fine?"

She nodded, offering the bowl to their nose. "Sure. They just need some TLC."

Tia slumped back, finding Faith's arms wrapping around her, head resting on her shoulder as her entire body pressed against her sister's. "Thanks for helping."

"Not much else I coulda done," Tia admitted, and Faith kissed the woman's cheek just next to her ear. "Still. Owe you one."

Leon didn't really see how interrupting their sex had accomplished anything. Tia wasn't the doctor and it had been a big load of fuss just to hand someone a bowl, as far as he was concerned. But he didn't let his irritation show, and watched quietly.

The new person was in rough shape, to be sure. Though he'd seen worse. Stragglers like this turned up all the time in some way or another, and you always had to scratch your head at the notion of how they survived.

Not that he cared. Watching the two "sisters" only helped inflame that other part of his mind which refused to die just because of an interruption. Moving up next to them, he murmured quietly, "Hope you're going to be able to handle another one." Another mouth to feed, of course.

Her eyes turned up to him and she frowned thoughtfully. "Better they get here now rather than in the dead of winter."

The last winter had been hard on them. They'd lost a few people to dog attacks, had a couple stolen by bandits, and two infants had died from a rather mysterious illness. It had been rough on the tight-knit community.

Doctor Benson looked to the three of them, their bodies huddled so close together as the individual finally stirred at the scent of the food, their hand grabbing for the spoon and moving to shovel it into their mouth quickly.

Faith watched Leon's movements intently, and subtly inched to be closer to him, her front still pressing against the distracted Tia. Her lips contorted into a rather scandalous smile at him before dropping to his groin, licking over her mouth rather blatantly before whispering back in Tia's ear as though nothing had happened, "I'll help you 'round your place all week and leave you all night. I mean, you'll still have them to care for, but I'll just go spend the night with Will an' Fiona."

Tia nodded, glancing back at the woman with gratitude in her eyes, "Next time somethin' like this happens, just get it yourself, alright?"

Leon caught the look, of course, and for a moment returned one of his own, one of those piercing dark stares the ladies loved so much.

At their talk he pushed himself between them both, an arm around each, though he pulled Faith into his chest a little more firmly. "I've missed you two, I gotta say." He kissed each of them on the head in a friendly, familial way. "Someday I swear I'll talk ya into moving to my place." He gave a warm smile.

He could tell Faith realized her preferential squeeze in the subtle manner that her body positioned itself against his, turning her torso just enough to let her breast rub against his chest. She smelled like sandalwood or some other natural spice, and she kept shifting herself against his form.

Tia seemed more sullen and distracted, though it was hard to tell for anyone that wasn't him. From the exterior, everything looked fine, but she withdrew just so from his hold, her eyes still upon the newcomer. She was lost in thought, and all but ignored Leon's words.

The rest of the crowd had dispersed slightly, going back around the cooking fire and to their fields or homes, though several mingled nearby, watching the newcomer as they devoured their food.

Doctor Benson removed the bowl as they finished, their eyes wide and seeking more. Offering them some of the flask at the hip, the doctor tested their reflexes and responses.

"How many fingers?"

"Two," the newcomer said in a strangely neutral

voice. As they slowly pushed themselves up into a sitting position, it became obvious why their gender was so hard to place. Everything about them skirted the line between feminine and masculine, but for their longer hair which could have likely been a practical issue. Still, there was no beard on their face, and the fullness of their lips was so delicious.

Leon watched the newcomer with feigned interest at first, though it did grow to genuine fascination. He knew better than to push or prod Tia in any way, she'd go however she wanted or intended, and that was that. So he rested a hand on her shoulder reassuringly, but devoted the bulk of his attentions to Faith, rubbing his large hand pleasingly across her back.

Leaning down to the petite woman's level, he murmured quietly, "I could convince you to come at least, right?" then gave her a teasing wink, his fingers rubbing below the edge of her tank top upon her bare skin.

"I'm sure with enough effort," she whispered back as Tia stood, moving to take the bowl away and discuss practical concerns with the doctor.

"She'd hate me if I let you, though." Faith smiled up at Leon, deviousness twisting her face and her voice to something nearly daring. "You too, probably," she purred.

Her beautiful little devious act managed to send a shiver down his spine, though he didn't show it through his calm exterior. Instead he locked eyes with her and gave a slow lick of his lips, his hand still rubbing along her lower back, brushing her shorts.

His manhood responded as he eyed the scantily clad vixen pressed up against him. "I'd never dream of separating you two," he remarked. "In fact, my dreams usually go the other way." With a wry grin he murmured quietly to her ear, "But then again... you are a tempting one," his voice husky and deep in her ear in such a soothing, reassuring manner.

She laughed, a little too loud, and Tia looked behind her at the two of them, seeming a bit skeptical. She never had been the jealous sort, and it had never been a problem in their relationship, at least from her part. Still, she had always seemed a bit cautious when the two of them were together, and Faith stood up at the glance.

"I'm goin' to see what Will an' Fiona are up to," she announced, though as she walked away her hips sashayed in such a prominent manner, her hands rubbing down over her pert ass and resting in her pockets.

Tia narrowed her eyes at Leon, confused, "What was that all about?"

Leon watched the girl walk away then turned his gaze back to Tia. With a roll of his eyes he crossed his arms over his chest, "Having a bit of fun at our expense," he said then smiled to her. "Anything I can do?" he asked, knowing there likely wasn't as he eyed the new addition to her camp. This is the reason he couldn't live out here. He wasn't a farmer or a caretaker. He built things, yes, but he was a man of action.

"Naw, I think it's just a matter of time. We should probably get them bathed?" She looked to the doctor for confirmation and she gave a slight sound of agreement.

"Bathed and rested, I'd say," she smiled, a twinkle of humour coming to her eyes.

Tia looked to Leon. "Would you carry them?"

He knew where she was referring to. It was an area just on the outskirts of town, a heavily fortified house with a man-made pool. They'd jerry-rigged it to heat rather easily, and used it as their bathhouse. It was one of the best protected places on their land, and as such was one of the places that many people saw fit to relax.

They'd relaxed there on more than a few occasions, usually spending some time there right before he had to head back home.

That was a task he could do. With a nod to her he unfurled his arms and bent down onto one knee. The strange newcomer looked like they'd be lovely, once they were cleaned off. He couldn't help but notice as he scooped them up gently in his big arms. Balancing them across his arms, with the head rested into the nook of his bicep and chest, he carried them easily to the bathhouse.

Leon didn't strain. He'd carried heavier loads just for barter across hours of open land, after all. Bringing them to the house, he laid the battered newcomer out, their clothes needing to be removed before they could be dipped on in the water.

Tia took to that, the mostly limp and unconscious individual slumping as she removed their shirt, their body emaciated and entirely flat chested. She coddled them as she tried to undo their pants, her fingers prying them down. They were already a couple sizes too big from the weight loss, and she quickly shed them of their pants and undergarments, revealing the male form nude and curled against her arms.

She looked to Leon once more as she shifted to remove the boots. "Will you put him in?"

Leon found himself staring, taking a moment to respond to Tia's request. He'd not seen such a lithe and delicate-looking man since before the whole mess ruined everything. Dipping back down, he scooped up the man, even more gingerly now—for some reason—and brought him to the bath. He dipped down, cradling the man's head in his hand as he lowered him down, gently letting him sink into its hot surface.

"There ya go," he muttered softly to the man, "nice and warm."

The stranger moved against Leon's body, reluctant to be let go. He seemed to crave human contact, but at the heated water they seemed soothed, a soft "ohh" escaping his full lips. His mouth parted, showing cosmetically straight and white teeth, as his lower lip trembled. His eyes remained shut, the water glistening as it lapped at his chest.

Leon let him go at least once he had arranged him carefully in the water. With a soft petting of the stranger's dirty hair, he smiled and looked to Tia.

"Got a fragile one here, Hun." It was said with warm humour, but he knew, of course, fragility was a weakness in this new age.

Tia's troubled look told him that she knew. Her lips were pursed to the side, staring at the new man in a fretful manner before she tore her eyes away, returning to Leon. "I'm really sorry we got torn away."

She wasn't apologetic to him; she was expressing her own desires.

Leon gave a gentle pat to the man's shoulder then rose up, smiling at Tia. "Me too," he said. He could be a bit overbearing at times, but with Tia he never pushed her to do anything. She'd only push back anyhow. "Been dreaming of it for a long time now, I can keep on dreaming a while longer," he remarked with a bit of light-hearted amusement.

Her nose crinkled, looking down at her hands, her breasts still so heavy and, as they were free from her bra, shifted easily with her motions. Her nipples even pressed against the light material, her own desire hardly dissipated. "Probably not a great idea to join him."

The stranger was sinking lower in the water, though it seemed controlled, letting himself bob down and get his hair wet before rising back up, some life and colour returning to his cheeks.

Leon stepped closer to her, slipping one of his arms about her waist, his hand resting on her ass fully. "Wouldn't make for a great welcome to the community if he woke up like that, no," he confessed, pressing the two of them together so that he could smell her once more. It'd been a nonstop round of sexual torture since that brazen vixen interrupted them.

Bending down he kissed her forehead. "Your sister and you," he began in a soft whisper, "could have more peace and security with me," and more time uninterrupted by the problem of others.

Her brows furrowed, her head tilting to the side a bit. "Leon," she moaned.

Tia wanted him. Hell, from the way she said his name, she might have wanted the same thing, but she shook her head.

"People need me here," she whispered, sounding so tired and defeated. It wasn't her usual manner of shooting him down. Her loneliness was pungent in the air.

"I know she'd like —" She stopped, noticing out of the corner of her eye that the man hadn't resurfaced in a while, and she brushed past Leon, quickly jumping into the water and moving to the man's front, lifting him up so that his head was above the water.

With a suppressed groan, Leon watched as yet another moment slipped past his fingers. He moved over to the side of the bath, watching as Tia soaked herself tantalizingly, and helped lift the man, positioning him safely again.

"Duties of a leader never end, huh?" he said to her good-naturedly, because the bitterness didn't need to be expressed for the both of them to feel it.

She was soaking, her white dress heavy and weighed down by the water, forcing more and more of her cleavage to be exposed. She looked so tender and vulnerable just then, the briefest flicker crossing her face as she moved around the man, her fingers pressing against his scalp and beginning to wash his hair. He leaned back, his head resting against Tia's large breasts, seeming quite content as he half floated in the tub.

"Pass me the shampoo," she sighed out loudly.

Leon watched this all, then gave a rather obvious groan of frustration before he grabbed the shampoo. Uncapping it, he handed it to her, this, too, being another thing they got from him, undoubtedly. "I can't help but think how much simpler it'd be if I just got you knocked up and you had an excuse to go look after our kid, without givin' a damn about the rest of the world."

"Maybe you should try harder," she remarked bitterly. It was obvious how much she was hurting, especially as she brought her fingers to the man's dirty blonde hair, lathering it as he moaned in pleasure. It sent a shock of derision through her that she didn't like in herself, but as he kept repositioning his head along her large breasts, she couldn't help but squirm.

"Stay still," she pleaded, and he tried to heed it, but he was obviously pleasured by the human contact, the feeling of someone caring for him, and his body responded in kind.

Leon watched the sight, the beautiful Tia scrubbing the grime out of the increasingly appealing man, and couldn't help but feel his frustration grow. In a soft voice, he added, "I mean, I just wish there was some way to simplify things, so we could run off together. That's all I'm tryin' to say, Tia. 'Cause... damn, do I want you." Hell, did he ever.

"Yeah," she sighed, her fingers scrubbing along the man's temples. His smile was only growing, despite obviously hearing the conversation between the two lovers. "But it's not that easy. It never is," she sneered, her hands working down to the nape of his neck, pushing him off her large breasts and revealing the soap-covered orbs floating in the water, barely constrained by her dress.

He reached into the water to take hold of the man and position him back safely again, and Leon's eyes were glued to the scene before him. "Should I just give you some space then to work? What's best, Tia? You know I want things as bad as you, but I can't be assed to give a damn about people other than you so much as you do."

Tears threatened her, and she really didn't want to have this conversation in front of this stranger. She sucked in her breath, letting her breasts rise up out of the water for a moment, her nipples still pressing roughly against the dress. They were almost exposed, but she didn't seem to care.

"I don't want..." Her voice quaked and she couldn't find a way to continue on. She obviously had it bad for him.

He took a deep breath as he watched her, both troubled by her distress and enflamed with arousal by her appearance. He'd stopped paying attention to the weary traveller, presuming him too out of it to absorb much of what was said, if anything. "Sorry," he said at last, "I'm a bit of a lout. Can't seem to shut up talking about what I want, even when I know it pushes what I want further out of my reach."

Her lashes descended, hiding her eyes from him for a long few breaths before she moved, rinsing out the stranger's hair, cleaning him off quickly before rising out of the water. Her dress clung against her form, between her thighs, her nipples visible through the transparent material.

She walked past Leon. "Get him out," she said as she grabbed a towel, offering it to the feminine man as he was removed from the soaking tub, warm and clean.

Leon was brimming with frustration as he hooked his thick, muscular arms into the water and lifted the man out. The wet, sleek feel of his slender form was something more of a tease to top it off. He cradled the man as he took him out.

"Careful now." He murmured, "I've got you," as he lowered him to his feet, to see if the man was able to stand again.

It took him a few moments, but he was able to get his footing as he leaned his nude form against Leon's front, getting him wet in the process. He was a fair bit shorter, and a lot thinner, and his tan seemed to only dim around his genitals, forming an obvious boxer's line. He leaned there for a few moments before Tia grabbed for him, wrapping him in the blanket.

"We'll get him back to our place a—" She stopped, realizing what she said, and quickly moving to the door, holding it open for Leon.

Leon didn't bother to correct that statement, instead scooping up the man in his arms again, without bothering to ask if he could walk back.

"Hear that?" he said to the man in his arms. "You get to stay with the most gorgeous gal in the whole town," he said with a toothy grin to the both of them, carrying him on out with a jovial air again.

# CHAPTER 5

She didn't live far from the bathhouse, just a few houses down. Faith sat outside, her brows furrowed in thought as she looked down at a book, flicking through it though she didn't seem too interested in reading it. Her knees were parted in the centre, exposing that smooth, slender flesh of her inner thigh, up to that dark, hidden part just beneath her shorts.

As they approached, she looked up, dropping the book. "Hey, Tia, have you heard from Fiona today? Or Will?"

She shook her head, opening the door to let Leon and the other man in. "Why?"

"I don't know. Their house looked weird, and it was locked. All the curtains were drawn and everything." It was an odd occurrence in such a free town, and obviously a cause for curiosity.

"Maybe they're not feeling well. Probably just napping," she sighed.

Leon had leered quite obviously at Faith's splayed legs, and gave her a cocky crooked smile as he passed on by, muttering, "Hey there, good lookin'."

He carried the man in his arms on past, then up the stairs toward the spare bedroom. He'd come to know the place very well over the years, and had no trouble navigating it.

He laid the man out on the side of the bed, and then began to pull back the covers before lifting him again and laying him there, "Not many people get this kinda treatment from me," he remarked with wry humour.

The man's eyes opened slightly, revealing a startling blue colour. He looked a lot healthier, if a bit worn, and his full lips turned upwards.

"Been a pleasure, Leon," he murmured out, rather sleepily.

Leon gave a hearty, but soft chuckle and tucked the man in, brushing a hand back over his forehead as he took a final moment to appreciate the man's rather gender-blurring beauty. "Rest well, no time for nappin'," he said before moving to leave and rejoin the women.

"I don't know. Will's always told me where he's goin' since he got here." Faith's voice rose from the storefront. "It ain't like him. He told me he was huntin' this mornin' but he was supposed to get supper with me."

"It's nothing," Tia sighed, her voice sounding so

tired. "He's probably just sick. Let it be." "Fine, but if he's dead, I'm going to be really pissed off you didn't do nothin' about it."

Tia's jaw tightened, her eyes suddenly hard on her younger adopted sibling, "You're acting like a kid, Faith. Get over yourself."

Faith's eyes turned up at Leon's entrance, and her entire body perked up for him. "Hey, Leon. You're all wet," she purred, her smile growing suddenly seductive. Tia turned to face him with another apologetic frown on her lips.

"Faith, it's time for you to go. We'll join you for dinner in an hour."

With a broad smile he strode on down the stairs. "Ain't the first time I've had some blowback from wetness I caused," he said. "Your sister's a messy one." He stepped to the two women, an arm on each shoulder again and kissed them each on the forehead. "Off again, are you, Faith?" he asked softly.

"Not if you don't want me to go." She smiled up at him hopefully as Tia bristled next to him. The younger woman was obviously taunting her, trying to get a rise out of her for the alleged slight.

"Faith's just pissed because the guy she's seeing is missing, so now she's looking for a replacement."

Faith's face soured as she looked to Tia.

"Shut up."

Leon put on a hurt look as he rubbed the two women's shoulders, "Seein' a fella?" he said. "And here I thought you two ladies were mine, all mine," he said in good humour, grinning once more, two of his fingers giving Faith a bit of a special rub along her spine down the back of her tank top.

Tia was obviously in no mood, and looking at the two, she shrugged away from him.

"I think it's best the both of you leave, then," she hissed, immediately moving up the steps.

Leon frowned up after her. "What's wrong?" he called out. "Was just messin' around!" He looked down to Faith. "What'd I say?" he asked in confusion, not removing his hand from the petite woman.

"She's just bein' a bitch 'cause I interrupted you two." She laughed, her voice carrying up the stairs as she began tugging his arm toward the door. "Come on, I'm sick of her. She's probably just goin' ta sulk all night."

# CHAPTER 6

Leon followed the small woman at her insistent tug, letting her lead the much larger man along. "Fuck," he muttered to her as they exited into the dark evening. "Think I ain't feelin' the tension from it too? I was balls deep in her when I had to pull out," he said crassly to the other woman.

"Who knows. Maybe she wanted you to follow and fuck her senseless." She shrugged, obviously undisturbed by the thought of leaving her elder hanging in such a regard, adding on quite crassly herself, "At least she has that naked guy you left there with her. Good job, stud." She smiled brightly.

She could be quite the little bitch when she wanted, her slender hand still tugging his as they walked through the night toward the back of the camp, away from the joyous sounds of singing around the campfire.

The thought was slow to occur to him, and as Faith brought it up he almost stopped and turned around then. Tia was very dear to him, after all. But he was no less stubborn than her, and she told him to fuck off.

As they disappeared toward the back of the camp the woman no longer needed to pull on his arm. He stepped in beside her, his arm back around her, his strong hand roaming down her back until he was cupping her bottom.

"Sometimes," he muttered in some mock disbelief, "I wonder if I didn't go chasin' the wrong sister." It was said in good humour, as Leon and Tia had known each other before Faith ever came into the picture.

She stepped away from his grasp, her smile only growing as she arrived at an out-of-the-way cabin. It was usually reserved for preserving meat and goods, but the lights were on and there were noises coming from within. It wasn't the same, joyous sounds from the campfire, but there was an aura of happiness. Faith kept sidestepping his advances now that they were no longer near her sister, and she pressed in the door.

The light was bright and there was a group of about five people, sitting on top of some crates. Leon recognized them as others from around the commune, though there was one new face—a redheaded woman that was curled up against a dark-haired man he knew only in passing. They interrupted their conversation as Faith joined them, and she immediately sat herself cross-legged atop the nearest crate.

"Leon, this is everyone. Everyone, this is Leon." They all nodded politely, though they seemed a little perturbed by why Faith had brought him here. They didn't seem to be doing anything that they shouldn't have been, but it was a strange behaviour for the normally openhearted commune.

The dark-haired man looked to Leon, then Faith skeptically.

"He's with your sister, dork. Why'd ya bring him?"

She smiled so brightly, her eyes up at Leon with some hidden promise. "He chose me tonight."

The man pushed his hand through his hair, letting it cascade back in his face as he brought his lips to the redhead's hair, kissing her gingerly and whispering in her ear. She got up, looking at the four others before brushing past Leon without a word and closing the door behind her.

Leon was annoyed with the rejection of his advances, doubly so with finding out the destination wasn't some private spot to rut, but he never let it show. With a firm, almost stern nod to the rest, he moved over by Faith, folding his arms across his chest and resting his shoulders back against the wall. "Little vixen stole my heart," he said dryly, looking down at her and not letting his curiosity about this whole thing show through his mask of utter confidence.

The rest seemed skeptical, but they obviously didn't care too much as they finally resumed their conversation.

"Well, if the babies are going to keep dying, it must be a sign," said a slender, olive-skinned woman with shiny, black hair. It went down her back, resting just above her bottom, teasing the bare flesh along her spine. Her shirt was cropped close to her rib cage, and her skirt was black and pleated. She was the only one among them that wore shoes, black sneakers covering her black socks from the floor.

She was smoking a cigarette of some type, and her eyes kept moving to Leon suspiciously, even as she led the discussion. "Maybe the dust wasn't able to kill all who were unworthy, or maybe there were some that only just passed the test, but they're not allowed to breed because of it."

Faith scoffed, shaking her head. "Aw, come on. Rachel's baby died, and she's one of the nicest people around here!"

"Yeah," agreed the dark-haired teen as he fidgeted on top of his crate, "but her husband's a real asshole. I don't know how he didn't get killed. I mean, really, you should see the way he treats the rest of us guys! We can't even look at her without him freaking out."

Faith smirked, her face focused on him, "Oh, well you're just so charming, of course he's jealous."

"Oh, shut up, bitch," he hissed, his eyes narrowing.

"All I'm saying is it must be a sign," repeated the Asian woman as she stood, patting down her bum of any dust.

A light-skinned woman sat in the corner,

doodling in her book and trying to avoid the conversation until the leader walked over to her.

"What do you think, Abby?" she asked, obviously interested to know the woman's opinion.

"Uh," she murmured, shocked by the attention and pushing back her black-framed glasses. Her hair was very fair, and her skin had a few freckles across her cheeks and her bare shoulders. "I don't know. It can't be nothing. There's been too many for it to be nothing, Celia."

Celia nodded triumphantly. "And who truly believes that Hannah and Alexander were taken by bandits? He was the strongest guy we had, and they had guns on them! There's no way." She shook her head, obviously solidifying her idea. "They left because they realized we were wrong. We're wrong to try to go back to how things were. They knew that we have to adapt and to become worshipers."

Faith smiled in a manner that showed she found it more comical than convincing, and the dark-haired boy scowled at her. "She's right, Faith."

She laughed, looking up at Leon. "Zach thinks everyone's right if they talk like they know what they're talking about."

Leon watched the dark-haired leader intently, studying her and absorbing the little secretive display here in quiet. With his thick arms crossed over his chest he looked imposing, but to Faith's words he looked down to her and crooked a light smirk.

The people of this "town" were all children in his eyes, their silly notions and all. He loved Tia, he did, but thought she was a little mad to want this, to want these people as part of her life. It was all a little too surreal for him. His dreams were a bit more simplistic.

"So," he began, his low voice carrying in the room very clearly, commanding attention even when he didn't intend it. "You think by worshipping... them, we'll have more luck knocking each other up?" he asked, no criticism in his voice, just plain questioning.

Celia stared at him, her arms crossing just beneath her small chest, the white tank top ruffling a bit. "Correct."

"Celia's always worried about that. Ever since she got here," Faith explained. She'd arrived the spring past, alone just like most of them, and had always been a bit on the fringe. Here she seemed quite at home.

"We know what's in our own hearts and that we've been accepted by Them, but we will never know what's in another's hearts or how They judged them to be. Perhaps They've changed their minds about this little camp. Maybe none of us will continue on our lines simply by being here instead of worshipping them," Celia hissed at Faith, her chocolate eyes dark to the other woman.

Faith uncrossed her legs, spreading them so that they hung off either side of the box. "Yeah, well. A dead baby is a good baby for me," she purred, her body arching erotically as her hips ground her against the box.

Flicking his gaze to Faith's display, he couldn't help but smirk. And throb. She was a gorgeous little thing, even if he didn't share her same sentiment there.

Leon watched the two women with great interest. He had his own theories on life now, and though he didn't intend to worship any damn thing, he at least sided with the dark beauty on how just lingering about in that camp wasn't likely to get them much.

Wetting his lips as he took a moment, he spoke again in his husky voice. "Anyone who knows a bit about me, knows I prefer to get shit done in my own way. Works well for me so far," he offered.

Celia suddenly seemed to show a good bit more interest, walking away from Abby and over to him. "Maybe Faith isn't so stupid for bringing you here," she jabbed at the other woman. It was pretty clear Faith wasn't well loved around the camp for a variety of reasons.

"An outsider can teach us much of the outside world." She turned her back on Leon, standing a pace or two away, and looked to the others in the room. "He has connections. He can find other believers, true believers, and help us to breed." She smiled, suddenly excited by the prospect.

"Children are life," she said pointedly to Faith, her eyes trailing over the woman's thighs and hidden vulva as she continued pleasuring herself with the aid of the crate, "and giving yourself up for anything less than that is a farce. A joke. A meaningless diversion."

Celia turned back to look at Leon, her voice lowering. "In that, I'd like to speak with you privately." Faith stopped her motions, her brows furrowing as she hopped off the crate. "Hey, I brought him. He's here with me."

Leon kept his pose, immobile and stony, as he watched Celia now, his interest upon her. As much as he wanted Faith, she'd been a brat, and turnabout was fair play.

An uneven smile slowly formed on his broad, strong face as he looked to the small darkly dressed woman, licking his lower lip in thought. "Yeah, we should talk." He turned his gaze on Faith again. "You don't mind, do you?" The glint in his eyes showed he was enjoying putting her back on the defensive, back to having to compete a bit for his attentions, as she had with Tia around.

"What am I going to do?" she whined, looking quite annoyed at not being lusted over despite her apparent disinterest in him. She was quite the tease, and hated having her power taken away from her. Reaching out, she grabbed his hand, squeezing it. "Besides, we're supposed to meet Tia for supper!"

Celia waited patiently, confident that she would have her time with him. The others merely watched, curious.

Leon gave Celia a hard stare, his dark eyes penetrating. With a look back to Faith he said, "You keep doin' what you were doin', and then I'll be back to get to you," and reached over to lightly slap his large, powerful palm against her ass, a cocky smile on his face.

Faith stood from the box and took a step forward, shocked by his spank, looking quite flabbergasted at his rebuttal.

Looking to Celia, he said, "Let's talk," firmly, as if commanding it.

"Tia's gonna be pissed!" Faith hissed out, as if suddenly she were concerned for her sister's feelings, her arms crossed over her chest angrily.

Celia, meanwhile, opened the door, leading him out into the fresh air and walking toward another cabin, not waiting for him to follow.

Before following after, Leon gave a brief sly smirk to Faith, whispered for her ears only, "Should've taken the opportunity when you had the chance," flashed her a teasing wink, and followed after the Asian woman to the neighbouring cabin.

# CHAPTER 7

He was intrigued by her the moment he saw her, and though he saw much of what she said was madness, that'd never stopped him before. Not with Tia, after all.

Opening the door, she revealed a rather small, plain cabin. It was intended only for two, and it didn't seem anyone else was home. Lighting a candle, she silently walked down the hall, opening the door to a bedroom and quickly closing the curtains. It was an action considered suspicious, yet she had no hesitation. Nothing about her movements gave a hint that she felt uncertain in any of this.

"Shut the door behind you. I don't know when my roommate will be home."

Leon did this dutifully, the tall, muscular man having no issue with the bizarre secrecy. He was a cautious man himself, after all. His home was a monument to that paranoia. Looming over her in the candlelit room, his dark visage was all the more imposing. "A lot of strong talk back there," he said lowly. "You surprised me."

"Faith bringing you surprised me. I don't know why she was there in the first place. She keeps showing up after she stumbled upon us a couple of months ago." Celia frowned, seeming quite annoyed at the other woman's actions. "Regardless, I'm pleased. You travel all over, yes?"

With a slow firm nod, he responded, "I don't take to farming, or sitting around. I go into the heart of the city, take the things others are afraid to go near. I trade with various places around, I give them those things I don't need or care for, and they give me the best of what they have to offer." He let his gaze roll down over her, studying her and her looks intently.

She was a fit young woman, and her scant clothes showed off her toned body. She set the candle down next to her bedside table, sitting atop the bed and crossing her short legs. Her skirt snaked up her thigh, teasingly high, as she bent down to untie one of her sneakers.

"Do you have information about other societies? Their birthrate and how many children they have growing among them?" she asked, her brown eyes moving up his body slowly.

She was definitely his type. With a slow nod to her question, he responded huskily, "That's easy enough information. Doesn't take much to get someone to start yammering to you about all the births and pregnancies in a camp when you pass through."

He didn't quite know what to make of the woman. He liked her, that's about all he knew, but he liked plenty of nutcases. He continued to stand immobile and tall, his bulky muscles easily outlined by his tight turtleneck sweater and the cargo pants that bulged with his thick thigh and calf muscles beneath.

She kicked her shoe into the corner of the room, bringing her other foot up onto the bed and unlacing that one, letting her skirt fall back around her black panties before she kicked that one aside as well, leaving on her black, knee-high socks. She shifted on the bed, cross-legged at her pillow.

"You can sit," she allowed, her eyes on his face. "Have you run across the cultists?"

At that, Leon came over, his heavy mass causing her bed to creak and groan beneath them both, creating a recess that almost sucked her toward him a little.

"Of course," he said, his hand resting near her leg, his thumb beginning to brush across her stockinged calf. He was intent to let this play out, see where this strange woman went with it.

"And what of their birthrate, hmm?" She tilted her head, the long, black hair falling over her shoulder and across her cropped top. "It's higher than elsewhere, isn't it?"

Watching her with his dark gaze, he was a bit enraptured with her. Perhaps the crazy talk helped, or maybe it was just the pent-up frustration of earlier, for he found himself nodding slowly. "Not many know," he said, his fingers feeling out her leg, moving up and past the edge of her dark sock. "They try to keep it hidden. Mask their power." Those broad fingers of his moved up across her bare thigh, achingly slow. "But not much escapes my view." A broad, sly smirk on his face.

She smiled, her crossed legs feeling so taut and muscular under his grasp. She looked gleeful at his words, sitting up straighter at his confirmation of her beliefs. She licked her lips, biting her lower one in as she digested it all.

"I knew it," she finally exhaled. "They reward their followers with the gift of eternal life through our kin," she explained diligently, her eyes excited.

"Do you believe?"

Leaning in toward her, his body looming a bit over her, he was grinning a bit as he spoke. "I was born for this life." His hard fingers brushed up against her skirt over those firm thighs of hers. "I was made to survive these wastes, and I embrace it." With his gaze locked on hers he leaned in, almost pushing back against her. "That's why you don't find me here with these fools. I live as the strong do. Independent."

She seemed so pleased with his response, her dark eyes focused on his.

"You're the best chance I have here," she confessed. It was a strange thing to say, something so crass in such an unsexual manner, despite the sexual underpinnings of her statement. "How long will you be staying here this time?"

With almost a growl to his voice, he said, "I'm

the best chance you have, period."

His hand slipped up her skirt entirely, rubbing her bare skin and then touching the band of her panties, fingering them as he began to push his chest to her, his face hovering but an inch from her own. "Two nights, tops," he said, his broad pecs rising and falling beneath his sweater as his breathing grew heavier. As cool and unsexual as she made it, it didn't inhibit his feelings on the matter.

"If you're strong enough to carry it through," he said, eyes partially lidded now, "I can take you away from here. Show you so much."

She shifted, her fingers hooking into her panties and pushing them down, moving them off over her socked feet and tossing them on top of her sneakers. She still kept on her thin shirt and her pleated skirt, her dark eyes focused on his face.

"I want your kid," she said, her words heated as her mouth moved to his neck, kissing him roughly. She even nipped at his flesh as her hands clasped his sweater, pulling him to her body, "I want you to fuck me 'til I'm pregnant," she hissed.

Such an odd way to request it, her word choice so bizarre. But it did the trick, for he pushed her down into the bed with his own motions, kissing her paler skin hungrily upon her neck in return. Grabbing her two legs, he pushed them back and wide, spreading her before he moved his hands to his own waist. His belt was undone and his pants open in a heartbeat, for he took her desires at face value, and wasn't about to miss another opportunity.

The massive totem of his own virility exposed

and throbbing immediately, he angled himself so that it rubbed down against her now exposed sex, trying to jam it into her as his two hands felt out her chest and kept her legs back.

She was wickedly slick, that trimmed bit of pubic hair doing nothing to hinder him as he slid into her body. She was so tight and pleasant around him, her entire body clinging to his. Even if she felt this was some sort of means to an end, she certainly didn't act it. She seemed, instead, hungry for his flesh.

She continued to kiss and nick him with her teeth, her slender legs easily pressed back so that they met the bed, her skirt flipped up over her stomach. Her breathing was already heavy, and she moved her hand, grabbing the candle and trying to hand it to him.

"Pain," she hissed, "is the purest form of worship."

Sheathed inside her he was almost too wrapped up in the pleasure of her cunt to absorb the meaning of her words. She was one sick little princess, he thought, but he was game. Before taking it, he pulled his sweater off over his head, and all the while his cock throbbed widely inside her.

With his chest bared, he took the candle in hand and let the light fall across the wide display of hard etched muscles, the pronounced markings of old scars and wounds. If she liked pain, perhaps she'd enjoy that sight, he reckoned.

In a low guttural voice, almost growling, he said, "You'll not find a better master of pain," and with a hard tug back of his hips, he then rammed his cock into her with a rough thrust. The stab of pain that accompanied it was alleviated only by the hot, stinging pain of wax as he tipped the candle so that a dribble of searing liquid ran down her inner thigh.

She hissed her pleasure, her head tilting back as she twitched, her cunt clinging to him tightly. Her hand went to her chest, flicking up the crop top and exposing her braless chest with the dark little nipples, hard and wanting. In the close light of the candle he could see there were some burns and cuts in various stages of healing along her normally hidden regions, the rest of her body delightfully smooth and youthful.

"Yesss," she moaned, digging his large cock into her further, feeling herself stretch around him. He was imbedded so deep around her with her legs pushed back as they were that tears sprang to her eyes and she craved more.

He didn't pause to admire her beauty, though he admired it all the same. Hers was a special kind, after all, rare in many ways, not the least of which caused by of her extreme behaviour.

With low grunts he continued to pump his hips into her, he gave it to her hard, for he relished the opportunity. As big as he was—as girthy as he was— he rarely got a chance to cut loose, even a little, with women. Though this was far from going wild, he hammered into her tight cunt hard, his balls slapping against her ass.

Licking his lips, he spoke to her in a commanding voice, "Give me a child, and I'll keep you swollen with seed till the end of your days," then tipped the candle again, another small dollop of wax landing, this time, upon her breast.

Her nipple hardened with the pain, her mouth dropping open in an "ahh." Opening her eyes, she found his, her breathing hard as she hooked her feet in under the headboard, her body rolling so that her ass was lifted off the bed, begging him to bottom out in her deeper and harder.

The woman was obviously no virgin or, at least, not a stranger to this type of pleasure. She took it willingly, her cunt quivering and tightening around his thick, black cock. Her hand went into his hair, grasping at it and jamming her mouth to his.

Mashing their lips together, he kissed her fiercely, bent over her twisted form he hammered down into her, striking the depths of her cunt, greeting the entrance of her womb with his bulging, wide crown. Grunting as he plunged his meaty shaft down into her, he felt his loins stir. It was all so much, and he wanted to pump her full.

Pushing the candle aside to the side table, he took hold of the bottoms of her thighs and ass, and he pistoned himself into her with a brutal pace. It had to have been excruciating for her, he thought, but he didn't let that hinder him. He continued with the harsh treatment as his broad chest heaved and he grunted loudly. "Cumming," he panted out, feeling his dick swell inside her, the fire travelling up its length as his balls tightened.

She seemed to derive more pleasure from that single word than anything he had said or done. She practically quaked against him in her excitement and the strain of her body, her eyes glassy with tears. A stupid smile appeared on her face between her gasps and whimpers, the pleasure crashing through her.

Her nails dug into his neck and shoulders as she rode out his orgasm, her pussy clamping down around his cock.

All the teasing and wait had been worth it, he decided, as he rammed his shaft down into her so hard and fast. The first heavy spray of his virile seed down into that waiting receptacle was satisfying beyond measure. Oh, he'd come inside that girl earlier, but he was so primed for danger he couldn't enjoy it at all.

This, however, he revelled in. He grunted and groaned loudly as he pumped her hard, making sure he squeezed out every last spurt, every last drop of his seed. With a loud, satisfying cry, he filled her with his rough thrusts as his fingers dug so hard into her flesh they'd likely bruise. He didn't even notice it, but as his thick black cock shot its load he had been cursing and muttering at her to "take it, take it all."

Her head twisted about on the pillow, writhing in her own, much quieter, pleasure. Both hands move to his ass, joining her socked feet as she pulled him within her deeply. She held him there, jammed within her sopping cunt, as she came down from her high. When finally she was able to speak again, her voice was a bit dry. "In the top drawer," she murmured, motioning to the night stand.

Opening it up revealed an assortment of illicit objects that he had no idea how she'd obtained. Razors, a dagger, and a very large dildo lay on top.

Looking at her assortment of toys, he pulled out

the large dildo, eying it curiously then looking to her. "Would've taken my time," he said, "if I knew you cared about more than carrying strong life." He flexed his still large, swollen dick inside her, forcing her vaginal walls wider for a moment.

She laughed, a short, stilted thing, as her eyes opened at him. "You'll have time before you go," she promised, her straight hair a bit messier after their tryst. "But in the meanwhile, I don't want to lose any."

The actual meaning of the thing then struck him, and he grinned a bit. "Good girl," he muttered approvingly. Carefully, he began to rise up, sliding his thick, veiny girth out of her, almost as obsessive as she about not spilling or wasting any.

Wiping what creamy white seed of his remained on his own dark cock into her folds, he then shoved the thick dildo into her hard, sealing it in place. With a lick of his lips he said, "More to come before I go."

She moved her pillow from beneath her head, propping her ass up and allowing it to tip her sex back. She was quite the little sight with her skirt and shirt pushed out of the way, revealing her wax-stained nipple and thigh, and the dildo-plugged pussy.

"First thing tomorrow morning. You'll be most potent then," she ordered.

"I'll be here," he promised with a wry smirk, watching her as he was already getting up and beginning to get dressed again. She was a sight to behold, alright, he mused to himself. It didn't take him long to throw on his sweater and do up his pants, nor did the little extra push he gave the dildo. "'Til then," he bid her farewell.

# CHAPTER 8

She let him see himself out into the chilly night. It had been an eventful day, especially for such a sleepy little hollow of such peaceful people. It was a crisp evening, and there was still light conversation coming from the direction of the fire. They were a social group, and spent so much of their time around one another.

Faith sat outside the cabin, looking rather sullen. She stared up at the sky, her thin arms wrapped around her knees, and upon his approach, her dark eyes turned to him. "Have fun?" she hissed hatefully. Apparently she hadn't quite mastered her jealousy as others in the camp.

Glancing back at the cabin he remarked ruefully, "That lady is nuts. Friend of yours for long?" He acted casual, as if nothing beyond a conversation with a crazy lady had just occurred, resting his back to the cabin beside her, putting his arm about her naturally.

"She's new." She rolled her eyes. "I tried to warn you. Fuck." Her eye twitched just slightly. "I'm sorry I ever brought you here. I thought it'd be a laugh."

"I thought it was pretty funny," he remarked wryly, his hand rubbing her back. He leaned in, speaking quietly, "Doesn't feel so good to tease now, does it?"

Her head turned away from him, shame burning her cheeks at his words. She quickly stood up, looking down at him. "We've missed dinner."

Seeing her stand up, he reached out, taking her hand and tugging her back toward him as he nonchalantly rested against the cabin. "Maybe we should do somethin' else then," he suggested, a slight curve to one corner of his smile.

Her confidence had been shattered, and no longer was she being the flirtatious young woman of earlier. Instead, she almost looked frightened, collapsing against his body and looking up at him on her knees. "Leon," she murmured. It was a mix of emotions, of reverence and fright, but mostly she sounded sober. "Tia's probably had some time to cool off."

Putting his strong arms about her, he held her comfortingly, stroking the back of her hair soothingly. He bent down and kissed her head. In a warm embrace he murmured to her quietly, "We can head back if you like, or we can prance off into the woods to play tag if you want. I don't care. Just glad I get to see you again anyhow."

She was all soft against him, no longer rebellious and in control. He had taken her down more than a couple of pegs, and her hands rested on top of his thighs, taking in a breath.

"I like you," she exhaled, her eyes on him, "but I don't want to get in the way of you and Tia. Not really."

"I know," he said, looking jovial and friendly despite his imposing stature. With his tender stroking of her hair, he leaned down. "That's why I want you both. All to myself. Forever more." He slowly broke into a big grin, though he wasn't joking. Not really.

"If only I could convince you two to come be mine."

"I go where she goes," she admitted, the prior bickering between the two obviously a passed storm, at least in her mind. "She's the boss." She squeezed his thighs, looking so vulnerable between them. He could feel her heart racing through her palms.

Squeezing his thick arms about her, he crouched down a bit, bringing him nearer to her eye level. Meeting her eyes with his own piercing, dark gaze, he touched a hand to her chin. "I love you. The both of you. Y'know that? But I can't stay here. Bein' a farmer or some shit. If only I could convince Tia... I'd take you both away and treat you both as princesses."

He leaned in, hovering just a fraction of an inch from her lips for a moment, before closing the gap and kissing her softly.

He could feel her lips tremble against his, and her hands squeezed tighter. Her lips were so soft and yielding against his, unlike the anger and hunger of the cultist he'd just bedded. Her lashes fluttered downwards and her head tilted just slightly, an exhale crossing his lips before she pulled back.

"I'll talk to her," she murmured softly, squeezing his thighs once more. "But we should go apologize. Well, I should."

He gave her a big, pleasant smile, said, "Perfect," and gave her cheek a gentle stroke. "You're beautiful, Faith. Maybe together we'll talk some sense into your sister, and all live happily ever after, huh?"

"Doubtful," she admitted, though she seemed a bit begrudging about that as she stood herself up again. "She really likes you, ya know. Always talkin' about you. Drives me nuts."

She dusted the dirt off her knees, waiting for him to join her before starting the short walk back.

Keeping an arm around her, he joined her, walking on back toward Tia's place, side by side. "Yeah, Tia's as stubborn as the two of us put together," he declared. "But the three of us belong together somehow, I believe." And he rubbed her back and spine gently.

"Might be right. I dunno, way things goin' around here," she sighed, her head hanging despondently. "Fuck, even Will's off and disappeared. No one's heard from him or his stupid sister."

With a reassuring squeeze, he asserted, "Talk some sense into your sister. Careful like. Then I'll take care of the both of you." Leaning over, he whispered to her quietly, "I got some old-world shit that'd blow your fuckin' mind, Faith," and flashed her a wink.

She laughed, though the sound was half-hearted as she knocked on Tia's door, waiting patiently for an answer.

"Like what?"

Letting the moment hang a while, he responded casually, though a bit coyly, "Oh, how long's it been since you seen a movie, Faith?"

She blinked, taken a bit aback before the door pulled open, and a freshly changed Tia stood behind it, looking more vibrant and refreshed. "Hey. I was wonderin' when you two would get back. Took ya long enough. You get supper?"

Her mood was restored to normal, and Faith was in her arms instantly, muttering her profuse apologies. Tia hugged her back, looking down on her with surprise, glancing to Leon. "You make her feel bad for earlier?"

With a confident, cocky smile, he gave Tia a secretive nod and wink behind Faith's back then responded, "I think it tears the girl up enough on her own, without my help. Never seen someone so stuck on another human being before that weren't at one time attached by a flesh-and-blood cord."

Tia laughed, kissing the crown of Faith's head. "Stop that now. You know I'm always going to love you," she soothed, moving the girl inside. "You eat?" She glanced to Leon, grabbing Faith some water.

With a shake of his head, he stepped on in, pulling his sleeves up over his arms. "Nope. Never had a chance," he admitted, brushing by Tia with a warm touch.

She smiled at him, leaning toward his touch

before whispering to him. "Do I owe you an apology?" she purred.

Faith smiled, backing away from the two and plopping down in a chair at the storefront desk. "He was just tellin' me he has movies, Tia. Back at his place."

He gave a big, cocky grin and kissed Tia on the forehead. "Would never hurt if done right. And yes, I do," he stated, arm about Tia, hand squeezing her hip and tugging her against him.

She smiled, resting her head against his chest. Her aggravation and hurt from earlier was gone, and her new outfit was far more casual; a simple nightgown that clung to her form, ending just below her ass. It was a pure white that contrasted nicely against her brown flesh. "We'll see what I can do about that, then."

Faith piped up, "What type of movies?"

"Anything here we can grab to eat?" he asked, rubbing his hand up and down Tia's side. "And what type? You kiddin', girl." He laughed, acting as if she were crazy. "You're talking to the best scavver in the known world. I've got it all. And if I don't got it, I'll get it," he declared confidently, puffing his broad chest out.

"Well, I know a certain scavver that brought me in a ton of canned goods, but I'm betting he wants something a little closer to home. You two stay put, I'll grab some stuff from the fire. Maybe... Faith, did you want to wake up our guest? See if he'd like something? I bet a home-cooked meal will perk him right up."

Faith nodded, taking another drink of her water. "Yeah, sure," she muttered, pushing the glass away and heading toward the stairs.

Leon watched the two women split up on their duties and moved over to the counter, taking the seat Faith so recently occupied. He took a drink of the water there and waited. He'd had an eventful stay so far, and the night wasn't even out.

It wasn't long before they reconvened, giving him just enough time to catch his thoughts. Faith pranced down the stairs, leaning against the desk casually. "He said he'll come down when it's ready. But that he don't have any clothes."

Tia entered just then, looking at Faith curiously. "Who? Oh." She put a pot on top of the desk. "Fuck, forgot about that. Well, I'm sure we can rummage somethin' decent up."

Twisting the glass about, Leon remarked casually, "He was small enough. He could probably fit in either of your things." There was no ridicule there, though he did find the notion interesting.

"Adorable." Tia smirked, bustling about to set the table. "But for some reason I don't think he'd like something like this." She motioned to her chemise, teasing. "Faith, go check the other bedroom. Joseph might have left something last time he stayed."

Faith sighed, but there was a flash of love in her eyes as she trotted back up the stairs.

Leon got up and moved to the table, seating himself and smiling at Tia. "You're lookin' lovely as ever," he remarked, reclining back in his seat, the wooden chair groaning beneath his muscle weight.

She smiled, placing a plate and a glass in front of him. "Thanks," she purred, inhaling deeply. "Are you still stayin' the night? I mean... there's still the extra room if..." She trailed off, unable to finish the thought.

With a pleasant smile, he stated, "Would love to, Tia. And as for what room, well... you know my feelin's. Wherever you want to put me is where I'll stay." He gave her a soft, but knowing smile. He had his jollies twice today, but would never turn down an opportunity for a third. Especially after so long without. Besides, it was Tia. She was different.

"You know what I want. Never changes, even when I want it to." She pursed her lips to the side. Faith seemed to have the good sense to stay gone a little longer than required, leaving the two to talk in semi-privacy.

Leaning forward in his seat, he reached out for her, taking hold of her wrist and hand in his, "Then I'll be stayin' right beside you." He gave a warm, desiring gaze. "I'd spend more nights like it if it were up to me."

"Me too." She leaned in, kissing his forehead. Apparently this cued Faith's re-emergence with the stranger right in tow, looking sleepy and yet somehow freshened. He smiled, and his entire face lit up.

"Look who decided to join us," Faith announced, glancing back at the attractive, young man. "Says his name is Christian." He pursed his full lips before smiling, good-naturedly. "Aw, she stole my line."

Leon gave a hearty chuckle and turned, eying the man openly. "Get used to her stealing something from you, whether it's your breath or your line." Standing up then he extended his hand to the much smaller man, "Leon, pleasure to meet you, Christian. Right and proper this time."

His shake was delicate, but his smile was not. It was all full lips and moon eyes before he forced his face away from the taller man. "Right and proper," he agreed, a bit bashful. "I guess I owe you a thanks." His eyes lingered on Leon's, hidden meaning passing behind them for a brief flash before he looked past him to Tia. "Both of you."

Tia nodded politely, finishing serving up the thick meat and vegetables. "Yea, yea, don't worry about it! Just sit down and enjoy your meal while it's hot and fresh."

Leon looked down to the other man's small, tan hand in his own large, dark mitt then released it, guiding him to the table before he took a seat. "Looks damn good, Tia," he said enthusiastically, being quite hungry at this point.

Digging in, he began to speak to the other man again. "And you'll want to save the bulk of your thanks for Tia here," he said, hooking his thumb in her direction. "I'm only a very honoured and fortunate guest, I'm afraid. She's the one you'll need to suck up to." And he winked to Christian.

Tia laughed, shaking her head. "No need to suck up. None at all." She smiled at both of the men, her expression changing to each.

Faith settled in, smiling at Tia pleasantly. "She's the best. Really." She looked to Christian. "She's been takin' care of me for over two years now and never complains about it. She probably should," she admitted, and Christian laughed.

"Well, I'm sure that's not true, miss," he responded in his light, airy voice, sitting between Tia and Leon, across from Faith. "Do you all... pray or...?"

Tia's lips curled into a smirk and she shook her head. "Not 'less it would make you more comfortable."

Leon, meanwhile, was already eating the thick stew and paid no heed. "Why pray when I'm already in heaven?" he said and gave Tia a big, appreciative smile and a rub of his stomach, looking more than satisfied with the meal.

She hadn't cooked it, but she looked pleased he was enjoying it regardless. Christian shook his head. "Nope, just wanted to be respectful," he assured her before helping himself.

They ate in relative silence, having had such a long day, and it already being so late. By the time they were done, the sounds outside had faded and the lights had begun to dim in the other houses. Tia looked between her three house guests and stood. "Well, you're all welcome to go get settled, if you wanted. I don't know if you wanted to sleep again, Christian, but it might be good to try to get your body used to normal hours."

He shrugged giving a little nod. "Yea, 'spose. It's a bit of a novelty being safe indoors during the night now, I gotta confess."

Leon gave a hearty chuckle. "You stumbled upon the right place to go to then. Hard to get luckier in stumbling upon a camp of fine people in this day and age," he remarked, casually studying the other man a while.

"A lot of 'em would as soon dump you further afield than take you in and look after you," he remarked, with more than a little truth to his words.

"Yea," Christian agreed, looking a bit sullen, his face contorting. He had existed outside of the camp for a long time, somehow. It was hard to believe such a tender-looking individual managed out there for any length of time, especially on their own.

Tia cleared away the dishes, speaking loud enough for the three of them to hear. "Well, you all get settled. I'm going to go tell the doctor what's happened and that you're alright. I'm sure she'd be worried."

Leon looked to Tia and smiled. "Never stops, does it?"

Rising up, he stretched. "I hear you got a clothes shortage problem Christian. I'd lend you some of mine, but... y'know, I assume you want to wear clothes. Not swim in them."

"Heh, yea." He looked over Leon's form, brushing his hand through his blonde hair. It was much more golden now that it was dried and free of dirt, though it still hadn't seen a brush. "Only had the clothes I came in with and they're pretty much disintegrated."

"He's a scavver, though!" Faith piped up. "Maybe he could find you somethin' when he goes out next." Tia laughed as she walked out the door. "Yea, give him an excuse to get back fast," she purred, shutting it behind her.

Leon gave a big, hearty chuckle. "Yeah, I could do that." He rubbed his chin, sizing up the man in an exaggerated fashion. "Though my services don't come free, of course. Always a trade to make. And you might not like my taste in style for ya." He reached out and gave Christian a gentle squeeze of the shoulder. "You let me know what sizes you take and I'll keep an eye out for ya."

There was something there, hidden behind Christian's calm façade, that told Leon he knew well about making trades and deals. Faith was studying the two men, and leaned forward from her seat. "He doesn't have nothin', Leon. I'm sure we'll get some stuff for you. Make it all fair. We always do, right?"

Leon gave another one of his friendly, warm chuckles and leaned over, kissing Faith's forehead as he kept his hand on the man's shoulder. "He can owe me, how's that sound?" Pulling up, he said, "Now, if you'll excuse me, I gotta freshen up." He head on to the washroom.

# CHAPTER 9

The closest one was just down the hall across from the kitchen, containing a large mirror, sink, and toilet. It was a wonder they had running water in these parts. Still, it was a pleasure. The candle instantly sparked his memory of earlier, and it glowed over his face in an eerie manner.

Leon went to freshen up. He'd had a long trek and been with two women. Before he spent the night with Tia, he wanted to take care of a few things. A few minutes passed before there was the lightest sound, almost like a scratching, at the door. He'd had enough time to take care of it mostly when he heard the sound however, and opened the door pretty promptly. "Almost done," he said in a quiet voice.

It was Christian, looking kind of lost. His voice was a whisper—"She's gone upstairs"—before he attempted to move into the room as well.

Leon was a little surprised, but he took it as he took all things. Stepping aside, he let the man in, looking him up and down casually as he set the door nearly shut. "Somethin' on your mind?" he asked quietly.

Christian looked suddenly confused, though it was harder to tell in the muted light, and his hand went to his hair, pushing it back nervously. "Ah... I thought..." he murmured, taking a step back, as though to leave, a small laugh coming from him. "Shoulda known better."

Pushing the door shut the final click, Leon rested back against the sink. "Hey, it's okay." He gave a light smile, looking the man in the eyes. "Don't worry. I ain't as mean as I look. At least, not around these people," he added with a wry grin, leaning forward a bit.

The bathroom was so small, and they were so close together. Christian licked over his lips, though his throat was still dry, causing his voice to come out with a bit more of a masculine husk than usual. "Just... you know, wanted to thank you and see... you know, about the clothes..." He trailed off, obviously nervous around the other man.

Leon reached out, rubbing his strong hand along Christian's shoulder and bicep. "Of course. I don't normally make special trips for stuff unless someone's a close friend, or offerin' a lot, but what do you have in mind, huh? And don't be shy. After you get asked to go fish someone up a dildo, or a whip, you stop givin' a damn about embarrassing requests."

Christian's eyes widened, and he shook his head slightly. "Oh no, nothin' like that. Just some clothes. Somethin' I can wear around, I don't even really care what at this point. I just want something that's mine," he whispered, still trying to keep his voice low, despite the dryness. "But we're not friends, and I don't expect charity. I figured... you know, that's why you removed yourself," he admitted with a flush.

Leon gave a warm smile. "You do what you gotta do, I understand that. It'd be a more than fair trade too, I reckon," he said, giving the man an obvious once-over to indicate what he meant. "But I don't barter for sex. Not up straight like that," he said calmly and plainly, then shrugged his shoulders. "I look out for the folk I sleep with, but that's not a trade as I see it."

"Oh, and I don't go scavvin' for just any ol' clothes," he said with mock indignation. "I'm the finest scavenger around. If I'm going to bring you clothes, you damn well better have something special in mind. Elsewise, ask any old fool to grab you some." He gave a warm, friendly look. "But like I said, I could see what I can do, and if you don't have anything to trade, well... you'll owe me."

Christian's hand went around the back of his head, face downcast. Despite the other man's calm demeanour, it was obvious that there was some shame or bruised pride lingering there. He leaned back against the door, taking in a deep breath. "Thanks." He returned his blue eyes to Leon's, studying him. "I guess you're staying the night, then?"

Leon nodded to him then stepped over, practically putting his arms around the man as he reached for the door. Pausing there, he brought his free hand up and traced a finger along the man's jawline, speaking to him up close, so that his low voice could be felt as well as heard. "And for the record, I ain't sayin' I'm not interested."

Christian's face snapped up, full lips dropping open slightly as a rush of relief washed over him, followed quickly by pleasure. A smile broadened his lips, revealing those white teeth once more.

Chrisian gave a quick nod, feeling almost trapped in the most delightful way by the other man. He nearly choked trying to speak, and simply resorted to nodding at first. After a few heartbeats, he finally managed out, "Just... let me know when... if..." He shook his head, laughing lightly at himself. "I'm usually pretty good at this, just so you know."

With a low, husky chuckle, Leon pinched the man's chin between his thumb and index finger. "I bet you are," he remarked with a toothy grin. Releasing the man's face he pressed into him, a bulge apparent as it prodded into his stomach. "You and I will work some stuff out, I'm sure. And in the meantime, if you can think of anythin' in particular you'd like me to get, let me know. Remember: special. I won't be gettin' you some old rags." He added pointedly, "Nobody I look after walks around with anythin' but the best. For the record." He then pulled open the door for him.

Christian let out a whimper and a sigh of relief, as though Leon had done something to him that was beyond mind blowing. He practically fell out of the door, looking back at the other man longingly. He swallowed, his eyes scanning over Leon's face and body, opening his mouth to speak just as the front door opened, Tia singing out, "I'm back!"

Leon gave the man a wink and casually walked past him, letting his palm rest against the man's chest briefly then trail on down across his body, nearly brushing his groin as he walked on past.

# CHAPTER 10

Heading downstairs he went to greet Tia with a mock glare, "Dammit, woman, you were gone an age!"

"You know how she is. We got to talking." She smiled lightly. "Marcia's doing a bit better, they're hoping she'll be alright in a few weeks' time. It's still pretty touch and go and she's really upset over losing the baby," she mourned. "Still, at least they have each other still."

Leon came on over to her and put his arm about her, pulling her in close and kissing her temple. "How about we go call it a night, huh? I'm beat, and I've barely had a moment alone with you, Tia," he said to her in a soft, weary voice. For he was indeed growing weary by this point. A long day of travel behind him.

She nodded, in full agreement as she began walking up the stairs. The other occupied rooms were all shut to the world as they made their way down the hall. Tia smiled at him gingerly as she walked to the bed, sitting down gently. "It's been a rough day, hasn't it?"

Shutting the door after him, he came over to sit himself down on the bed beside her. He stretched out, reclining and placing his arm around the voluptuous woman with a big heave of a sigh.

"Well, I dunno about for you, but I trekked through miles of sodding ruin to get here, so yeah." He gave her a big, cheesy grin as he rubbed his hand along her side, brushing against the underside of her breast.

She gave a soft chuckle, resting her head against his shoulder. "Yea. I won't be offended if, you know. I have to wait. Even if I was teased and tormented for most of the day by your presence and... the coitus interruptus that is my sister."

She stroked her hand along his thigh, down along the knee and then back again. "She can be a brat, but she really has a crush on you, I think. Don't be... I mean, she's never..." She admitted softly, rubbing at her temple, "I mean she'd kill me if I told you, but she's all talk."

With a low, husky chuckle he gave her side a squeeze, in the process pressing the heel of his hand into her breast. Leaning over he gave her neck a kiss, speaking to her quietly. "Don't worry. I have a crush on the two of you anyhow, so it's mutual."

With a wry smile, he added, "And keep you waiting? Tia, I wouldn't dream of it. I was balls deep in you when I had to pull out, and now I've got you to myself again at last, you think I can just fall asleep now?" He gave a laugh. "Yeah right."

Her lip twisted in a curl, her posture relaxing further as she nodded. "Good," she murmured, moving off him and staring at him quite seriously. "I actually had an idea I'm sure you'll love. See, Faith is kinda stuck on this Will guy, but I think she's probably... nervous. You know how she's always been, she always puts on this show and acts like she knows what she's doing. But she really doesn't, and I think it's been getting to her a lot more seeing this guy, since of course he kind of expects it." She inhaled, shaking her head. "To get to my point, finally... I'd kinda like to show her. Introduce her to things, and let her experiment in a less emotional setting. Let her make mistakes, figure things out, and do so with... two... trusted adults."

Leon saw where this was headed long before she approached anything approximating the point. He knew what a free-loving sort Tia was, part of what he adored about her, even if it made her seem crazy at times. Leaning over to her, he gave her a kiss on the lips. "Sounds right. The right thing to do, I mean," he said firmly. His demeanour was calm and rational, but already his manhood was stiff, despite its frequent use that day, throbbing a bit wildly at the thought in fact. "Three of us are somethin' special anyhow, huh?"

"I'd trust you with her"—she smiled, kissing his neck lovingly—"one-on-one, but I just think she'd feel a bit too pressured. To try to put on a show and make you feel like she knew what she was doin'. I want her to be able to relax." She kissed along the line of his sweater, tugging it with her teeth. "I think it could be something she'd remember forever."

His hand slid to her breast entirely, pressing his palm to the large mound fully and beginning to knead it as they started to kiss and explore one another. "I love the idea," he said lowly, "you and me, teachin' a sweet and curious Faith what she's been pretendin' to know all along." He gave a light laugh then bit her earlobe, squeezing her breast. "Sounds perfect, Tia. Well... if only I could take you both back to my place for it, it would be."

"Don't start," she warned, but even then she had a smile on her face, shifting to straddle his lap. "My, my. You like that even more than I would have guessed," she teased, kissing the corner of his lip, her chemise riding up around her hips and revealing the bare skin beneath. "I guess I have gotten kinda greedy with you lately. I just... you don't get here often," she apologized, her chocolate eyes begging for his forgiveness.

Feeling her seated upon his lap, and his cock, he gripped her hip in one hand and her breast in the other, holding her firmly in place as he felt her out. "Mmm, you know, you are the perfect woman for me, Tia," he said in a deep, somewhat gravelly voice after all day. "Too perfect. Because though I could have you, and almost everything else I wanted on top, you're just too much of a damn individual to get that one last thing from you." He gave her a hard kiss on the lips. "And I think all three of us will remember the night, not just her, Tia love."

Her hand went into his dreaded hair, her nails trailing against his scalp and down his neck. "Every time you come back, I want us to make this work, but it never does. Not for good." Her teeth tugged his lower lip, her nose rubbing against his. "You don't know how bad I wish I could leave it all, just spend my days with you, learning to do what you do. But I really believe in what we're doing here. I think we can make a difference." Her teeth moved to his ear, tugging it gently. "But there's always now. Always tonight."

With a shift of his hips, Leon pressed up against her with his groin, his fingers moving back to sink into her ass. "Let's pretend for one night then," he said softly, "that we're sticking it out together. Because I love ya, Tia"—he kissed her neck then lifted her, turning about and laying her back on the bed— "and I want you."

"I love you too," she admitted, her thighs crooked around his hips as she shifted, somehow managing to grab her nightgown up over her body, tossing it into a pile in the corner of the room. It left her body so delightfully bare, the light-brown skin so smooth, despite the roughness in her hands and the strength in her arms and legs. Her breasts were so large, they parted with the newfound freedom, her nipples puckered atop them. She smiled at him, looking so passionate and loving toward the man she obviously cared deeply for. Despite her free-love lifestyle, she knew what she had with him was different.

The feeling was mutual. Leon was a self-involved

man in many respects, and had no time for monogamous love, or devotion to something other than self, but for Tia, he was softer around the edges. Taking home of one of her now free breasts, he parted his mouth, about to dive down and suckle it, but instead rose up, pulling off his sweater and tossing it to a corner of the room with disdain before lowering himself down, bare-chested. With her heavy breast in hand, he kissed about it, licked around it, before clamping his lips to the areola and nipple, suckling on it hungrily.

Her moan was in good humour, the end turning into a gasped laugh as she pushed her breast harder against his mouth. "You said you wanted to do this the second you got here." Her hand pressed him to her harder, encouraging his languid attentions as her stiff nipple was teased by his adept tongue.

He lapped at her, suckling at her breast hungrily despite the man's massive size. Tia's greatest physical asset was her generous chest, and he loved to revel in it any chance he got. He had no answer for her, as he continued to assault her teat, before finally pulling off his mouth. "And you have no damn idea how hard it was to not drop to my knee, tug down your dress and start on 'em right downstairs before everyone," he declared before devouring the other breast, too, squeezing and rolling the flesh of the first in his hand, letting the saliva-slickened nipple poke up between the ring of his thumb and index finger.

Her day had been long and emotional, and he was giving her just the attention and release she'd been craving. The ability to lie back in her bed and have him lavish attention on her was just what she needed, and it was so quick that she was breathing heavily. The scent of her arousal already permeated the air, and she writhed under him eagerly. Her lower lip trembled and she bit down on it, silencing a loud moan as her back arched.

He wasn't often, but Leon could be a tender and caring lover at times. And as he lavished his oral affections upon her breasts, he lowered one of his big, hard hands down, rubbing the dark digits along her slit in a pleasing manner before trailing back up and parting her labia. As he curled his tongue about her nipple in his wanton suckling, he began to rub her womanhood, stoking its fires as he prodded and encircled her clit.

She didn't bother trying to hold out on her moaning for long. Instead, she felt the absolute need to express her gratitude to him, and after a few moments, the room was thick with the sounds of her pleasure. As his finger glided across her slickened sex, her legs encircled him, her head tilting up to look down at him affectionately. Her words of praise, her compliments and expressions of love and fondness, mixed their way into her moans and sighs.

Tugging back on her teat, he let his dark eyes meet hers a moment as he brought his free hand down. It was a bit of doing getting his belt and pants undone, but he managed it without so much as having to pause his dual ministrations on her, fingering and suckling. Worming his way out of his last garments, he recommitted himself to her body, tugging on her teat harder and letting his thick fingers dip into her cunt with their skillful motions. He wanted to make Tia squirm and writhe, remind her of all he had to offer this night. Maybe that's part of what drove him to be so good for her, to make her see just how great he could be for her and sway her mind.

She was almost shaking beneath him, his ministrations bringing her to the brink before toppling her over with a loud cry, her head tilting backwards and her eyes clenching shut. Her body writhed and shuddered as he continued to manipulate her body, and it was nearly too much. Still, she demanded he not stop, and it wasn't long before there was a warm gush coating his hand, quickly soaking the bed as she shook beneath him.

Leon simply grinned with her tit still in his mouth. He loved the way Tia came, always such a warm, slick mess. He prolonged the moment, continued to provoke her oversensitive body in its heightened state before he unsealed his lips, letting her nipple snap back into place, and raised his digits to his mouth, licking her juices from them. He rose up, his back straight, letting the heavy length of his veiny girth rest along her slit as he eyed her.

She was in a daze, that ecstasy on her face so obvious. She was halfway between heaven and earth, and as her eyes worked over his body, she looked much closer to paradise than the hell on earth. She adored him, it was so obvious. "Did I tell you how sorry I was for earlier?"

Sucking the last of her juice from his pinky finger, he slid it out of his mouth and gave her a half smile. "You don't have to," was all he said, pulling back his hips and letting the underside of his cock drag along her cunt, until the wide tip was positioned at her entrance. Resting his hands on her thighs, he pushed them back and lined himself up before giving a single, swift push, knowing her body so intimately well as to be able to use the exact amount of force to tweak her sensations just right, giving a lewd groan of his own pleasure in the process. After her orgasm, she was left so slick as to be easily penetrated, even by his large organ.

He could feel the aftershocks of her orgasm, her pussy contracting around him so pleasantly. She was a woman who enjoyed sex, and foreplay, but wasn't necessarily promiscuous. As far as he knew, she'd only had a couple other partners at the commune, though they were no longer in the picture. One of her partners was actually the man that was earlier kidnapped by bandits, and it had come as a rather hefty blow to her. He was actually convinced, for a while, that she'd leave to be with him full-time after the loss. It was what had brought their relationship to the ground, but this trip had shown him her forgiveness and interest in continuing, if nothing else. Her legs wrapped around him as she encouraged him in, though he needed none of her guidance. Her hands went to his strong shoulders and her head lifted, silencing her own moans against his mouth.

He'd been with two other women this very day, but now was the time he took to savour and really enjoy it. No need to rush, or do anything but revel in their two bodies mingling. Tugging back his hips and pushing in, his powerful body rutted into hers with an increasing intensity. Leon knew just how to amp it up, though tonight, with her excessive slickness, there was less need to worry about easing her into his size or pace. Pistoning into her cunt he kissed her hard and rubbed his hands up and down her body, coming to rest upon her breasts and work their flesh as he fucked her.

She was so responsive to touch, and her body arched and moved against his as though they were dancing together. They complimented each other so well, her breasts and ass so soft and round, his body so hard and sculpted. Both a beautiful brown tone, though she was far lighter than he. Both young and still in their prime. She trembled against him, her body still so sensitive from her orgasm, and another tremor passed through her nervous system, her breath hitching.

Pulling back from their intense kissing, he let his fingers curl around her back, so that he was holding her almost completely about her waist now. He held her body so, like she was utterly under his power, shaping and directing her with his strength as he hammered into her harder. He was breathing heavily himself, though he took the time to watch her through lidded eyes, enjoying the wet slaps of their bodies striking one another as he kept it up, ratcheting up the intensity continually.

She likely wouldn't have been able to handle or enjoy it so much if she weren't so aroused. The teased entrance of earlier had really worked a number on her, and his skilled ministrations of her body only warmed her further. Her body was primed for him, and the slight discomfort he did bring her was warmly received by the murmurs of pleasure she expressed. It wasn't long before she shook against him once more, her sensitive body so primed for pleasure.

Leon had stamina to spare usually, and after this day it was doubly so. He took her through another climax, and before she knew it, had her bent over, ass in the air, face mashed into the bed as he took hold of her hips and was pumping into her cunt from behind. He even gave her round ass a few slaps as he huskily praised her body and spoke about how long he's been dreaming of this moment.

After her multiple orgasms, she was putty in his hands, so easily melded and convinced to whatever he wanted. She had already soaked him, and the scent of their sex was everywhere in the small room. Her breathing and their physical activity had already caused the humidity to rise, and sweat glistened along the small of her back as she struggled to keep herself up on shaky arms.

His muscular form was glossy in the dim light of the room, the contour of every muscle, the line of every scar outlined all the more by the thin sheen of perspiration. If this were the first night of many together, he'd have been more careful not to wear her out and leave her sore, but he wanted to make the most of this, and so through each position, each hammering he gave her, he savoured her body. Breathing heavily, they eventually found themselves off the bed entirely. He had her legs in hand and was pumping into her, her back to the wall as they noisily humped against it. He kissed her face and neck, muttering, "Dammit I wish I could have this with you more often."

She was exhausted, her mind addled by her orgasms. "I missed you," she moaned, "I missed you so fucking much."

He gave a low growl at her words and husked out his agreement. The other two occupants of the home were no doubt well aware, by now, of just how much fun the two were having together, with their noisome exercises. Grunting he eventually took her back to the bed, pumping his cock inside the now puffy and battered sheath of her cunt as he spooned in behind her, their bodies intertwined, thick limbs all about her. "I need to finish," he groaned out into her ear, his hard, authoritative voice so needy for once.

She nodded her agreement. She had always, in the past, preferred he cum elsewhere, insistent against getting pregnant. She cared for so many, she had argued, that she couldn't afford to take time off just for her own selfish desires. Not when the father wouldn't even be around. Her legs tightened against him, though, trapping him deep within her. His absence had certainly stirred something in her.

It wasn't the response he was expecting, not at all. In fact, only a lust-addled mind let him utter the words in the first place instead of pulling out and cumming as usual. But the tight clench of her cunny walls was more than enough, and after their exhaustively long lovemaking he squeezed her whole body in his arms and moaned aloud. With a shuddering intensity he spasmed inside her, flooding her depths with his thick seed, the orgasm seeming to last an eternity after so long of a buildup.

Her entire body quaked, knowing the risk she was taking. But she was taking it with him, and something inside the back of her mind was positively delighted at her lack of self-control—or the change in her mind. She held him so tight, as if she were afraid of losing him. She wanted him near her so badly, and nothing about him being finished lessened that fact.

Long after he was done, his member twitched and spasmed inside her, drooling just a bit more of its pearly-white essence. And Leon never pulled away, just held her in his thick, comforting arms protectively. It was a special night, he realized that, and squeezed her across her breasts and chest, kissed her neck and nestled in against her. He didn't want to break the magic of the moment by doing or saying anything that would endanger it.

They somehow found sleep, enwrapped in one another's bodies, surrounded by the scent and fluids of their copulation, messy and content. It was as deep of sleep as either could hope for, warm and protected in the safe commune, in one another's arms. When finally dawn broke, Tia stirred with the sounds of the camp, her body feeling so delightfully sore as she slowly nuzzled into Leon, not wanting to wake.

# CHAPTER 11

The gentle nuzzling awoke the giant of a man, and he blinked at the bit of light that was beginning to seep into the room with dawn. Still entangled, he squeezed her body against his and gave her lips a firm kiss as he stretched out his thick, cramped muscles after a night of sleep. "Best night of my life," he muttered in a gravelly morning voice.

She refused to open her eyes, even as she agreed with him. "I don't wanna wake up," she moaned, rolling onto her back and glancing at him with a small smile. "Wow, so... that was all real, mm?"

Grinning a bit, he leaned over, nudged into her cheek, pushing it out of the way before kissing her neck again and then propping himself up on one elbow. "Damn well better be," he said, looking over her gorgeous form in the morning light.

Her hand rose up, stroking along his strong jaw, taking in a deep breath. Her eyes were lidded, and she looked so peaceful and calm. She had a glow about her that screamed of her happiness. "When are you leaving?"

With a roll of his shoulders he took a deep breath, his chest swelling. "I dunno," he said. "Gotta talk some business with someone this morning, but no more than twenty-four hours at most," he said, looking to her with a bit of disappointment at the thought of leaving her side.

She nodded, looking instead grateful just at the extra time with him. She had obviously been assuming that he'd be leaving today, from the way her arms draped around him. She glanced toward the half-curtained window, then back at him. "When do you gotta leave?" she purred, her eyes only partially opened, "And when will you be back?"

With a wry grin, he squeezed her body against him. "Promised to meet 'em first thing," he said. It wasn't uncommon he met with people in the community for private "commissions" or to deliver some package or letter. "But we should meet again before I go, even if I end up taking off today." He brought his face down to hers and kissed her on the lips. "We could meet up again this morning."

She kissed him, though it was a bit chaste and embarrassed. "Morning breath," she explained as she pulled away, covering her mouth a little. The apples of her cheeks rose up, even as her smile was hidden from him. "You do what you gotta. I'm gonna see about gettin' breakfast goin' for my two wards. I'll talk to Faith... maybe... before you go? I mean, she has her boyfriend and I don't know when you'll be back next. And you know how fast things move around here."

He'd forgotten all about that! Getting up, he started gathering his clothes, which were flung to the four corners of the room. "Now for that, I would stay the extra night," he said, shooting her a sly grin. "Count me in, Tia," he declared.

She smiled, looking so relieved as she got up, grabbing her discarded baby-doll and pulling the silky white material over her head. "Thanks, Leon." It was as though he was truly doing her a large favour, gratitude apparent in her tone. "We'll be around all day, probably getting Christian set up with some clothes and introducing him around. You find us when you're ready."

With a nod he set about getting dressed and cleaning up. As crazy as his appointment was, he didn't want to show up without a bit of cleaning up. Once he'd tidied and freshened, he set off, however, hands in his pockets as he made his way across the little community of cabins toward the one he'd trysted with the woman last night in.

It was still just post-dawn, and though there were some people around, he didn't run into anyone he knew well and they just let him on his way. However, there was a head peering out from a window in the cabin he'd met the cultist the night before, and the door immediately opened, revealing the petite Asian. Her eyes narrowed at him, her arms folded under her chest. "Where have you been?" she hissed, looking over him crudely. "I hope you're potent," she added on. She was quite the crass young thing, and she was wearing the same outfit as yesterday, though she hadn't bothered with the socks. The black crop top peaked at her puffed nipples, her pleated skirt just landing beneath her ass as she turned to walk into her bedroom. "Be quiet, my roommate is still probably sleeping, lazy brat."

Leon wasn't fazed by her outburst. He just took in the woman's physicality, noting her aroused state, and followed her on in. The moment he was within grasp of her, his hands went to her hips. "Don't you worry," he murmured deeply, "the job's probably already done after last night, but I'm plenty virile." He pushed himself in behind her, the pronounced bulge of his cock against her rear. "Came over as soon as I could."

"Yea, well, you better be fresh," she stated boldly, but her body soothed at his touch, her ass grinding against him slightly. "I confess there's so much more variety I'd like to do with you, but that will have to come about later. For now"—she swallowed back her hesitation—"we should simply focus on ensuring our shared lineage. I suppose now that you know a bit more about me that this can be more adventurous?" she inquired, her nails scraping along the backs of his arms, resting on his hands. "You were, after all, quite delicate."

He found that amusing. Oh, he'd had more to give, to be sure, but he'd never met such a small woman able to take quite that much from him even. His powerful hands gripped her tighter, taking control of her body and grinding her back against his cock harder. In his commanding, dark voice, he muttered into her ear, "If you can give me a strong heir, I'll take you away to my lair, breed you, and explore every depraved act imaginable. That is a promise." He bit her ear, tugging it roughly before letting one hand move up beneath her shirt. "A strong, healthy, attractive son or daughter," he reiterated into her ear after letting it snap back.

She nodded, quite amicable to the idea. She pressed her body against him, encouraging his rough manhandling of her body before she turned to face him. "I'm pure in the eyes of the Gods, and they will reward me. Should you be up to their vision of the future, I accept your offer." She put the blame back on him. She locked the door behind him, heading to her bed and sitting down on it, her legs parted and up on the mattress. "Do you like us to be undressed for this or what?"

"This is fine," he said, watching her intently and already unbuckling his belt. He liked a woman in a little clothes during sex. "When you give me an heir, we can move on to things like pleasing outfits and the like." And with that, he pulled out his cock, thick, black, veiny, and wanting, as he moved between her legs atop the bed. "We'll have to be quiet?" he asked, remembering the roommate as he took hold of his dick and rubbed its mushroomed tip against her slit.

She shrugged, looking in the direction of her roommate's room. "Eh, who cares." She glanced back at him, her eyes dropping to his cock. She seemed to excite at only the sight of it, her nipples straining the top further. "You know, you're quite blessed," she informed him rather matter-of-factly. "The capability to cause pain must be a splendid reminder of your power."

Something of her was perhaps beginning to rub off on him, or he was just playing the part, for he gave a simple nod and said, "It is." Pushing the bulging head to her labia, he took hold of her two legs and pushed them back, taking control of her body more freely now. "This'll be your first child I take it?" he asked then with a brutal thrust, the likes of which he'd never opened on any woman before, he impaled her on his weapon harshly, jabbing into her very depths with such force.

She let out a squeal, her hand steadying herself against his arm as she held onto him, feeling her body fight his impalement, despite her arousal. He was so large. Pleasure rippled through her, intertwined with the pain. "Fuck," she murmured, her pussy so taut around his large cock. "You last longer in the mornings, right?"

She didn't answer his question, he noted, but he gave a simple laugh to hers in response. With her legs bent back, he instead gave the only response appropriate: the immediate and unhindered pistoning of his dark-brown shaft into her tight little cunt. The way he had her bent back, the two of them could see it plunging down into her so deep and rough, and he took advantage of the view. He watched each time as the dark organ thrust her pink folds out wide, and it encouraged him to go harder, faster. Gripping her ankles so tight they would undoubtedly bruise, he grunted animalistically, and could feel the heat build beneath his sweater. Damn, he should've taken it off first.

She was as enraptured in the view as he, her dark eyes focused on it and her facial expression revealing her enjoyment. She was so wet for him, but it did little to aid in his brutal thrusting, and she enjoyed watching her delicate labia grow darker with the increased blood. They could even see as she began to grow puffier, the light hair she kept there doing little to hide her body's natural response. The unpleasant pain in her ankles only made her feel more at home, and she forced her eyes away from his pistoning shaft for a moment. "No kids," she murmured before staring back at their sexes interlocking.

The fact that she hadn't had any kids didn't surprise him. Although, well, the timing of her response to his long ago asked question did, at least. Grunting in response he continued the hard pistoning, pounding down into her with an ever increasing intensity. He kept at it for some time, until finally he grew tired of the position. She was right, his stamina was greater in the morning than usual, and he was going to enjoy this time with her more than the last. Slipping back, but not out, he pulled his sweater off again, his dark broad chest, scars prominently on display, and he took hold of her and got off the bed. He pushed her to her feet and twisted her about, forcing her to bend over and press against the wall for support as he began to pound into her from behind, each strike jarringly shaking her as he battered her womb.

It was deeper —so much deeper—and she began to scream and cry in earnest, yet her body responded in quite the contrary manner. She met him with every push, even as it caused her to scream. She had to go up on tiptoes, and even that wasn't enough to keep him at a comfortable height. She stepped back, into his feet, lifting her up another inch or so, her ass pressing so tightly against his body. She was so tiny and thin that he was able to pound her so deeply, and she loved every second of his brutal assault.

In this position he enjoyed the change in view, his hands able to grip her about the waist so that his fingers touched, encompassing her narrow width entirely. The sound of his cock thudding against her flesh inside, the loud slap of his balls hitting her mons, it was delicious when mixed with her squeals and cries. His cock swelled inside her thickly, and he slapped her ass with a loud crack, instantly leaving a dark-red handprint. "Dammit, I'm gonna breed you so hard, bitch," he said, and then with his free hand he grabbed her hair and yanked back, twisting her face about so she could see the hard look on his own. "And if you're real fuckin' good, I might give you a special place in my harem." He was getting a bit into this, to be sure.

She ate it up, that strange look on her face as his hand tightened in the long, black locks one of pure ecstasy. She had surely found her calling at his hands, and the more he lost himself to it, the more her body tightened around him, as if in reward. She liked being made to feel so small around the brute of a man, both physically and emotionally.

Bent over her as he pounded her flesh with the sort of reverberating smack that sounded like fist punching a slab of meat, he licked her cheek and growled loudly. She was encouraging a side of him probably best left alone, but he was eating it up almost as much as she was. With another loud slap on her petite ass he gripped the flesh after and groaned in pleasure. He wasn't near done, the poor woman in having such a long pounding ahead of her. Continuing on, he eventually had her face jammed into the bed, his hand on the back of her head as he used his free hand to lift her hips to keep her at just the right height to stab down into her cunt with his wildly throbbing dick.

She was such a willing plaything. She had instigated this, bossed him around, but now that he was filling her, there was no more sass. She hadn't the time or the energy for it. Instead, she was crying out for more, agreeing with his cruel words and begging for his seed. She wanted it, and she wanted him, and it was so abundantly clear that she didn't give a fuck about anything else. She wanted the pain his body brought her, that clarifying, purifying emotion that intensified her pleasure.

He'd lost all track of time plowing into that tight body of hers, but he still was utterly fascinated by the sight of his thick, dark cock pummelling her now rosied labia. With his hand gripping her skull, he commanded grimly, "Beg for it," as he felt his heavy balls slowly begin to tighten with impending release. His finish was near, but he wanted her to bed some more. Her cavalier attitude about the whole thing amused him, but now he wanted to hear it on her panting, needy breaths. "Beg me nice and good or I pull out and blow it on your whorish face," he threatened.

Her entire body shook with his words, and immediately she started sputtering out, "Please cum in me. Fuck me and knock me up. I need your cum," she whimpered, and it wasn't a play for her. It wasn't a joke, or a fun game. The amount of truth and desperation in her plea was authentic, and the way she enunciated "your" spoke volumes. She had chosen him, and she needed him alone.

He wasn't really going to pull out of her, but that was what he needed to hear to really satisfy him. The genuine panic and need in her voice. With a few extra hard thrusts, bruising the poor girl's pussy for a long time to come, he grunted and groaned like a wild beast as he rode out the last of their rutting. To the very end it came on hard, his whole body shuddering and shaking as he quaked with orgasm, his cock thickening with each gush of creamy seed deep into her, and a loud gravelly "ahhhh!" punctuating the air repeatedly until he was emptied.

She was just as desperate and needy as the night before that not a drop was wasted, and she pressed back against him even as her body screamed with agony. But oh, how she had enjoyed it. Her skirt was flipped up with the rutting, revealing the soft curve of her behind, that tantalizing view of his cock shoved between her thighs. She pressed her legs against his, but she was unable to vocalize her needs.

Leon took a moment to enjoy the view of her

body so weary and battered, her ass cheeks bright red from his palm strikes. Once he'd done that, he reached over to the spot from last night to retrieve her "instrument" for her, not needing to be told.

"You're gonna swell up real big," he predicted with a grin, imagining the small woman carrying his child.

She shook with eagerness at his comment, her tiny little body impaled by his. "When can I see you again?"

He spoke to her a little differently now, authority in his voice stronger than was there before, possessiveness eeking into his words. "I leave tomorrow morning," he stated, stroking his rough fingers along her side, hip, and ass before he pulled back in the same careful manner, wiping his cock off into her hole before stuffing it full again with the dildo. "I'll come by on my way out of town to ensure you're seeded," he stated.

She nodded, slumping her body down and leaving her ass in the air, the black toy filling her where he'd so recently been. She didn't move from the position, obviously hoping the strange tilt might help her chances.

"Thank you. I'd really like that," she murred, more submissive than she had been earlier. Where before she had been bossy and commanding, their most recent tryst had allowed her to trust his understanding of the situation.

Standing back up, he admired the strange little woman, her physical form, and her dedication to her odd ideals. It didn't take him long to dress again, even at his slow, casual pace, but he moved over to her and sat beside her a moment, rubbing his hand over the painfully sensitive flesh of her battered ass cheek.

"You've not been with any other man as of late, I assume." He continued without waiting, "and if you continue to do so, if when I come back through town you're pregnant, I'll take you away. Out of this town, away from these people and their silly ideas. And you'll get to live like you were meant." He said all this in his husky, postcoital voice not as an offer, but as a detailing of a plan already set in stone.

She nodded hazily, her dark eyes studying his handsome face, flinching just the slightest bit at the attention to her pained behind. Licking over her lips, she managed out, "I look forward to it."

# CHAPTER 12

He stood up then, and with a final look at her bent over like that, he simply left the room and headed on back out. The morning was likely gone now, he thought, but he was starving, and needed to make it to lunch.

Sat outside on the stoop was the girl from the night before, the redheaded woman from the hidden meeting. She looked up at him skeptically before returning back to her book, letting him get on with his day with no further comment.

It wasn't quite so late as he thought, but the rest of the morning was a tizzy of excitement and planning as he struggled to get all of his jobs lined up for the next visit. Most of the previous day had been eaten up by unplanned events, and he had a host of eager tradespeople wanting little favours and deals.

By the time he finally broke away from it all, he'd just finished dinner and was headed back to Tia's general store.

She was tidying up from the day when he entered, and her big smile told him all he needed to know. Her voice was a lot lower as she walked around to him, dressed in a beautiful baby-blue sundress that clung to her breasts.

"I've spoken with her"—she pulled him into a hug, her large breasts pressing against him—"and she's excited, I think. Embarrassed, but excited. She went and got a bath and just got back a little while ago," she explained. "She's upstairs in her room, but I think we should use mine. The bed is larger."

Leon put his arms around the busty woman, tugging her in and holding her close and kissing her on the lips as a husband would. "Give you more memories to think back on when you're falling asleep in that bed too," he remarked with a wry smile, his powerful hand giving her ass a firm squeeze. He was already twitching to life at the thought.

She laughed, a sparkle of excitement in her eyes before she tried to quiet his voice. "Did you maybe want to go talk to her first? See how she is? It might be easier for you to kinda get a feelin' for how she's goin' to be."

With a warm smile and a nod, he spoke huskily as if a father taking on some responsibility—"I'll do just that"—then gave her a full kiss, parting their two lips to push his tongue into her mouth. All the while he stroked her side and kneaded her ass flesh, taking his time with the kiss before he broke it off. "We'll call for you when we're ready then."

"You guys can just barge in. I'll be in my room." She smiled, biting in her lower lip and tasting his lingering saliva there.

He chuckled and gave her bottom a pinch before he moved on, heading up the stairs toward Faith's room. It was hard to contain his excitement at the prospect, but Leon did a remarkable job of it as he approached her door to knock lightly. "Hey, it's me, sexy," he called in a casually suave manner, laying it on a bit thick to lighten the mood.

She didn't just call him in as usual, instead walking to the door and opening it slowly. She was still in her jeans and tank top, but her skin was freshly scrubbed and her hair was still drying a bit, dripping down her back. There was a bit of wetness where it had soaked the material of her top.

Her smile was slow and cautious as she pushed open the door, letting him in and closing it behind him. "Hey, I'm sorry about her. You know how she is."

With a hearty chuckle he moved on in, making himself comfortable in his slow, steady manner. He sat down upon her bed and leaned onto his knees, watching her with a smile. "Does it matter if we finally got what we really want?" he said in a sly, conspiratorial tone that was as much joke as serious.

She shrugged her bare, olive shoulders, joining him on the bed, sitting herself down cross-legged. It was as if being called out on her teasing had taken the wind out of her sails, and instead she was just... normal. She glanced at him out of the corner of her eyes, her smile quirking her lips.

"You don't think it's weird?"

Chuckling at that again, he leaned over enough to put his arm about her, tugging her to him with that extreme ease his great size and strength allowed him, nestling her to his chest. "Everythin' is weird since the fall," he explained quietly, then kissed her head, "but nothin' about caring for you or Tia feels weird to me, Faith."

She nodded, moulding her body into his and obviously feeling a bit more comfortable at his reassurance. She took in a deep breath, unable to look at him as she asked her final question.

"You won't think differently of me?"

Wrapping both of his burly arms about her, he gave her a tender, loving squeeze, his hand stroking up and down along her hip and thigh. "Certainly won't love you any less," he stated assuredly, then added for humour, "but it is only fair. You've seen me in all my glory more than once, and I never get the same treatment."

She laughed, her head dropping down as her shoulders jostled. "Yea, well. You're an easy guy to walk in on," she responded slyly, looking at him curiously. "So we're sure, then?" she mused, the words seeming as though they were an affirmation of her own convictions.

Lifting his hand from her thigh, he gently took her chin and tilted her head up toward him, holding her gaze with his own dark eyes awhile. "Damn sure," he stated firmly, then leaned in, head tilted, and gave her a warm kiss on the lips, a milder version of what he gave to Tia just moments before.

It quickly became apparent just how nervous she was, that thin wall of confidence she had so recently built coming tumbling down. She trembled against him, her lips so soft yet almost unresponsive, uncertain. She tasted so delicious, though, like she had just eaten something sweet, and her body smelled exquisite as he got in so close to her clean flesh.

Leon didn't back down right away, though. He lingered there, his mouth and tongue massaging her lips and giving her time to adjust before he pulled back slowly and squeezed her in his arms again. "I love you, Faith. You've got nothin' to be ashamed or frightened of with me." He gave her a wild, disarming smile. "We don't have to do a thing until you're ready."

She was breathing heavier by the time he released her, and her face was already flushed hot. She licked over her lips, so similar to what Tia had done moments before, and her eyes caught his. She was burning for him, yet she trembled with uncertainty and fear. Above all else, she did not want him to think less of her.

Trailing her hand to his face, she stroked over his jaw so lovingly, her thumb rubbing against his flesh before she nodded.

"I trust you."

With a broadening smile, he touched his forehead down to hers and stroked his thumb over her cheek and neck. "Good. Because there aren't many in this world that I'd give everything for, and you're one of 'em." He leaned in and gave her lips a kiss, just at the corner this time. "We can stay in here, just you and I a bit longer, if you want." His hand trailed down, lightly grazing her neck and shoulder.

She breathed a bit heavier, uncertainty crossing her face. She was obviously considering the feelings of her adoptive sister, and she licked over her lips as she thought. That tiny pink tongue running along the beautifully sculpted lips, she seemed so unaware of her own beauty and power.

She had spent so much time putting up such a powerful front, and it had all crumbled because of him. She squeezed his knee. "Will she mind?"

With a big, uneven grin he rubbed his hand back over her thigh, his thumb between her legs as he felt her. "She can wait. And when you waltz in there on my arm ready to pick up where you and I left off, she'll be confused as hell." He leaned down again and kissed her lips plushly, then again. "Besides, I like my alone time with you."

She trembled, her hands going up to either side of his face, holding him so near to her as if she didn't want his mouth to leave hers. She breathed against his lips, her eyes hooded, "I just wish she didn't think I couldn't do this on my own. I wish she trusted me."

As she held his face, he slipped his own hands around her body, rubbing up her back and holding her in turn. He continued to give her his moist, warm kisses, their lips smacking lightly. "She just wants your first time to be special. Where you've got nothin' to prove to anyone. But frankly, I'm glad it's an opportunity for you and I to share somethin' so close, Faith." His own voice was husky, low, and soothing.

She blinked, having not thought about his rebuttal, but her smile grew as he continued on. She nodded, becoming more adept at returning his oral affections. She mimicked him in slight manners, each time leaving shy and returning more boldly.

"I just need some time to warm up to the idea," she murmured, and for a moment there was a flash of the old, familiar Faith. The vixen that lay beneath the inexperience.

Rubbing his hands over her more and more aggressively, feeling her out as they kissed, him, too, seeming to heat up to their activities, he worked his lips back from hers across her face toward her ear. He murmured to her there softly, "I thought for sure you and I would've ended up together sooner than this. You damn near drive me wild, Faith."

She laughed, the sound soft and embarrassed, nuzzling her skin against his. She seemed to just want to feel him, to experience his body for a while; the heat and the warmth and security that his form brought her. "I was scared," she admitted, the sound so small from such a usually brazen woman.

"I wouldn't have guessed," he responded truthfully in a husky, gravelly voice. Kissing his way down her neck, his strong hands rubbed about her still, moving from her back to her sides, his thumbs beginning to push up around and over her breasts. "You're gorgeous Faith," he said deeply.

She wore no bra. That much was obvious as he roamed her back and sides, the swells of her breasts so firm and tantalizing. Her nipples poked against the fabric of her top, and her breathing grew more shallow.

"Thanks," she murmured, her hands running along his arms, then down to the tops of his hands, holding him against her. "I always liked you. Figured Tia... woulda been pissed, but then she came and talked to me today and... I dunno. Was weird."

He pulled back a little, though his hands never ceased to feel and rub her as he looked her in the eyes. With another moist kiss he asked, "Once we've done this, we can meet, just you and I, in the future. Do it our own way, y'know?" With a broad smile, he kissed her again. "And I've always liked you too."

She kissed him back, sucking on his lower lip exploratively, her arms slowly moving to wrap around him. She was slender, though still healthy, and quite tall. It made her curves look more subtle and drawn out, and the way her small clothes clung to her was exquisite. She managed to look so casual and sexual all at once.

"What's going to happen?" she murmured, her pulse pounding.

Continuing to kiss down her form, his thick lips puckering and peppering her shoulder and neck, he spoke to her in his steady, strong voice. "You and I are going to stay here, touching and doing whatever we want, until you decide you're ready to go into the next room. Then you'll not need to worry about a single thing, Faith. Because Tia and I will show it all to you." His thumbs brushed against her stiff nipples purposefully, then he moved down, kissing them over her top before rising his head up with a confident smile.

She nodded, her breath catching in her throat for a moment before it exhaled with a moan. "Okay," she agreed, her lips quirking into a smile. She relaxed against him with sex off the immediate table, and she allowed herself to get more into his motions, suddenly feeling the fabric of her shorts and top to a degree she hadn't before. She was growing aware of sensations she hadn't noticed, and the warmth and confidence of his body kept edging down her barriers inch by inch.

Shifting, Leon slid one arm about her back, then pressed into the kiss more deeply than before. His tongue delved into her mouth, and he pressed her whole body back, supported by his arms. He made out with her back atop her bed, the thing groaning and creaking beneath his weight as he used his free hand to feel her chest, stomach, and down to her hips and thighs. He took his time exploring her, holding himself back to ease her into things.

Her body yielded to his, her skin so smooth and fresh from her recent bath, feeling as though it had been recently lotioned—not such an easy task after the fall. Her arms wrapped around his thick neck as she kissed him back, growing more comfortable with the motion and following his movements. They were already so warm, the heat in the air growing noticeably the longer they made out.

With a low groan from deep in his chest, Leon felt his own need rising as they slowly made out. His cock was straining against the confines of his pants, and it pushed him forward, urging him to touch with his own fingers betwixt her legs, rubbing over her own sex in a careful manner at first. He was cautious in stoking her fires, but his strength and masculinity was so abundant.

She gasped, and for a moment it felt as though she might try to bolt. Her entire body tightened and tensed, but his skillful fingers didn't leave her scared for long. After a few moments, she relaxed against the bed, but her lidded eyes stared up at him.

"I think it's time," she murmured.

Raising his head up, he gave her a broad smile, eagerness on his own face as he continued to rub her sex, tracing its outline through her pants.

"Almost wish we didn't have to go over there," he said, but he slipped back up off her, and held out his hands, taking hers and pulling her up with gentle ease.

She was a bit bashful, a full flush over her body as she accepted his hand and squeezed. "We don't, but I'd like to," she admitted. She was closer with him now, not straying far from his side even as she walked to the door and opened it. "I want to do this right."

He gave her a proud smile, and put his arm around her, resting his hand on her hip and walking out into the hall together.

"Can't wait then," he said, leading her down the hall to Tia's room. He didn't bother to knock but pushed open the door to lead Faith on in.

Tia was sat on her bed, still in her light-blue dress, and her eyes darted up from her notebook when she heard the noise. Placing it aside, she stood up, the room lit by a few candles, a light scent of natural flowers in the air. She looked so beautiful, her brown hair pulled off her shoulders and piled at the back of her head.

"Hi," she uttered softly, as though she were not wishing to break a spell. "How're you feeling Faith?"

Faith smiled as she looked up at Leon, then back at her "sister." "Fine. Just... didn't want to get too carried away," she added on, squeezing Leon's hand.

Tia walked over to her, shutting the door behind them. "Well, you're safe to get carried away here. It's all up to you. We'll take it slow, though?" she asked, more than told, and Faith nodded.

"I was enjoying..." She flushed, looking away.

Leon leaned over and gave Tia a kiss on the lips before turning his full attentions to Faith again, squeezing her hand back and then rubbing his hand across her stomach. "We both were," he agreed, giving a big smile and pulling the smaller woman into an embrace again, holding her against his chest.

Faith enjoyed being coddled by him, and her fingers rubbed along his chest as Tia reached out to take both of their hands, guiding them to the bed. "Well, I don't have to interrupt. Just, whatever you want. I can show you if you have questions on how to do something," Tia encouraged, looking at Leon. "If you wanted to just keep going." Tia smiled, sitting on the bed, her legs stretching out along the seam with the wall.

Faith looked at Leon as she sat atop the bed, her eyes inquisitive.

With a broad smile to Tia, Leon helped guide Faith to the bed, climbing atop it with the two women, arms still around the less experienced one. "Well, you have seen me and Tia at it more than once," he remarked, looking to Faith with a glint in his eyes, "but you've never really seen it in motion, have you?" He leaned in and nuzzled the woman's neck before kissing it. "Like to see a bit more first?"

"You guys always stopped when I came in," she whispered, a smile sneaking to her lips that revealed a bit more of her intentions on such entrances. Her heart pounded against her chest, craving closeness with the man even as she nodded.

Her expression was one of delicious joy, of excitement and pleasure that she had a hard time containing.

Leon's look began to match hers, and then with a soft suckle of her neck and a kiss of her lips, he slowly untangled himself from around Faith and looked to Tia.

"I think we just got a request," he said, and standing up, he pulled his sweater up off over his head, tossing it away as he bared his broad, hard chest. He took his time, methodically removing his belt and pants, but it all came away quickly nonetheless.

Faith was enraptured, finally having the time—and the approval—to stare. She was hungry for his body, her eyes scanning over him, focussing on the differences in his body from the others around town. She seemed enthralled by his scars, those marks and flecks that marred his beautiful chest, the delightful hue of his body titillating her.

Tia matched his slow motions, stripping herself

out of the blue dress and letting it fall beneath the bed. Her body was so much shorter and more curvaceous than Faith's, and suddenly the young woman's eyes went back and forth between them. She had obviously seen her older "sister" nude many times before, but so rarely in this context.

The centrepiece of Leon's body, his thick, sizeable cock, stood out with its aching stiffness. Moving toward Tia, he took her into his arms in a smooth, comfortable gesture that spoke of their long familiarity. He gripped her ass and held the back of her head as they met in a deep, passionate kiss, and almost immediately he began to push her back to the bed, the two of them moving to crawl atop it.

Tia's arms immediately wrapped around his neck and body, her hands slowly wandering down his back, scratching at him lightly. She moaned against his mouth, her legs spreading and leaving room for his thighs, his cock pressing against her mons lengthwise.

Faith crept closer until she was very nearly touching them, lying back as she watched the two lovers position themselves.

Leon made somewhat of a show of it, though he didn't have to change much. Breaking from his deep, passionate kiss with Tia, he lifted one of the woman's legs, providing Faith with ample view of their two groins, pressed together. Looking to the younger woman, he spoke in a gruff, almost commanding voice.

"Take hold of it, guide me in," he directed, though it was hardly necessary, of course. His practiced hips would've angled himself to impale her with ease.

It seemed to work, though, the shy girl being given a direct task and following it through to the letter. She swallowed as she touched it, feeling the strange hardness covered by the soft flesh. She didn't want to stop touching it, but slowly she rubbed the swollen tip down over her sister's folds, past her clit, and to the wet, willing slit beneath.

Tia whimpered, her eyes closing as she felt him so achingly near. She had made this out to be such an exercise, something for Faith, but she couldn't help the pleasure she voiced.

Leon's meaty shaft throbbed and swelled at Faith's careful, inexperienced touch, the veiny shaft pulsing wide. Bending down, he kissed Tia's large breast, then began to plunge into her cunt slowly, letting Faith get a full view of it as his girth spread those lips wide about his dark width.

With a groan of pleasure, he pushed down until he bottomed out inside her, giving a satisfied sigh as his balls rested against Tia's ass. Then again he pulled back out in such a fashion as to let Faith savour the view.

It was a slow, exquisite torture for all of them, but Faith was fascinated. She shifted her body to get a better view, absorbed in the sight of the slick petals swallowing that pulsing, veined shaft. She licked her lips, feeling her own body tighten and relax in desire and anticipation. Her breathing was heavier, and she could smell their sex in the air.

Tia glanced at the other girl through heavy eyes,

her nipple glistening with saliva, and she throbbed against Leon's cock.

Holding himself up on one thickly muscled arm, he kept Tia's leg up and back as he began to rut into the woman beneath him at a budding speed. His heavy sac began to slap wetly against her flesh beneath him as he angled himself just so to hit her in the right spot, repeating the motion with such fluid perfection as his taut muscles were so well practiced in doing.

His gaze slid between the two women before he said in a husky, sex-laced voice, "That'll be you soon," and bit and licked Tia's calf.

She hadn't realized when it had happened, but she felt her hand pressing against her clit through her shorts, rubbing it absently. Her breathing was so heavy, her breaths so shallow she felt as though she might faint. The sight of watching them fuck was... exquisite, and it felt so naughty. She still remembered a time before the fall, before the commune, and those taboos had stayed with her.

They caused her to lick her lips, and she slowly looked up over Tia's body, watching as the heavy breasts jostled with each thrust. She wanted to touch them, and before she could stop herself, her hand was pressed against the nearest breast, as if to still its heavy motions.

Tia whimpered, looking at Faith with devious eyes.

Leon gave a deep, approving groan at that sight, very much liking the two women touching one another. In reward for the sight he began to pump his hips faster, harder, fucking Tia more aggressively as he gave a throaty growl of desire. "Damn good tits, aren't they?" he said.

Faith's hand retreated, as if she were caught doing something she shouldn't have been, her heart thudding harder against her chest as she nodded, frowning a little bit. She had obviously become intensely self-conscious, but the feeling faded, and her hand returned, and she looked at Tia.

"It's okay?" she asked.

"Mmhmm." Tia smiled, encouraging as always, even as her face contorted in pleasure. "Anything you want, little one."

With his back arched, Tia's leg in hand, he was really pounding the woman now, setting her fleshy mounds to jiggling and rocking more aggressively. It was his way of urging Faith on, and of course, giving Tia more of what she craved, by fucking her with his exquisitely large and sculpted dick.

Grunting huskily he let Tia's leg rest against his shoulder and reached over, lightly stroking his palm over Faith's hair, down her back. "Why don't you get undressed."

Faith's skin prickled with his touch, her head craning into it as if she were a cat being stroked, and she looked to him curiously. She realized, all at once, the speed he was thrusting into Tia and her throat closed off for a brief moment, drawing her lower lip into her mouth and biting down.

"Holy fuck," she murmured, letting the lip pop back out, then staring at Tia's face and seeing only pleasure, pure and sublime. It must have done something to her, because she was quickly bouncing off the bed, shedding her clothes instantly.

She had shaven.

It was recent, and there was a few shades difference in her skin tone where her pubic hair had once protected her, another leftover taboo from the old world. Razors were notoriously difficult to get and keep sharpened, but somehow she had surprised them both.

Her breasts were less than a handful, but firm, topped with perky nipples, and they stood out against her chest. She glistened between her smooth, shaven thighs, and she moved back onto the bed into position next to Tia, looking between the two.

Leon towered over the two women, and he was easily able to reach over and stroke his hard hand across Faith's bare breasts and down her chest across her stomach. He gave the younger woman such a lusty, appreciative look as he ogled her body, letting sight of her fuel his cock pistoning into Tia. Then with a throaty, groaning voice he asked, "You ready?" His fingers moved down to touch across her bare slit, feeling its slick dampness for the first time directly.

Her legs shifted and she rolled further onto her back, her thigh falling away as she shook her head. She seemed shy to ask for it, but she was a far sight better that most first timers, as she actually did. "Just touch for now?" she pleaded.

She was so beautiful, her hair spilling around the pillow, the dark tresses forming a sort of halo around her. She was so smooth and slick to his hand, but he was so large. Tia reached out, grabbing her hand softly in her own, an erotic smile playing on her lips. "Just him?"

Faith took a moment before she nodded, and Tia accepted it well, as usual. She squeezed Leon's arm, rolling from under him.

Leon felt the cling of Tia's wet cunt slip from him regretfully, though he quickly turned his attentions back to Faith with a broad, wanting smile. Moving over her, his glossy cock pointing out, he stroked one hand over her smooth chest, the other dark fingers continuing their toying with her cunt. He kissed down on Faith's breast, skirting her nipple and teasing her areola as he began to expertly finger her, stoking her loins hot. "You're damn wet," he murmured deeply.

Her slippery vulva had already wettened her thighs, the outer labia shining a beautiful shade of deep pink. Her entire body was hot, desirous for him, and she found herself arching toward his mouth, her nipple almost hurting as it stiffened harder against his expert mouth. She never thought this would happen, and seeing his full, black lips enclose around her olive breast was almost too much for her.

Hands clasping the sheets, she writhed beneath him, her entire body electrified by his touch as Tia hung back, watching the two of them as she rubbed at herself.

Leon's dreads fell against Faith's smooth flesh, tickling her sensitive skin lightly as he began to slowly build his kisses into soft suckling, working her nipple into his mouth. The thick digits below, meanwhile, continued their motions, encircling her delicate clit and bringing the girl almost more pleasure than she could handle. His own cock, still carrying a glossy sheen of Tia's honey, pulsed with desire. Even though he knew it'd be inside another cunt soon, it was ravenous for more thrusting.

He gave a throaty growl again and pulled back on Faith's nipple as he suckled, before letting it snap back into place and kissing it.

She toppled forward slightly, bracing herself before she fell back to the mattress, her back arching. Her entire, young body was attuned to his, and she grew more and more desirous for him until she finally uttered, "Okay," her breathing so hard it almost didn't sound like a word.

Tia moaned, though, signifying she'd heard the young woman's request and was pleased with it, her brown fingers rubbing her body eagerly, her free hand rising up to cup her own large breast.

Leon didn't need clarification. He simply took hold of Faith's legs, arranged and moved her as he saw fit, and climbed over her. He was slower, more careful than he was with Tia, if only for the sake of not overwhelming the woman. But once over her, he rested all his weight on one arm, the bicep bulging out as he did, and stroked the backs of his fingers across her cheek. "Take hold of it and guide it in at your pace," he instructed.

Her trembling hand returned to his wet, hard member, holding on to it more tightly and inadvertently pulling back on the foreskin slightly. The sensation took her a little off guard, and her head lifted off the pillow, glancing down at his cock just long enough to see the head push between her inner labia.

She sucked in a breath, seeing that dark tip prod against her pink folds, then stop, forced against her barrier. She winced, but her hand didn't falter, and she tugged him forward slightly.

Leon expected her hymen to be broken by some accident in the past, so he was surprised to feel it impeding him. Leaning his face down, he kissed her plushly on the lips, "It's better if we do this part quick," he said and looked into her eyes for confirmation. With her hand still lining up his shaft, he didn't waste much time, not wanting her to tense up, and he pushed down steadily, forcing his way through that thin wall with his large, dark tool so that it plunged into her a couple inches in the process.

She gasped, her eyes rolling up in her head at the sudden feeling of pain, and then the residual feeling of fullness. Her hands clutched the blanket, and she shifted, trying to find a comfortable position. It wasn't easy, however, as he was such a large man. She glanced down, seeing the thick rod piercing her, and felt her body squirm with the idea.

She had so recently watched him glide into another woman, and now he was within her. A sudden smile and burst of confidence flooded her body and she tilted her head to look at Tia, her eyes bidding Faith over. Tia shifted, all at once ignoring her own pleasure as she curled in against Faith, her top breast spilling onto the other woman's arm and chest.

"Okay," she murmured again, and suddenly

Tia's lips were all over her adopted sister's body, beneath her ear, down her neck, over her collarbone. Her kisses were so smooth and sweet, so seductively soft and wet, and Faith moaned, finding her pain assuaged.

The sight made Leon want to start plowing into Faith's virginal cunt then and there, but his muscles merely twitched all across his chest and ass, and he instead began to push more of his length into her. Reaching as deep as he could go, he began to pull back and slowly build up a motion in her. It was a gentler repetition of what he'd done with Tia, his massive cock throbbing within her wantonly, begging for more as he pumped the poor woman full.

It was almost unfortunate that he was her first. Being so well endowed, he certainly was raising the bar for her other paramours. Still, considering his competition was the man who only yesterday interrupted the plowing of his sister, there was some sweet justice lingering there. Faith's mouth turned and found Tia's, soft and tentative at first before she gained more confidence.

Her hand ran through the other woman's ponytail, urging her closer as the two women kissed, their mouths slowly working together, then pulling away in a sensual dance of tongues and lips. They stared at one another, Tia looking hungry for more. She understood his resistance, and rewarded him for it with a brief run of her hand down his side, cupping his ass gently.

Leon's ass was so hard and well rounded, solid muscle there bulging out, it pressing back into her hand as he seesawed his way back and forth with the increasing action. He was breathing heavily now, lustily watching the two woman.

Reaching over he touched Tia in return, rubbing her shoulder and back. He was in control, he felt, and had these two gorgeous women before him, trading between their deliciously wet and tight cunts. He gave a loud grunt of satisfaction, his other hand moving down and taking hold of Faith's hip and waist as he fucked her harder.

She yelped a bit at the sudden increase of tempo, her breathing stuck again as her heart pounded faster, but Tia was there soothing her. Silencing her with a kiss, she trailed her lips up to the other woman's ear, suckling it gently. In between, she murmured soft reassurances, nuzzling along the outer edge of her ear.

Leon's dark hands stroked over the two women then, feeling out both their bodies, stroking their chests and breasts, while taking time to look down and enjoy the view of his cock plunging into that once virginally tight cunt.

In a husky, lust-ridden voice he groaned, "You're both so damn gorgeous."

They both moved beneath him, shifting so sensually together in their arousal, brown lips working over the slender neck, the high cheekbones, and the beautiful, perfect breasts. Tia flicked her tongue against the aroused nipple, teasing it with her tongue before biting it. She gave it a slight tug and Faith's body moved exquisitely as though being played by a puppet master.

Leon couldn't help but groan in arousal at the scene they were making, his cock swelling inside that already stretched taut cunt, pushing it out wider. Meanwhile he reached down, trying to get his fingers at Tia's sodden cunt, slipping his thick digits inside to finger her as he continued to rock into Faith with such remarkable skill and precision.

His whole body stretched and bulging with glossy muscles in the dim candle light, his dreads bounced, and he looked quite the dark Adonis.

Tia's thigh fell back away from his hand, leaving him unimpeded as he thrust his rough fingers into her silken pussy. She sighed against Faith's breast, the cooling saliva puckering her nub further.

Faith moaned, her eyes squeezed shut. She was in an area between pain and pleasure, even though he was being quite gentle with her. He was just so large it was hard to really be that gentle.

Her lower lip trembled, and she sought to quiet herself once more on Tia's lips.

He kept the same even pace on Faith, building the girl up to some satisfaction methodically as he restrained himself. But with his hand in Tia's cunt, he began to bang the thick digits into her hard; he knew what she could take, and what she had so abruptly taken from her when he had to turn his attentions to Faith, so he was doing his best to make up for it, one of his digits slickly rubbing over her clit as the others dipped inside her.

She was absolutely sodden around his hand, though she was obviously restraining herself for the sake of the younger woman. Still, her lower body acted independent of herself, grinding against his hand as her thigh fell to the bed.

She kissed Faith's lips, her tongue exploring the other woman's mouth curiously, tasting his saliva and her strawberry-scented breath. Their mouths were hot pressed to one another's, and they shared breath between them.

Leon's body was tense. His balls were tightened somewhat from the scene before him and a release he was holding at bay. He knew the girl's first time wouldn't come easy, and he was committed to making it something to remember, but he found himself hammering his hand into Tia harder without even realizing it, some coping mechanism as he watched the two women writhe and kiss one another.

The brutal thrusting was welcome for her, though she was finding it harder and harder to focus on the other woman as her own body began betraying her with shocks and spasms of intense pleasure. Her hand wandered up over Faith's chest, squeezing her breast tenderly and finding herself wanting more. Her kisses were more frantic as the fire began to build along her body, and as her hand ran into Faith's hair, pressing their lips together more tightly, she felt herself explode.

As Leon watched Tia erupt about his hand, he brought the other down across Faith's body and began to stimulate her clit, rubbing his thumb over it. He knew it was a long shot, and the woman likely had about as much as she could take, but he was stubborn. Watching as his dick pumped into her narrow cunt, he worked it so smoothly, grunting needfully all the while.

Faith was overcome by emotions, her pink tongue swirling around Tia's, then retreating as she gasped. She looked up at Leon with a cross between confusion and alarm, but it was quickly stamped out by something far more primal. She gulped down air as her body twitched and, seeing this, Tia quickly brought her mouth back down to the woman's nipple.

She sucked in just the right manners, finding just the right pressure to pull against the taut nub, teasing her along with Leon. Briefly she paused. "Maybe go down on her," she murred before returning to the girl's chest.

With a loud, masculine grunt, he yanked his dick out of her, creating a slick noise. Slipping back, he moved down onto his elbows and knees, over the edge of the bed, and moved her thighs. Eying her puffy labia, he brought his lips to her sex, tasting her feminine folds mixed with the musk of his pounding cock. He began to move his tongue up over it, prodding and provoking her clit as he worked his mouth against her, dark eyes peering up over her form.

Her eyes were clenched shut, but as Tia's hands worked over her, and their collective mouths paid worship to the recently deflowered's body, she trembled. Her entire body was abuzz with new sensations, and the feeling of his wet tongue against her wetter folds sent chills through her. She writhed, but her heels begged him closer, positioning herself just so until suddenly her eyes shot open and she cried out.

Tia didn't stop sucking her nipples, even as the woman convulsed beneath her, licking that smooth, delicate skin, kissing and sucking the puffy nipple into her mouth so eagerly.

While below Leon did much the same, relentlessly tongue lashing her sensitive clit in his frenzy to get the sweet Faith off. He stroked her inner thighs in such a contrastingly gentle fashion as he rode out her climactic release, watching it all over the rise and fall of her body.

Their insistence kept her cumming long after she should have stopped, and her entire body felt so numb, and yet so alive. She writhed beneath them until finally she could take no more. She cried out, loudly, "Stop!" and immediately Tia pulled away.

Leon was slower to acquiesce, but finally did, licking around his mouth, clearing it of the honey as he stroked Faith's soft inner thighs. He gave a satisfied, almost smug, grin to the two women. "I think she liked it," he declared.

Faith was panting and struck dumb with the power of her orgasm, still struggling to catch her breath as Tia backed away, stroking the woman's hair lovingly. She kissed her forehead, but there was nothing sexual in the motion any longer. The moment had passed between the two of them, and now she was once again the older sister caring for her younger.

She pushed back some matted hair from the wet forehead and cooed softly, "You okay, lovey?"

Faith nodded, a half smile crooking her lips, but when Leon's head was finally removed from her thighs, she closed them and curled up slightly. Tia's hand trailed over her body, caressing her softly. "I'll go get you a heating pad for the pain," she murmured, quickly excusing herself from the room.

Leon watched Tia leave, then climbed up atop the bed, stretching out beside Faith. Stroking her hair and lower stomach gently, he spoke to her in a soft murmur, "I wasn't too rough on you, was I, Hun?" He gave her cheek a kiss tenderly.

She obviously didn't have a frame of comparison, but she shook her head, curling tightly against him. She wanted to be held and lavished, the discomfort of her first time finally fully striking her now that she was removed from pleasure.

Leon simply wrapped his arms around her and held her in close to his chest, coddling her against his broad physique. Kissing her temple, he murmured reassuringly, "It's alright. It won't be like this ever again. Just the pains of the first time."

She nodded against him, and only a moment later Tia returned, a bag of hot water instantly finding its way to her lower stomach. Tia curled into Faith's back, her arm draped over the two of them as she nuzzled and kissed Faith's hair. "You're a woman now, my sweet Faith. Nothing left to fear."

Leon gave Tia a private smile between the two of them at that, then leaned over, kissing her on the lips as he held and comforted Faith in his arms. He was still rock solid and wanting, but he was tender with the woman and put that aside as they slowly drifted off to a thick, warm sleep. Tia gave him an apologetic smile for his lack of an orgasm, but the way Faith was curled into him, it was impossible to tear her away.

# CHAPTER 13

He couldn't linger long in the town, and after paying a short visit to Celia, he was headed off through the forest again. It was just an hour or two past dawn, and he had a good meal in his stomach and a lot of reminders of the life he could have there. A life filled with people who love and lust for him, who feel safer with him around, and who miss him terribly.

Yet there always came a time that he had to leave, and strike out on his own once more.

No matter the loneliness of his life right now, and the pangs of missing the people back there, he couldn't live like them. Not all the time, it would drive him insane trying to be a farmer.

Sure, he could be useful in regards to protecting them, too, but that also wasn't the life he had in mind for himself. Standing around, patrolling, and keeping watch over a small community not his own. He'd feel like a servant. And with the world in ruins, that's one thing he'd never be. What he'd said to Celia on that matter reflected his true thoughts. He was thriving in this life, as grim as it could be, and he wouldn't settle. He determined that long ago.

So with his stop there done, it was time to head back to his place. It was about half a day's travel by foot to his home, and he'd have to stop there before heading back out for another rendezvous or expedition to scavenge in the city.

The most he saw on the way back was a deer, though it looked slightly off. Some of the animals did, now, as if they, too, knew of the old gods and what used to lie beneath the earth. Almost maniacal in some manners, yet the graceful dawn let him pass unthreatened.

It was nearing evening by the time he finally got back, the sun already starting to dip below the horizon and casting an eerie glow along his paradise.

His home wasn't much to look at from a distance. Elevated upon a sort of hill with a ring road about it, the building was formerly a massive, suburban construction box store. Now, however, it looked burnt out, the ring road locked with vehicles going both ways, bumper to bumper or rear-ended into one another.

It was all carefully constructed facade however. The vehicles were positioned by him, painstakingly, when gasoline was still able to be found. Together they formed a wall of sorts, deterring a lot of would be intruders who were daunted by scaling the near vertical slope and climbing the jagged mess of vehicles. He'd scorched the brick himself, and though the glass was busted, he had a near invisible, tar-coated box behind the windows to keep out the elements.

It was important for his trips away to make the place look as uninteresting to scavengers, looters, or the wild things as possible. And who would bother to climb that hill, scale that wall of vehicles, just to loot a burnt-out old construction supply building when there were tons of empty buildings all about?

The doors were all well barred and secured, too, with fake "rubble rooms," he called them, behind each exterior door, in case someone did batter them down. So breaking through the big metal doors got you little more than looking upon charred-up rubble that barred your way yet again.

The only genuine access point was a service tunnel hidden in some obscure point. He'd camouflaged it well with foliage and branches, though the big metal vault-like door would be enough to deter most anyone even if they did know it was there.

The old door took several keys to unlock, but entering in, he covered the entrance and shut it up. The long dark tunnel that led up into the building itself would've been treacherous, if not for the fact it was perfectly straight and uncluttered. At the end there was a faint glow-in-the-dark indicator that allowed him to know the stairs were there. Though it was unnecessary, he took pains to make sure there were no signs or sounds of intruders. Satisfied at last, he hit a switch, and the whole of the building lit up. Albeit dimly. The lights exposed a mysteriously strange world of his own construction. The building was massive, easily able to house more than the community he came from, the old steel shelves that were used to hold up heavy metals and lumber now mostly supported a latticework of makeshift chambers, each a "home" in their own right.

It was a scaffold village, suspending on wood and metal, with walkways suspended eight feet in the air. The purpose was also fuelled by his paranoia. It was another security measure, both against intruders and potential flooding, keeping him, and any who might join him—which was nobody right now—safe from the damages, with a high perch.

A trained engineer, he had made it all work, and the lights were powered by old solar panels he'd scavenged from the store itself and placed upon the roof. He didn't get much power from them, but with all his time away, it was enough to allow him to keep the lights on when home, with extra to spare.

Moving to a hidden nook, he pulled a rope and let a ramp come sliding down from above. One of the hidden access points, he climbed on up, heading to one of the "buildings" within his building. He moved about frequently, also for security, but the last place he'd stayed in was still where he'd kept his favourite change of clothes and a store of food.

It was a long day of travel, and he was ready to eat and relax. He'd do just that, too, after he'd checked everything and climbed atop the roof to make sure the solar panels and water collectors were in place and functional.

His home was exactly as he left it, leaving him to spend his night peacefully alone. With all the business of the preceding days, sleep found him quickly, and it wasn't until dawn that he woke once more. After the fall, most individuals had returned to their natural rhythms of following sunrise and sunset, their bodies adjusting quickly without the false lights.

By the time he set out for the city, the sun was just peeking over the forest. The route to the heart of the city seemed straight forward, but with roaming bandits and wild dogs, not to mention any other manner of large animal, it still required caution.

He had his favourite places in the city, hidden stores and abandoned homes, but after so long it was getting harder to find things in a good condition. With his skill, however, he always managed something.

The city was large and urbanized, densely packed in the middle with high buildings and large stores. Some of it had been cleared out with the rise of the "Government," the self-proclaimed police of the area. The Traditionalists, like Tia, took to more secluded places, and anyone such as he with a taste for individualism got the hell out of their grasp as quickly as possible.

Glorified bandits, they were termed.

Leon had in mind things to get, for his own use, for trade, special requests. Before leaving Tia and her crowd he'd met with the man to go over what it was exactly he'd like. With any luck, it wouldn't be too hard to get, not for Leon anyhow. He knew his way around, and with all the clothing stores and abandoned dressers and closets in a city this size, what he wanted was out there. Somewhere.

The going was always slow though, because he didn't rush things. He took his time, agonizingly so, gun at the ready, always scanning the area ahead. He was a big man, but that didn't keep him from creeping ahead stealthily on his way to his first target, one of the ritzier clothing stores.

Christian had still obviously had troubles thinking in such terms of what Leon could get for him, only requesting a few clean pairs of rather simple, though attractive, clothes. A couple of button up shirts and pants, a jacket for winter, some boots, and undergarments. He obviously wasn't thinking big, and it was Leon's chance to impress.

As he turned the block toward the upscale stores, however, there was a howl let loose. A few miles away, he knew from experience just how these packs moved and how far their howls were based on the way they bounced off the building. Another responded.

After their masters died off and could no longer care for them, the dogs of old returned to being beasts. Worse than that, he would bet whatever those damned things were, those gods from elsewhere, had done something to them. They were ravenous monsters now, and he knew better than to risk encountering them.

With a quick scan, he looked about, trying to find the best place to slip into and hide, to await their passing.

At the last moment he saw an outside stairwell leading up to an opened window in a tall building. Scrambling up it, he could see the three dogs converge beneath, sniffing the air for him. Large, vicious-looking things, he could almost see a red glow in their eyes before he ducked in the window.

It smelled inside. A rotted corpse sat at a computer console. It was obviously an office space prior, likely of the store below. The room he first entered was small, though only occupied by that one body, likely a middle-management sort, by his dress. Against the closed door, however, there was the sound of scratching. A shadow moved along the bottom as whatever it was out there paced, scratching on the door at regular intervals.

It was a closer call than he'd have liked. These damn mutts could cling to a scent persistently, and he'd rather not have to try taking them out. Guns were noisy, but knives were dangerous, requiring him to get up close. He wore thick clothes in layers, his trench coat, sweater, and layers of leather padding keeping him pretty safe from bites. But there were no guarantees, not even with his riot armour looted from a police station.

Satisfied the pack was kept out, he began to search about as best he could, trying to find some way to another area of the building, or out entirely, a route the dogs couldn't follow.

The room was in a corner, having two rather large windows including the one he came in through. The door likely led to a hallway, and were he able to get through whatever animal was out there, he might be able to move freely within the building. The scratching continued, however, growing louder and more insistent. A soft whining came from the beast, though there was no howl or bark to address the pack. It could be anything, though he knew from experience it was more likely an escaped house pet or a fox at this point.

He wasn't about to just sit around and wait things out. That wasn't his way. Hearing just the one on the other side, and peeking beneath to try and gauge if he saw the shadows of more than one dog's legs, he stood up.

Sliding his hunting knife free, he slipped his trench coat off. The heavy garment, he judged, would allow him to throw it over the dog, blinding it and rendering it unable to hurt him, and then he could pin the damn thing down and stab it. It'd probably mess up his coat with blood, but hey, that was the least of his worries.

The moment the door opened, whatever it was on the other side scampered away, frightened by the sudden motion. He only caught the tail end of light orange fur as it slid out of view and around the corner. With nothing else impeding his way, he was free to head down the stairs and into the department store below.

Struck off guard by the sudden departure of the animal, he slung his coat back on and moved ahead. With the rifle over his shoulder he had his hunting knife in hand, fighting ready as he pushed on to search the rest of the building as quickly and quietly as he could for a way out.

The rest of his scavenging was uneventful. Walking through the upstairs of the building, he found a stack of books abandoned in a corner of one of the offices which he quickly pilfered. He was able to easily procure a large mass of men's clothing, not to mention a few lovely dresses for women.

There wasn't a soul to be seen, leaving the city eerie and wild feeling. It was surreal, walking the barren streets and not hearing a single person. To not see anyone walking between the stores. It was always a little unsettling, but as the day grew later, he knew not to tarry.

Another pack of dogs were walking the streets just before he got home, but with his keen listening and evasive maneuvers, he was easily able to avoid drawing their attention.

He'd lucked out, he realized. Though he'd had a narrow brush with danger, it had paid off immensely. But he needed to rest, and plan.

His routine was so steady. Head into the city. Grab what he could. Return home to his empty nest. A cat had found him on his third trip out, following him home and begging for scraps, his black frame thin and emaciated. He had a strange limp, likely the cause of his kindness to a human and his inability to hunt.

He couldn't help but sigh at the sight of the poor thing. Though in the end a combination of loneliness and pragmatism won out; he'd keep the cat and care for it. With the limp it'd probably be a lousy hunter, but hey, the rats probably wouldn't know that right away. She might serve to scare the things off.

It was a week and a half before he saw something out of the norm of Bandits and Government. His usual trek was impassable, a large black bear family threatening him down a different, strange path. Through the edge of the forest that surrounded the town, it was almost as if someone had formed a road, but it was so small and indistinguishable. If it hadn't been for his skills at tracking, he'd never have seen it.

# CHAPTER 14

Pangs of missing the women back at Tia's town were pushed aside, as he got down to business. Following the trail, he set out with great caution to determine if this was something to be concerned about or not. Any new encampment of people was something to watch out for.

It curved away from the city, and for a few moments he thought he had lost it before he heard a light voice. It sounded as though it were a woman, singing. As he neared it, he could hear the words to some old world song that was far older than the voice that sang it so emotionally.

Coming upon a very small clearing, he could see her back as she hung up some clothing on a line. She was dressed in a light skirt and an airy top, her black hair pulled to the side in a ponytail. Her shoulder blades were visible through the almost see-through top, and he could see them tense, her motions stopping as she turned to face him.

Wide, black eyes bored into his, her bangs swept to the side across her arched brows. Her lips turned downwards, and she immediately grasped the gun from the holster on her thigh, pointing it at him.

Her English had an Asian accent to it, though she spoke it fluently.

"Don't come closer."

Leon hadn't had his gun pointed at her, so entranced by her singing was he, though at her alarmed demand he lowered it further. "Hey," he said in a smooth, calm voice, "it's okay." Taking his second hand off the rifle he tried to look as harmless as he could, though it was difficult, being six and a half feet tall and a mountain of muscle garbed in police armour and a trench coat.

"I was just investigatin' the trail," he explained softly.

She hissed, her beautiful face contorting in annoyance. "Fuck!" she exhaled. "Where'd you pick up on the trail, huh? I don't have anything here for you to take." Looking around the clearing, it was likely true. A small wooden hovel and a fire pit were hardly cause for celebration, and she stepped toward him with her handgun raised. "Show me."

Slowly he brought the rifle back around behind him, slung over his shoulder by the leather strap. "I ain't a bandit, nor a crook," he stated firmly. "And as for where I picked up on your trail... fine. This way," he said, turning and beginning to walk slowly.

Watching her, he began to move along at a slow pace. "I was just curious as to if I had new neighbours... and whether I should avoid 'em," he explained in the same deep, soothing voice. Though he couldn't help but be amazed by the pale, petite woman he'd just stumbled upon, her obsidian hair in such a stark contrast. She was like something out of a movie of the old world, he thought to himself as she pointed the gun at him.

"Neighbour?" she asked, her voice going a bit high with fright before she regained her calm. "You live around here?"

Her shirt was buttoned up the front, but it did nothing to hide the fact that she was nude under the transparent shirt, her black skirt landing at the middle of her thighs.

Leon kept a calm exterior, didn't show that he was nearly ready to drop to his knees before this woman already, so beautiful was she. Continuing on, he nodded slowly. "My place isn't far from here"—he glanced back down the path—"though it's a lot harder to find, so I'd be surprised if you knew it." Pointing ahead, he said, "I stumbled on it just ahead."

She looked around the trail, lowering her gun only just then looking up at him. "What about it gave it away?" she asked, her voice still stern but a lot softer now. It was easier to see this woman singing in her front yard as her guard was slowly dropping.

Clearing his throat, the tall dark man spoke quietly. "I was driven off the main route I take by some bears," he explained. "And I've got my share of tracking skills, so I noticed the forest here was a bit...

off." He looked to her—"The name's Leon by the way"—and gave a light smile, very faint.

Her lip curled slightly as she rubbed her forehead, brushing the black bangs from her eyes toward the ponytail at her side.

"Well, I guess it's time to move on then," she murmured, looking a bit crestfallen at the prospect. Seeing as how he hadn't yet hurt her, she lowered her gun to her side, letting it hang there limply.

"Adrianna," she responded in turn, looking back toward where he'd pointed out as his general location. "How far away are you?"

Her voice was so lovely. The more calm she became, the sweeter and softer it grew. It was so lyrical with her accent that it was hard to pay attention to the words. He could simply listen to her speak all day.

Stopping, he turned and faced her completely, his smile growing without it even intending to, he was so taken with the woman, her looks, her voice. "Well that's a shame to hear," he said, one hand up at the strap of his gun, keeping it there behind him, the other at his side. "Would've been nice to have a neighbour that's not a bandit, a wannabe boss, or a rabid dog for once." He cracked a bit of a wry grin. "And I'm barely a stone's throw away. In fact... I'm a bit embarrassed I didn't notice you here sooner, within so short of a walk of my place," he admitted.

She frowned, her gun slowly pressed back into the holster. "Don't think I can't get to it in time if you try anything," she warned him, beginning to move back toward her cabin. "I just got here a couple weeks back. Was a wonder I wasn't found sooner if you could find this place. No offence."

Her attitude and crack made him bust out into a chuckle. Before she was gone too far he called out, "If you're interested, before you leave, I've got things ta trade." He put on his most charming grin, with a bit of humour to it.

She stilled, turning back to him curiously.

"What type of things?"

She didn't look much like the material type of individual, living ostensibly on her own in a shack with barely anything in it, especially if she was a nomad. But nomads always needed a few things — clothes, protection, shoes.

Seeing her interest piqued, he took a few slow, tentative steps closer so they were back to casual speaking distance again. "You name it," he began. "Books, clothes, food. Though," he said with a certain degree of confidence, "my speciality is findin' and repairing old world tech." With a shrug of his shoulders ,he explained, "You name it, I've probably scavenged and repaired it at some point. Guns, radios, even TVs." Holding up his hands in mock surrender, though, he said, "But I ain't carryin' all of that on me right now, if you're thinkin' of robbing me. Just a warning."

"I think I'd notice if you had a TV strapped to your back," she quipped, but her lovely voice made it seem like such a delicious reprimand. "I do not have much to trade in return."

With a jovial chuckle, he responded, "The opening line of every shrewd negotiator." With a grin, he added, "I know to be wary with you then." He looked back down the path toward her place. "Since I've already seen it, did you care to care to have a look and discuss back at your place? You can see what I've got on me, and if there's somethin' you need, we can discuss that too."

"That is fine. I will be gone from there quickly," she spoke in her singsong voice, seeming a bit more uplifted, if nothing else, as she headed back through the trail. She obviously knew it well, and her heavily traversing of it is likely why it was easy for him to follow, even though she was so thin and small.

Returning back to her hut, she opened the door to let him in, revealing a small one bedroom with a table and a bed stuck unceremoniously to either side of the shack. There was very little room, and it was hard to even understand who put this house here or why.

Sizing up the tiny place, he moved to the table, slinging his gun off and leaning it to the wall in a careful manner, so as to not alarm the woman. "You certainly didn't pick the glitziest place in the neighbourhood," he said. "No wonder you didn't stick out."

Pulling off his backpack, he put it onto the table, and began to undo the straps. "You must be tougher and more capable than you look," he said, giving her a pointed once-over that was more sexual than it appeared, "to survive on your own like this."

She was a single Asian woman living amidst a sea of bandits and bullies, of rabid dogs and wild animals, and it was easy to understand why he would have underestimated her. Still, as she sat across from him and crossed her legs, her hands rested atop her knees and she looked serious. If there was anything about her that stood out beyond her beauty and intoxicating voice, it was that.

"If we're less capable than we look, we die," she assured him, her bangs landing just below her sculpted brow. "And so. If I'm to travel, I will need supplies. Many."

He couldn't help but look down across her leg as she sat there like that, but then perhaps that was her aim. "Fair enough," he said with a firm nod, liking the woman and her self-assuredness more and more.

Seating himself at her little table as well, the chair groaning beneath his weight, he pulled out a pile of goods from his backpack. He hadn't taken much with him.

"I was on my way to go scavving," he explained, "not on my way back, or out to trade. So I ain't got much on me." He pulled out the food supplies he was taking with him, things in tins and sealed canisters, easy and light for travel, but nourishing. Tinned sausages with a twist-off lid, fruit cups. Things that were worth more than gold in the wastes of civilization. He ate a lot, though, to keep up his muscle, so it ended up being quite a bit. "And like I said, I got things I can get and bring back here within a few hours if you can make a tempting offer."

"As you can clearly see, I do not have much to barter. You may have thought you were otherwise calling my bluff." She leaned forward, her arm leaning against the table.

"Still, I've told you what I will need. I think it is only fair you let me know what you might find useful. Perhaps something might fall into my lap while you're out collecting the rest of my supplies."

With a wry grin at that, he chuckled briefly. "I see." Nodding slowly, he pulled a few more things from his backpack; a very sturdy, well-built compass, a few extra knives, watch, thermal canteen. "Shame you're movin' on so soon." He reached up and stroked his chin, looking over at her.

"I ain't got a lot of need for much of anything," he said, "mostly I trade with some of the farmers and the like for fresh vegetables I don't make myself. Or the occasional hard-to-find odds and ends I need for repairing gadgets and the like."

He let that hang there a while, not wanting to get too explicit yet.

She looked over at the wide array of items, her fingers tapping along the edge of the wood. How did she grow her nails out so long in the wild like this? She touched the edge of a knife blade, hefting it in the air and moving it about to test its weight before settling it back down.

"I am fine for food. What about bullets?"

He nodded, slowly. "What calibre? I've got all kinds, but I only carry the one with me. Though I don't usually trade in ammo and guns lightly. I don't like to arm potential trouble, if you get my position," he said smoothly. He looked to the handgun, having already recognized it of course. "For that one?"

She nodded, her thigh shifting to allow the gun to come into better view, with the side effect of exposing a lot more of her leg. He could almost barely see the cusp of her ass as she tilted in the chair. "Since I will be moving, you should trust I will be no trouble."

He didn't want this woman to move, he realized. Though he wanted to slap himself for giving a damn. That kind of thinking got you killed. "That I can do," he said easily enough. "You're trained in it, I take it? Or at least well practiced?" he asked, genuinely curious.

"I will not kill you while loading it," she reassured him as she leaned forward, her hand cupping her chin, fingers pressing against her lips thoughtfully. "Other than that, I usually have everything I need. But since you will not trade lightly, what will it cost me?"

The fact he could see through her top was making this agonizing on him, constantly distracting him from thinking clearly. Pulling his helmet away, his thick dreadlocks falling down to the sides of his face, he scratched his head in thought. He was a strikingly handsome man himself, of course, his smooth, chocolate complexion flawless, his jaw wide and masculine. Full lips, dark piercing eyes. He was known to make ladies swoon with his protective, capable manner.

But she was doing a number on his confidence it seemed.

"I don't know what you have," he said, trying not to look over her body, "though if it's true what you say, and you don't have anything worthwhile to trade..." He shrugged. "We could work out a deal to benefit us both."

She nodded at him, her lips quirking just so. Fuck, she was gorgeous. She leaned back in the chair, straightening her skirt once more, though she did nothing to move it further down her legs. Her new pose only did more to try to tantalize him toward her bare breasts, only slightly hidden beneath the dark, transparent shirt.

"How long did you say it would take?"

"A few hours," he said quickly, not willing to show more weakness than necessary to this woman. "I don't carry handgun ammo on me," he stated. "I stick to my rifle for the most part." That was true, it was what he trained with the most.

Sitting back in the chair, it creaked beneath his weight, and he folded his thick, muscular arms across his chest, looking across at her, a firm façade hiding his reverence for her dainty features, her pale beauty.

"Then I will stay here until nightfall and see what I might find to barter with," she agreed, standing up from the table. Her breasts were almost perfectly in his line of sight, and just out of reach. They were so perky and well rounded, small enough that she didn't need a bra yet large enough...

It had been almost two weeks since he had seen another woman, let alone touched one, and there was something about her body language that was off-putting. She was so close... He could smell her and it was almost like French vanilla, a light, warm fragrance.

Shaking those thoughts from his mind, he replied in his own satiny voice, "I'm sure you will." He pushed his things back into his bag, and looked around. "Shame again that you'll be movin' on. A friendly neighbour that's open to trading would be a welcome change of pace." Closing it up, he remarked, "Normally I gotta hike most of a day for that." His dark eyes travelled down her form again as he hefted the back, slinging it over his shoulder.

"I'll be back before nightfall," he said.

She followed him to the door, looking after him as he made his way toward the city, and as he moved past the clearing, he could hear her singing once more. An eerie, dark song that reverberated through the trees and filled the air with her soft, sweet voice.

# CHAPTER 15

It was strange. His head pounded, the sensation growing the further away he got. Her song echoed in his ears, the melancholy beauty of it, and he wanted to please her. To find these bullets and just get the fuck back to her. The trek took too long, even though he didn't see anything along the now deserted paths. Not even an animal moved into his way.

His movements were faster as he tried to reach his home sooner, ignoring the headache that throbbed at the back of his eyes.

Arriving back, he had to chastise himself several times for not being careful enough, but overall he was just struck with the urgency of needing to do something for her. He took the bullets, then grabbed up a few extra things. Foremost one of the communicator radios he'd repaired, stuffing it into his bag and hurrying on back.

The prospect of being near to her made his headache dim, moving out into the still afternoon. It felt as though things were finally looking up for him, some idea formulating in his head that he couldn't quite put his finger on. Still, he knew his luck was about to change, and had a strong suspicion it was tied into this strange, gorgeous woman.

# CHAPTER 16

By the time he arrived back to the squalid hut, he was feeling joyful and positive for the first time in many days. She was no longer outside, her clothing pulled in off the line, and a candle burned in the hut. It flickered and elongated her shadow from wherever she was in the room, but there was no more singing. It was simple silence as he knocked on the door.

The seconds passed torturously as he waited for that brass knob to turn, but when it finally did and he smelled her heavenly scent once more, his muscles instantly relaxed.

"Ah, you're back. I was getting afraid you'd stood me up."

She was the most beautiful woman he'd ever laid eyes on, he realized. Some nagging part of his brain told him he was being stupid, and not careful enough with this woman. She could've been waiting for him to return to shoot him and take the bullets.

That part went silent before long, though, and he continued smiling to her. "Stand you up? My only neighbour? I couldn't bear to do it," he said, letting his backpack slip off his shoulder so he could hold it up.

She let him into the room, a bag settled on top of her tiny cot. Obviously all her worldly belongings were shoved into there, though it really wasn't large. She settled back into her seat at the table, a mug of some herbs placed just in front of her, half drunk.

"I'll be leaving at dawn," she assured him, and he suddenly was wrenched with a feeling that he simply could not let her leave. He thought of his plans, of having a kingdom of his own, and with her he could attract so many more, surely.

Moving to the table, that knot in his gut, he laid the backpack down and began to pull out the ammo boxes. "That's a shame," he began, "a real shame in fact." His own dark gaze flitted to her. "You must move around a lot then? Never staying in one spot too long? Must be rough."

"I only make it a few weeks before someone finds me, usually. Sometimes months, but never in the winter. Spring and fall are usually the only times I'm able to really make a place home." She leaned in, still wearing the translucent blouse and her skirt with the gun strapped to her thigh.

"It gets very lonely."

As if in a daze he slowly sat himself down, looking to her. "I know exactly how you feel," he stated, pulling off his helmet and laying it aside. Shaking his dreads free to their natural state hanging loosely about his head, he continued, "Gets tiresome. I gotta admit." He licked his lips. He wanted to blurt out something pathetic, but struggled to make himself not. He was gonna work this coolly if he was gonna do it at all.

"I can imagine. How big's your place?" She crossed her leg again in that subtle, meaningful manner, exposing the strong outer thigh toward him as she moved to sip her tea once more. "Did you want any?" she asked as she placed the mug back down on the table, and the smell was almost as divine as her.

He nearly laughed, because his place was a town in itself compared to her shack. "Big enough for you, me, a dozen others and then some," he said, his eyes flicking to what she was drinking. Common sense and his natural caution told him to say no, but part of him couldn't let himself distrust her. "Sure."

She shifted to the small area that served as the kitchen and the pot that steamed on the counter, going to fill the mug at its side. It was already prepared, apparently, for his arrival, and she stirred it before bringing it back to him.

"It's hot," she warned, licking her pink lips thoughtfully. "The bigger the place the lonelier it is, isn't it?"

With a slow nod and muttered thanks he took the mug. "It is," he said and peered around. "Guess that's the reason behind your setup. But for me"—he shook his head and raised the mug just before his lips—"I wanted to plan. For kids. Lots of 'em. A fine woman to help me lead a crew. Though none of that has materialized yet," he said, blowing on the hot liquid. "I'm too picky." He took a sip at last.

"Shame," she murmured, mimicking his motions and taking another sip. "There's so few around, it's hard to be picky. I can empathize, though," she added on, her voice taking on that melodic hint, mixing with her foreign accent. "And yes. I live small because I don't wish for a constant reminder of the singularity of my existence."

Looking her over pointedly atop his mug he lowered it to the table. "Woman like you would have her pick of all the men in the ruins of civilization," he said pointedly. "Woman like you looks like she'd have been a supermodel before the fall." He wet his lips, barely able to restrain himself from asking her to stay with him in the most blunderingly amateurish way.

"Beauty isn't a virtue in these ruins." She tilted her head slightly, her side-slung ponytail dipping away from her head, her bangs following suit. "Bandits, bosses. Imagine how little you like being neighbours with them then ask yourself what they might see me as."

Lowering his eyes, he gave a weak sign, showing he understood. "What about a lone scavenger?" he asked, the words just blurting out without him thinking about it. "Able to look out for you at least. Keep you hidden and safe," he tried to salvage this massive proposition to a woman he barely knew. Though part of him wanted him to mess it up; he couldn't trust her with his home location anyhow!

"You aren't like the others," she cooed, taking a long sip of her tea before pushing the bottom of the mug away, disinterested in the stems. "You haven't tried to hurt me. You've brought me ammo to defend myself," she said certainly, no question in her tone.

"You want the world to be a better place."

Her words were like sweet balm to his nervous brain, and he smiled widely at her. "The ammo is yours," he blurted out, "to take, regardless. I look out for the people I care for"—he nearly choked at that pathetic line—"and I'm starting to like you."

"Just starting to?" she asked curiously.

She was unlike any woman he'd ever met before. Her calm demeanour was off-putting, and the casualness of her confidence was amazing. She seemed to have everything in control, able to handle any misstep along the way, and her smile lit up her face as if it were some reward that he had strived for an eternity.

Leon merely gave a shrug, a sort of boyish shrug that seemed to indicate he was out of his league. Though the large, strikingly handsome man should've known better. "Keep 'em regardless of what happens. But," he began, hesitating for just a split second, "if I might somehow talk you into stickin' around..."

"How would you do that?" she inquired, her dark eyes staring at him from under those black lashes. She brushed her bangs from atop her brows, quirking them at him.

He sat back in his chair, sniffling a little as he thought. Crossing his arms over his chest, he responded. "There's a few ways I might try," he began, trying to sound confident, though he had trouble being himself around her. It wasn't natural.

"I know I could offer to take you to my place. It's secure, ain't never been uncovered by anyone in all the time I've been there. Well defended. Hidden." He cleared his throat. "But I realize that's a risky proposition for a lady on her own. To put her trust in some man she just met to come stay with him like that, so..." He trailed off, trying to gather his thoughts before giving her an alternative.

"So it's just you in this castle on the hill, secured from bandits and bosses and other nasty Tribals," she mused out loud, looking down at his mug skeptically. "You are there to defend all night?"

He looked to her abruptly. He'd never said where he lived exactly. Dammit, he must've been careless, let her see where he was headed. Swallowing, he shrugged. "I ain't there all the time, it's true. I go out during the day to scavenge mostly. And I do go on trips to trade about, sometimes away for a few days. But... the place ain't never been discovered while I'm away. Ain't never had so much as a small animal get in while I was away." His throat was dry with worry that he'd fucked up and given away too much. That she might shoot him down!

She leaned back in her chair, uncrossing her leg and then recrossing it in the opposing direction as she stared at him thoughtfully. "I see. How long have you been there?"

He was riveted by her every movement, the crossing of those long, pale legs of hers like watching a sensual dance. Dammit, he was losing his mind.

"About two years now," he said, licking his lips. "I can stay home more. If I had reason to. I don't need to scav or trade as much as I do. It just keeps me occupied," he offered, trying to curb his desperation.

"Everyone needs a hobby," she conceded, standing up. His height allowed him to be almost just at her breasts, and he had to look past those perfectly shaped globes to see her face, or so he justified. They poked against the shimmery shirt so tantalizingly. It was strange she wore such a tempting item when worried about what the bandits might do to her.

Her hand reached out, lightly cupping around the back of his neck, squeezing him there. "I wouldn't mind settling down for at least a few more weeks. I sense a lot of potential around here."

Swallowing as she worked him so proficiently, he stared up at her. "Give me time at least," he began, his usually authoritative voice a bit quieter, more gentle, "to convince you what you might get from sticking around with me." Gods, he felt like a boy again before this beauty. He was even rubbing his palms into his biceps nervously.

"I can afford you a week to see how things will be. If I don't like it, well, this is not a contracted agreement," she purred out in her singsong voice. She sounded so docile, yet so commanding all at once, as if he were really convincing her and she was finally relenting, despite the fact that she was obviously working him over.

"Will you be home this week, then?"

He nods slowly, though he had been planning to

go visit Tia. "I will be. For you," he added on. Then, to snap himself out of his stupor, he reached into his backpack and pulled out one of the radio communicators. "I repaired this," he stated, laying it before her. "We can talk from my place to yours. You can get in touch with me any time if there's trouble," he stated. Having thought about this on the way back. He'd repaired several of the things in case he ever set up some aid in his home base.

She looked down upon it thoughtfully, then back at his face. She still stood over him, so temptingly, her hand stroking the back of his thick neck. "I thought you were going to take me back to your place," she mused. "Unless your place is so large I'll need to speak with you through one of these. Still, I admire your forethought."

His eyes widened, he'd been so wrapped up in having to convince her into this he didn't realize she was agreeing to come back with him already!

With a broad, toothy smile, he reached out, resting his dark hand on one of her pale knees. "No that's—" he broke off. "You can come back with me right now. If you don't mind a bit of travel in the dark," he stated, eager to please.

"With you, I think we'll manage." She smiled that slow, tantalizing smile. How was it possible that so much of her mood shifted with his? That cool, calm demeanor lightened by just the upturn of the corner of her lips, as if it were some great reward for him.

"I am already packed."

He stood up at that, putting his things back into his backpack and shouldering it. "I'll take your things for you," he insisted. Whatever hold she had over him was irresistible. He couldn't shake it despite his best attempts. "It's a long trek, I don't want you to get there tired."

"Thank you."

She grabbed their mugs, dumping out the remnants in the small sink before tossing them, the spoon, and the pot in her bag as well. It was small, but quite heavy and seemed a bit jagged and bulky. Grabbing just enough ammo, she unholstered her handgun and reloaded it—it had been half full previously—then kept it in her hand at her side as she opened the door, waiting for him to lead the way.

Hoisting her things, he flung them over his shoulder and then set out. Despite the odd circumstances, he couldn't have been happier than he was then.

The trek back wasn't bad. The extra weight of her things wasn't that much, really. He was used to taking more on his long trips to trade, after all. As they approached the hidden entrance way to his home, he felt an irritating sense that he was being madly irrational, but he shrugged it off. "It's through here," he said, leading her to the camouflaged entranced and beginning to clear away the bramble that kept it masked.

She had been silent the trip back, and she was no less so now as she stepped through his hidden corridor, still letting him lead. She holstered her gun once more as they stepped into the secured location, a statement of her confidence in him.

Sealing everything up behind them, he explained

his defensive measures to her in great detail. He was a bit proud of his work, and it came through as he guided her down the corridor.

She took it all in with great interest, listening to him intently. She kept step with him, walking so closely that her arm brushed against his a few times.

"I see," she murmured. She was thoughtful and reserved, but didn't seem displeased.

Coming to the end of the corridor, he paused. "But aside from the security, here's the best part." She couldn't see the grin on his face for the darkness, but then the lights went on. All about them the dim, low-energy-consuming lights went on, illuminating a world of elevated homes, suspended on steel and hard wood, all in a neat and well-ordered fashion. "Welcome to your new home," he said cheerfully.

For a moment, he swore she was awestruck, but then the fleeting look disappeared, replaced with calm approval as she looked about. She felt so small in such a large place, and her eyes went up to his. "You have spent much time working at this," she stated.

Grinning, he gave her a nod. "Oh yes. As you say, we all need our hobbies. And aside from scavving and trading, this was my main hobby. Makin' this place the perfect defensive base." He licked his lips and gestured for her to follow. "C'mon. I don't keep anything down here on the ground floor," he stated.

Moving ahead, he went to one of the hidden nooks and pulled a rope within, causing one of the ramps to slide down perfectly as he'd engineered it to. "When it was a construction place it also sold some furniture," he explained, "so there's tons of big beds and the like." This was the first time he'd ever shown anyone his home, and he was revelling in the opportunity to show off his work.

She was quite interested in his revelations, even as she did her best to maintain her posture and confidence. She didn't let up, even for a moment, to let him think he had the upper hand.

The thought struck the back of his head he should be grateful that she was here to allow him this moment. A strange thought, but as she smiled at him and revealed those white teeth, he knew it was true.

Returning her smile with his own, adoring look, he led her to the largest of the suspended "homes." "There's a store of food in here already. And I've got clothes and things about. Women's clothes, I mean. Though"—he turned to her as he laid down her pack inside the door, then his own—"I don't know how much of it will fit your very petite body." His words were adoring. It all seemed to fit in place now. All this preparation, it was building up to giving HER a place to call home.

She nodded at the compliment, her eyes fluttering just slightly to make her wide eyes seem more inviting.

"And this is where I will stay, then?" She quirked her head to the side. Her bangs hung off her face just so, the beautiful hairstyle doing so much to accentuate her pale, Asian beauty.

Nodding to her with that same stupidly happy look on his broad, brown face, he said, "Unless you prefer another. But this is the best," he said, looking around, the place bigger than her own little shack of earlier. It had to be just to fit the large king-size mattress. "It was mine, but"—he looked back to her—"there's no need to share, if you don't care to." Why was he being so dumb? Part of him could at least acknowledge he WAS being dumb.

Walking around the room, she inspected it, lifting herself up on tiptoes at one point and accentuating her thin but shapely legs, that swell of her ass facing him before she turned, walking back toward him. He could smell her French vanilla scent, and he leaned in a bit closer.

"Where would you stay?"

He spoke softly, almost in a trance. "Wherever would make you feel safest," he said, his voice warm and concerned. He only cared for this sensual beauty before him. His cock was rock hard, though he was oblivious to it bulging through his worn pants.

The way her eyes dropped spoke to the fact that she wasn't, but she maintained quite calm. There was a bit more sensuality in the way she walked away from him, though. The slightest of exaggerations in the sway of her slender hips as she went to the bed, sitting upon it and unstrapping her weapon, putting the gun and the holster on the side table. The area that it had so recently been was red and raw from it rubbing all day, and she propped the heel of her boot against the table, looking at him.

"Do you have lotion?"

Watching her every movement with such rapt attention, his mind was already thinking of rubbing away that mark and soothing her before she even asked. "Be right back with it," he said, instantly leaving. He had to do it all perfectly, had to make her realize this was the place for her. As he went, he shed his outdoor things. The heavy trench coat, bulletproof vest. When he returned with one of the bottles of lotion he had stored for trading he was down to his boots, pants, and one of his favourite turtleneck sweaters.

"It's the best I've got," he said, moving toward her, dropping to his one knee and beginning to uncap the bottle of almond-scented lotion.

She had barely budged from her seat, though her eyes had wandered over almost every inch of the room, taking it all in. It smelled like him, and when he finally dropped to his knee before her, a smile was widening her lips. "Good," she praised, the word so singsong and beautiful. It wasn't just the praise, it was the way she said it as she waited patiently for him to start rubbing the lotion into her thigh.

Her skirt was pulled up, almost above her hips, and he glanced at those tight, white panties cupping her sex so lovingly. Just the merest sliver of it visible, but it was so much more than he deserved, he knew.

His body was wild with it all, gazing upon that perfect glimpse of womanhood. He knew, could feel, that she was so much better than him. He was fortunate to be allowed this, and he squeezed the lotion out onto his dark hand, laying the bottle aside and reaching out to her thigh. Reverentially he paused, then moved in, slowly beginning to rub the lotion into her reddened skin. Though his body throbbed with desire for her, his thoughts were only of wiping away this blemish and soothing all her hurts and worries.

"This should help you," he said softly. "I've got more. And can get as much of this sorta thing as you need, if you choose to stay," he explained.

"That will be helpful," she admitted. Her thigh was so soft, the flesh pulled taut over her lean muscles. She shifted it, resting the hook of her knee over his shoulder, her body lying back on her forearms as she stared at him.

He could swear there was a hint of desire running through her, something in her facial expression seeming so familiar to him, yet so foreign.

He'd never felt so hard in all his life as he knelt there, her leg over his shoulder. He gazed up at her barely covered cunt openly, seemingly unable to show shame anymore as he rubbed his thick finger tips into her smooth, perfect flesh. She was perfect. She was the sort of woman a world should be built around.

Smelling her, his mind was abuzz, and a memory of what it was like when he was separated from her for the trip to get the bullets surfaced. "I want you to stay," he said huskily. "I'll do what it takes to convince you to stay. Be my matriarch here. Help me make something... meaningful," he stated, swallowing with anxiousness.

Her lips quirked at the choice of his words, and the heel of her boot dug into his ribs. "Is that what you want?" Her hand reached out, cupping his jaw and stroking her thumb against the rough, dark flesh.

Her hand contrasted against his so much, and she stared at it for a brief moment.

Both his hands were wrapped around her thigh now, rubbing, massaging, the lotion and his purpose for this forgotten now as he sought rub away all bad sensations from her and replace with the strong feeling of his soothing hands. Nodding to her words, he licked his lips, ignoring the feel of her boot dug into his ribs. "Yeah," he stated. "In time I'll recruit others. But you will be their boss," he said, "and I'll be your protector."

His eyes nearly shut as he revelled in the feel of her petite, pale hand rubbing over the stubble of his jaw. It was heaven to be touched by her.

Her tongue licked up toward her upper lip, staying there for a while as she continued to rub him gently. When she retracted her hand and placed it back on the mattress, he yearned after her.

"I will see how this works," she agreed, her knee tightening around his shoulder and dragging them closer together by only the slimmest of margins. "Would you like that?"

A look of relief washed over his face at her words. Smiling broadly, he placed each hand on the outer skin of her thighs, soothingly stroking her. "I couldn't ask for more," he stated almost dreamily. He was smitten. No, it was more than that, and that annoying part of his mind that was resisting him was finally fucking off against the chorus of desire for her.

He gave a reverential kiss to her inner thigh, knelt closer to her quim now after her tug. "You won't want for more, I promise, Adrianna."

She nodded, though she frowned at his kiss, removing her leg from around his neck and crossing her legs tightly. Her knees dug into his chest as she stared down upon him from the mattress.

"You will behave," she told him, and he knew he would.

"Stay with me the night," she finally ordered after a moment of silence. "However, you will behave."

The thought of spending the night with this woman and doing nothing should've been agony with how hard he was, but he nodded obediently, looking rather crestfallen at having her legs and that gorgeous sight between them taken away. "Of course," was all he could say other than "I'm sorry." Remaining there, knelt before her at the edge of the bed.

"You may get undressed," she commanded, looking at him sternly. His kiss had soured her mood, and she seemed much cooler.

He could never have imagined himself behaving like this. The old Leon would never have, but he felt different now. Not himself, someone else. He obeyed immediately, pulling his greyish-blue sweater off over his head, revealing the broad, well-defined muscles of his upper body. Those wide shoulders, the sculpted toning of his chest and abs, marred only by a bit of nicks and scars.

Continuing, obeying her absolutely, he unbuckled his belt and shed his cargo pants, the heavy garment going to the floor revealing his thick thighs, narrow hips, and the steel-hard cock, so impressively large as it stood out above his heavy set of balls.

She refused to take her eyes off his face, and as the final bit of his clothing hit the floor, she uncrossed her legs. "Now me," she purred. She stood up, her body poised before him, the buttons on her blouse begging to be undone.

There were no more thoughts in his head but obeying this goddess before him. Quite literally. Moving his strong hands to her boots, he carefully undid the zippers down the side, one at a time. He lifted her feet and very carefully removed the footwear, laying them aside with such worshipful care, as if they were relics of a saint.

He wanted so badly to touch her beautiful, pale legs, lick, kiss, bite, and rub them. But he didn't dare. He moved his hands up, undoing the buttons on her blouse slowly, carefully, revealing more of smooth stomach, until at last he peeled it away and those gorgeously formed breasts, unclothed beneath, were exposed to the air. It took immense willpower, or something else altogether, to keep from cupping and squeezing those perfect mounds.

With her blouse off, he went to her hips, undoing the zipper he found there, sliding it down off her legs and lifting each foot to get it off completely.

All it left were those panties, the white morsel of cloth nestled between her thighs. And he took extra special care with them, curling his dark fingers into the fabric and rolling them down off her as he revealed her pinkened labia. He stared at that sight as he finished his task, stripping her down to nothing at all and laying her panties aside with the same meticulous care.

She barely breathed as he undressed her, but her eyes were stuck on him with rapt attention. She bent when he required, positioning herself in front of his body. Her hands didn't even shake.

Though her fear of men was well founded in most of the remaining world, with him she didn't even tremble. Her skin was so smooth, and her tight nipples begged to be sucked, but instead all she said was, "Crawl into bed."

Her voice had returned to that lovely, dulcet tone, no more anger or annoyance present. He had pleased her!

The hulking black man did as told like an obedient boy, climbing onto the large king-size bed and making room for her. He rested back against the ample number of pillows, propped up on his elbows as he lay there. The pose did wonders for exposing his masculine physique, leaving little to the imagination as his thick, throbbing cock rested against his lower stomach, his sac against his two thickly muscled thighs.

As imposing as he could be to look at in all his glory, he simply lay there watching her, waiting for more of her beautiful words to instruct him. To just speak to her was bliss.

She moved atop the bed, grabbing the blankets and pulling them down as she slid on top of the mattress, her long legs poking down into the sheets as she lay there, just inches from him. He could smell her, but she pulled the blankets back up. Her hand went to her hair, pulling out the side ponytail and placing the elastic on the night side table, leaving her dark, black, lightly curled hair to fan around her head.

Her eyes fluttered shut, but her lips opened, a familiar tone coming from her. It was a lullaby of some kind, though he could only assume it was in her native tongue, for it certainly wasn't English. There, with the woman lying mere inches from him, smelling and looking so heavenly, he found sleep despite his hardness. It remained, throbbing against him as he slumbered.

# CHAPTER 17

A strange sensation lifted him from sleep, though he had no idea how long he had rested. It could have been seconds or hours, but the feeling of weight on his body was apparent. He tried to move his arms, but found them useless at his sides, his legs equally so. Even opening his eyes was a struggle, but when he did he found the room basked in a pale pink light that didn't seem to have a source.

Atop him sat his new roommate, and he could feel her pussy around him, though he couldn't lift his head to see it. She felt so divine, though. Slick and tight, her speed just right as she coaxed his body to pleasure. Her hands were on his chest, he could feel, and with each motion of her hips he could see her firm breasts jostle.

Her eyes bore into his, a nearly sadistic smile

curling her lips as she noted he was awake, and her inner muscles gripped him tightly. A soft song came from her, though it barely seemed like her lips moved.

He should've been alarmed at this all. Nothing about it was right or natural. But instead all he could think was how grateful he was that this was happening, even if it was only a dream. The cling of her tight cunt about his massive cock was beyond perfect, he decided, and he groaned lewdly, smiling thankfully up at her as her beautiful, ethereal voice filled the room again.

He wasn't bothered by her sadistic smile, not in the least. His cock throbbed inside her and he could only hope she was enjoying it as much as he was despite his inability to move.

The way her hips rolled and glided over his thighs, the press of her hands to his chest were all such wonderful sensations, even as her nails dug into his flesh. Her black curls framed her face so perfectly, and her eyes turned toward the ceiling.

It was hard to tell how long she had been fucking him, but her pussy was dripping and had already coated his cock, the thick honey running down to lubricate his thighs and heavy sac. Her mouth began to move, catching up with the song, and upon that final syllable, when all became quiet, he came.

It was powerful, the sensation starting in his toes and running up and down the length of his entire body as though it hadn't just been his cock that she had been caressing and pleasuring. It was beyond compare, beyond anything he had the ability to reason, and his mind went blank, filling with blackness.

By the time he came to once more, she was no longer in his bed, her ponytail holder disappeared from the side table, though her clothing remained folded at the side. He was struck with panic, at first, at her disappearance.

Something in him, though, spoke to the fact that she was not gone.

His erection still throbbed between his legs, smooth and clean, and he couldn't be sure it wasn't all a dream.

# CHAPTER 18

He got up immediately. He wasn't panicked, feeling she was here, but he still wanted to see her. To be sure.

Without dressing he exited the room, leaving the door open as he looked about the dark hall of his home. He wanted to believe it really happened, all of it, despite what scary implications there were behind it. Something in his mind felt broken, and he was no longer able to think anything ill of her for certain, only meekly question at the recesses of his mind.

She was standing at the top of the steps, overlooking his kingdom. She was so delightfully nude, that smooth curve of her bottom so lovingly pronounced above her slender legs. Her black hair was pulled back in her side ponytail, the curls just barely touching against her shoulder.

She turned toward him, her smile touching the corners of her mouth.

"Sleep well?"

Nodding vaguely he approached her, wanting to be near her, climbing the ramp to the top level of his multilevel base with her. Looking down at her as he approached, he managed a soft, "Was it a dream?" His voice an eerie murmur.

"Was what a dream?" Her head tilted to the side, but he could swear she was laughing at him behind those dark eyes of hers. She stared only a second before averting her eyes. "What do you have for breakfast?"

Looking over her petite frame, so light but appropriately padded in the right places, he was so smitten. He felt his erection would never subside.

"What would you like? I have some preserves from the village," he stated, talking about the jams and pickled vegetables he kept from them. "There's also a bunch of old-world things. Cereal even. Though not much milk left, it's been a few weeks since I traded," he stated, willing to give her any of it. All of it.

He almost forgot his question, but it came back to him. "And I meant... us, you and I. Did we have sex?"

The nature of what happened hardly seemed describable by sex. He was unable to resist, or do anything after all, and she had obviously initiated it without his consciousness even.

She tilted her head to the side, looking at him intently. "Of course we did. You wouldn't stop touching me, feeling over my body as I tried to slumber. Perhaps it was the drowsiness that let me succumb to you, but"—she moved closer to him, pressing her small body against his large, bulky frame—"maybe the loneliness had its role to play as well." She lingered there for a few moments, his cock pressed between her stomach and his pelvis before she stepped away.

"The village?" she asked, her curiosity piqued. "Where?"

He knew that never happened. He wouldn't have dared touch her again without her approval, not after the last time. But she said it had, so somehow he accepted it. It just seemed right to, feeling her pale form against his dark skin like that.

"It's west of here," he said softly to her. "I do regular trades with them. They don't want the techy stuff so much, so I just bring them simple things, they generously give me fresh foods and the like, so I'm not eating only old-world tins and packaged grub," he explained.

"A good deal for you both, then," she cooed, her hand trailing down his arm gently, her fingertips almost tickling him. "When are you leaving for there next?" She tilted her head softly in question.

Smiling down at her with such pleasure at her touch, his manhood twitching in response to that voice of hers, he said, "When would you like me to?" Nothing else mattered, he decided, but pleasing her.

"Soon. I will come with you." She smiled, as though she were gifting him with something amazing. Her hand moved along his bicep and down to his hand, guiding it to her hip. "They have something that belongs to me."

He more than eagerly placed his hand on her hip. He wanted so badly already to put his arm around her, after all, but didn't only because he feared upsetting her again. He'd do anything to avoid upsetting her again.

Brightening at her offer to come with him, he asked softly, "Are you sure you wish to risk going out? I could get anything they have of yours and take it back to you. You can count on me." He was being absolute honest and determined.

She looked at him, considering his offer for a while before she finally nodded. Her voice came out far more singsong than before, almost melodic in her manner of speaking. "They have my sister. I wish for her safe return to me. She was taken right after the fall and I have not known where she has been until very recently."

It was a cryptic response; she seemed to have no interest in the village yesterday, despite living only a few hours away from it. Not to mention there was only one person in the entire place who could possibly share a blood relation with her.

That didn't deter him, though, and he gave a broad smile. "Celia," he said softly. "I know her." He looked absolutely enchanted to be able to divulge that information to Adrianna. It meant he would be able to please her, and nothing mattered more.

His powerful, dark hand gripped her hip firmly, "I will bring her right back, Adrianna," he said in his low voice, the authority gone, and only devoted worship left. "Don't worry, I won't disappoint you."

She nodded, stroking his hand against her hip tenderly. "We will eat and you will leave. How long do you typically stay?"

He looked absolutely in bliss, she was touching him, and he was touching her. They'd made love. "On average a couple nights, it depends," he said honestly, his strong fingers kneading her flesh at her hip. "Is there anything else I can do for you before I leave?" he asked eagerly.

She smiled and shook her head, leaning up and kissing along his chin on his strong jaw. "We will speak before you leave. For now, we will eat."

# CHAPTER 19

After he'd prepared her a breakfast—breaking out the special foods he'd been saving for a spectacular occasion, such as bacon fried on a gas grill—he tidied up and explained to her the workings of his manner, all the little traps, tricks and such. "The solar power isn't enough to keep everything going twenty-four-seven," he said as he wrapped it up. "So be careful with how much you use," he warned.

He was all smiles, dressed back in his travel clothes, gun over his shoulder, backpack stocked for the trip. "Are you sure there's nothing more I can do for you before I leave, Adrianna? Or anything else I can get while away? I want this to be YOUR home, no matter what it takes."

She took in a breath, exhaling against his chest as she stood just in front of him. It felt almost tingly, even through the thick, protective material he was wearing. She traced something against his chest and shook her head.

"Just act natural. Be yourself. Do not frighten her," she warned, reaching up to touch his face.

"I will protect our home while you do this task for me, and when you return, all things will come to you."

Something about what she'd said or done made him shiver. "You'll see I'm the best man you could choose," he stated, for the first time in ages some of his old firmness coming back to his voice, "and you could not regret that choice." He almost bent down to kiss her, but stopped before quite doing so. He hadn't been given permission, after all.

She smiled and stepped away from his intentional kiss, the action so smooth it barely seemed like a rebuttal.

"Be safe," she bid him. "I will be here when you return."

Those words soothed him, and he set out. Unable to keep himself from looking back frequently, even when the building itself was but an increasingly smaller silhouette to his back.

Once he met the entrance to the forest, though, his attitude took a dramatic shift. He felt like his old self once more. He still desired to be with the woman he'd left at his home, but it was no longer equal to his love for Tia and Faith. He still wanted to help her, but it was just as much as he wanted to help others.

He still wanted her to stay with him, but as a part of his plans. He was no longer a pawn in hers.

Still, there was a compulsion to see this through to the end, and as he hiked through the eerily silent woods, his trading goods strapped to his back—at her insistence of seeming normal—he was able to properly reflect on her presence in his life, and his home.

It was disconcerting, to say the least, seeing the world again as he had, only now such dramatic decisions having already been made, and so carelessly at that. He couldn't fathom what had possessed him to behave as he did. It seemed bizarrely unnatural, and a shiver went through his spine.

He could even feel a bit of worry that he'd return to find his home robbed or burnt down—for real this time. But he pushed that aside, he'd do this, as he normally would, and not just because Adrianna had told him to. He was looking forward to seeing those women he cared for with Tia.

# CHAPTER 20

The trek was uneventful, and when finally he came to the clearing that indicated the start of their perimeter, he could hear the same sounds that had greeted him when he left, though they seemed somehow more sombre. He remembered that Tia had mentioned that a woman was ill after miscarrying, but that she was on the mend.

He couldn't see anyone he cared to speak with, though many familiar faces looked at him as he made his way through the camp.

The unsettling revelations that came to him after leaving his home troubled him still, and he wanted some answers. He wasn't one to wait around, after all, so he went to see Celia. She would be expecting him anyhow; he'd told her to after all. So he headed straight there, intent on letting himself in if able, avoiding the more open areas of the little village, so that he wouldn't stumble into Tia first. As much as he wanted to see the woman, he had to have some sort of resolution first.

The door was left unlocked, and pushing himself into her room, he saw her sprawled on the bed, her legs kicked in the air as she looked through a fairly heavy-looking old book. She gasped and shoved it between the wall and her bed, sitting upright.

"Don't you knock?" She scowled, wearing the same clothes as she was last time. It was easier to care for clothes than to have a wide array of outfits, and it suited her so well. Her face was a bit red at his intrusion but as she got up from the bed she looked up at him earnestly. "It's too early to tell, you know."

He had laid that matter aside for the time being, his mind so wrapped up in the odd happenings with Adrianna. Though at her words he couldn't help but frown a little. It'd been nearly a month, so he was hoping she'd know something.

Unshouldering his bag, he put it down by the door and shut it behind him. "Let my excitement get the better of me," he said, trying not to let his disappointment show. He sized her up. "No clue at all?" he asked, stepping near to her.

"Even if there was, I wouldn't jinx it by telling you," she said, her words only slightly acidic as she moved up toward him, staring upwards and letting her long, black hair cascade down her mostly bare back. "Come to make sure?" She smirked, her flush returning to her cheeks, but looking less embarrassed and more excited.

His own worries of the past couple days went away, and he reached out, sweeping the small woman up into his muscled arms and lifting her off the floor. Pulling her up nearer to his height he kissed her lips hard. "Yes," he said in a gravelly, authoritarian tone that he'd almost thought forgotten. "And more."

Her eyes widened a bit, then narrowed eagerly. He could practically feel her arousal at his manhandling of her, her mouth eagerly parting against his.

"Like what?" she purred, all but begging for more.

He kissed her again, shoving his tongue deep into her mouth before pulling back. He was nearly crushing her in his arms. "I came to take you back with me," he husked. "If you aren't with child yet, you will be before long in my home," he promised. His strong hands stroked her spine, and he didn't give her opportunity to argue. "And it'll be a better environment for you. Keep you from being troubled by other people's nonsense. Focus on the one thing that matters." The words rolling off his tongue so roughly.

Where his eagerness had seemed so strange and false with Adrianna, her eagerness with him was all honesty. Her arms wrapped around his neck as her mouth met his, again and again. Pulling away, her heart beat steadily against his solid chest.

"I really hope you have a decent fucking setup," she warned as her mouth trailed to his neck, biting him roughly. "When do we leave?" She hadn't been this eager last time to leave, so perhaps she did know something she wasn't telling. Or, perhaps more simply, she enjoyed him far more than the commune.

He returned her gestures in kind, though his larger mouth kissed and bit at her neck more roughly, more widely. He gave a soft groan, feeling himself harden so in his pants. For though he had sex with Adrianna not long ago, he still felt oddly unsatiated. Huskily, he murmured into her ear as his hand cupped her ass up in under her skirt, squeezing the cheek hard. "Be ready at sunrise tomorrow. But we might have to wait until the next day," he told her. "Be ready either way. And don't worry," he added, nipping her earlobe and tugging it, "my place is far better than anything this village has to offer."

"Fuck me before you go," she begged, her teeth skirting his skin, nose rubbing against his earlobe. "I haven't been with anyone else and there's only so good I can feel on my own," she murmured.

She was offering him a chance to work out his aggressions and regain the control he had lost last night. She was so sweet and supple, so light in his arms as she clung to him hungrily. It was almost as though she were addicted to him and had gone too long without.

He hadn't intended on leaving without having her. He needed her right now, he felt. As strange as she was, as demanding as she could be, she did give him the rush of feeling in charge that he'd lost the past two days.

Pulling back and meeting his dark gaze with hers, he stared a moment, gauging her honesty, then lunged in, kissing her hard. His hand in under her skirt curled in her panties, yanking them crudely to the side to expose her sex as he walked her to her to the wall, pressing her back to it.

Without so much as removing his trench coat, he began to work his belt, loosening it immediately and preparing to slip his pants open. His deft hands had them open in so little time, and she could quickly feel the heat of his large, brown cock brushing against her pinkened flesh. His breathing was so heavy with desire, he felt he was ready to ravage her.

Her body wasn't yet slick for him, but she tried to shimmy down on that huge cock, her entire body needy for him. Her hand reached between them, guiding his stiff member back and forth over her tight slit before he could feel her body heat.

He drove her to the brink, and the way the slender woman acted around him, he felt like such a hero. A big, brutal hero that she wanted more and more of. "Push," she moaned against his flesh, biting down on his clothed shoulder. "Hard."

He should be more careful, he thought for a brief moment, in case she was pregnant. But her pleading pushed him beyond that concern, and he instead had to do it. With a groan he was shoving that dark crown against her still unwettened folds, putting such force into the act to jam its wide girth into her pink little labia.

With her crammed to the wall, he pressed a palm against it, bracing himself as he gripped her hip and shoved. It would be cruel to enter a normal woman this way, but here she was, holding him, guiding him in and egging him on to do it.

She cried out in earnest, her hold weakening as she braced herself against the shooting pain, but she never told him to stop. Something about the way she was begged him not to. She wanted this, the pain, the violence. She wanted him to dominate her, even as she bossed him around and told him what to do.

He knew all this, instinctively, and as her cry warbled she silenced herself by jamming her mouth against him, passionately rubbing her tongue against his.

He knew better than to stop. He kissed her back hard, pushing his large tongue into her mouth as he crammed more of his thick black meat into her tight little pink cunt. It was hard going, her vaginal canal tacky and resistant, but he forced it in more and more, groaning into her mouth with a sound that reverberated up from his chest.

He needed this, and he kept her pinned to the wall tightly as he gradually impaled her in the most painful fashion possible, his heavy clothes still covering most of him.

Her legs wrapped around his hips, hooking her nude knees around his flesh as she writhed against him, her body hesitant to accept the pain she so craved and desired. The longer he strained against her pussy, though, the more moisture arrived to aid him. She was getting turned on by his brute force, and her tight little body hugged his so hard.

"Fuck," she murmured in his ear, and it wasn't certain if she was cursing or commanding him.

Either way, he did it, he began to pump his powerful hips, tugging back out of her without leaving, then pushing in. He began to make headway like this, going a bit deeper into her each time, working more of that growing dampness along her folds as he pumped his dick into her.

He was groaning lewdly, his deep, husky voice loud, heedless of the noise he was making as he rutted the sweet little Asian girl before him. He only broke the series of grunts and groans to kiss at her, or murmur into her ear, "Breed me a big family, you fucking bitch."

She squeezed him, her nails digging into his sweater as she moaned loudly, the sound interspersed with whimpers of pain as she kept tugging him into her over and over again. She couldn't get enough of him, even as he split her body apart. She was so tight against his member, as if her cunt were begging for him to cum.

She bit his neck rudely, suckling the dark flesh between her pink lips, licking his skin so eagerly.

Her tight cunt was working him toward that end, milking his thick dark dick so thoroughly he couldn't help but shudder and quake with growing pleasure. "Fuck," he cursed, muttering into her ear such coarse language as he pumped his cock into her at an ever-increasing pace. For each bit of lubricating slickness she gave, he balanced it out by striking into her harder, rutting into her more painfully, and he could feel it working upon his loins, bringing forth his own release, closer and closer.

It was painful. Her body was tense and she kept crying out, but there was so much desire in her tone. Even with how brutal he was being with her, she still wanted it. Wanted him. Her head tilted back and struck against the wall as she let out a loud moan, the muscles in her throat looking so enticing. That amazing skin tone, so smooth and vibrant, exposed to his hooded eyes.

His dark sac tightened up against him and he could feel his release impending. He was pistoning his black dick into her so hard and fast now, and he could feel the fire tracing its way up his length as he called out, "Cumming," in his gruff, gravelly voice.

She had little time to react to that, though, before he was thrusting up into her for the last time and exploding his load deep inside her, thick streams of his seed pouring into her depths, filling her. All the while he tossed back his head and let out a tremendous groan of satisfaction.

She let out a shout, the words muddled with varying emotions and nonsensical words as her pussy clenched against his cock, begging him for every last drop. She panted roughly against him as her entire body started to slacken, her muscles spent from clasping around him so roughly the entire time.

"Fuck," she murmured, and it definitely was not a command this time.

With her jammed up against the wall by his hard chest, he kissed her cheek hard, then took hold of her, cradling her small body in his powerful arms and lifting her away from it. He brought her to her bed, and gently laid her out there, though he didn't pull out, he instead laid himself atop her, careful of his great weight as he nestled there, kissing her neck and cheek in quiet.

She breathed against him, her entire body seeming so much warmer beneath her little outfit. Her legs still wrapped around his waist, though more relaxed.

"Fuck, I should have told you Gina was out," she murmured, her head tilting back. "Whatever, we'll be in your place in no time and we can do whatever we want." Her lips twitched in a smile, and she hugged him with her calves.

He began to chuckle, and the sound rumbling from his chest grew louder. The little woman was so... "Audacious," he said. Kissing her fair-skinned cheek he felt his cock throb inside her and remarked. "We could've fucked on her bed too. Damn."

For the first time since he met her, he took his time, nestled atop her, stroking his rough, strong hand along her thigh and side, enjoying the moment.

She laughed, taking a lot of pleasure in his snide remark. "If you hadn't left me for so long, maybe I'd have had enough brains to suggest it," she offered, her socked heel rubbing down the back of his thigh before resting her foot against his ass.

He kissed her lips again, producing a loud smacking sound as they made out a while. Breaking from it, he asked curiously, "You're not going to miss this place, are you? No family or friends about?" he probed as his mind got back to normal.

"They're all ready to chase me outta here anyways," she admitted a bit nervously. "They've been saying I'm unstable and that I'm to blame for Will and Fiona, but I don't know how. They didn't even show to the meeting that day."

She lifted her head, kissing his thick lips, softer than her usual manner, "Fuck them all."

He felt a bit of worry at first, but then he couldn't help but smile widely, grinning in fact. He reached up, stroking her cheek with his dark hand. "Fuck 'em," he reiterated, then kissed her lips again. "You'll be mine, all mine, and never need see nor worry about them again soon," he reassured.

Carefully, he shifted a bit, his cock still lodged inside her. "What happened to those two anyhow?" he enquired casually. "And why think you had anything to do with it?"

"They killed each other or something. I don't know. He mighta killed them both for all that stupid Doctor can tell." She shrugged. "Or the other way around. I never did figure you could trust new ones with guns, but no one listens to me," she moaned, her legs pulling him in closer, and there was a strange flicker in her eyes as though she was getting off on talking about their deaths.

"They're having the burial today but they think that because of what I was saying at the meetings, I drove them to it." Her little smirk touched her lips and her cunt grasped him tighter. "Maybe I did."

He was alarmed by her words at first, though he didn't show it. He pushed the thoughts away; he had no idea what really happened, after all. Something about that insistent tug and squeeze at his still mostly turgid dick also helped distract him, and he kissed Celia's lips once more, despite her morbid reaction.

"You're downright nasty to the core," he said in his masculine husk, his cock unable to help but responding to her actions with a throb.

"It's a nasty world," she moaned, not taking insult at his words as her eyes fluttered closed. "We just have to worry about us surviving on," she murmured.

"It's their world, now. Even if they left it, they'll be back for the strong that can manage through their test, and crying over some stupid twins I barely cared about isn't going to help me." Her pussy squeezed him again and her hips positioned slightly so that he pushed in just the slightest bit deeper.

His body responded despite her morbidity, and he put it to use. Gradually he began to tug back his hips, then push in again, pumping his thick cock into her cum-filled cunt slowly, his hand still on her cheek, stroking her smooth light skin with his dark flesh.

"It is all about us now," he agreed, throbbing.

"Damn, I wish there were more of you," he groaned. "A nice twin sister or somethin' so I could double the breeding I get out of you," he remarked casually, fishing even as they rutted.

She laughed, her head tilting to the side as she felt him push into her soaked cunny. "You couldn't handle two of me," she murred, her head turning back to face his, her eyes lidded. "I think you could barely handle me," she teased, her breathing faster.

"I think she got jealous," Celia continued, "He was dating your friend, and he and his sister were really close. Apparently their dad died a few months ago leaving them alone and they were always together until they finally got here last month. You ask me, them being out there in the fucked-up world by themselves, there's no way they weren't shagging."

He gave her a harder thrust. It was some cheap way of trying to punish her for her callous disregard for those lives she spoke about, but it was futile, of course, as she'd only like it.

His voice lower and harsher with his postcoital state, he continued to rut her, albeit slowly. "Nothin' wrong with that," he remarked. "Times have changed, after all. If you've got any family left at all, it's amazing enough."

"Keeps the bloodline pure, if anything," she agreed, her mouth silencing him for a moment before she pulled back. "Most weren't so lucky. Maybe the gods would prefer families to be close knit like that, but I never had a brother and father died when I was a girl."

"Maybe we'll change things," he said, his pace of humping increased now so that his dark balls slapped against her ass beneath. "What about sisters? Got a sister out there for me?" he remarked with a toying grin, licking his lips hungrily, both for her and the information he wanted.

Her hooded eyes gazed at him, a little confused by his prying before she shrugged. "Did, but haven't seen her in a while, so I don't know if I do any more," she admitted, her cunt squeezing him a bit harder before she squirmed. "Ugh, please don't tell me you're going boyfriend mode on me."

He gave a gruff laugh as he continued to pump messily into her cunt, breathing a little heavier now. "You're my pretty little prized breeding mare," he replied, his hand rubbing down from her cheek to her neck, closing his hands about it and squeezing lightly. "Got it?" he demanded roughly, a glint of mischief in his eye.

She didn't protest, nor did she confirm. It seemed as though she wanted this, and didn't want to say anything to mess it up, even as a smile passed her face to make way for an "oh" of panic. Her cunt trembled around his member, and her body arched against his.

As the slap of his hips striking between her thighs grew louder, he clenched his hand about her neck, the powerful fingers making a ring about her, closing off her air entirely. With clenched teeth, he lunged near her ear and repeated bitterly, "Got it?" All the while never taking his gaze from hers.

Her head finally nodded, her face growing dark and her vision dimming, yet all the while her body responded in a way it never had before. He'd never felt her body squeeze him so tightly, and the rocking and spasming of her body was caused equally by her orgasm and her struggle to breathe.

It was far too soon for him to climax again, it was impressive that he could keep himself rigid still, but he pushed his own cum deeper into her as he thrust, all the while that hard gaze upon her. When finally he loosened his hold on her neck, he gave a groan and began to reach to the side, pulling open her drawer. "Best remember who you belong to now," he stated firmly.

She coughed a few times, but he could swear that love and respect gleamed within her eyes as she lay back on the bed. She nodded meekly, quiet now that he had literally taken her breath away.

Pulling the now familiar dildo from her drawer, he brought it in between her legs, and in a quick maneuver slid himself out of her cunt and rammed the new object in his cock's place hard. Grinding on the end of it with the heel of his palm he relaxed back beside her, his cunt-slickened cock resting against his clothed stomach.

"Be ready to leave this dump by sunrise," he commanded. "You've got a long life of getting fucked and popping out kids for me ahead," he remarked rather harshly as he moved to get up, "so don't start disappointing me now."

She nodded, seeming so small against her bed, but the way she looked at him with her widened eyes and her slack mouth, she could only be feeling one thing for him.

# CHAPTER 21

Leaving Celia's place, he couldn't help but ponder the odd woman. He had a good grasp of her, he thought. The whole rough act with her proved that. She seemed to eat it up, though he never meant it.

Still troubled by the odd occurrences with her sister, however, he headed on to Tia's place next. He was hoping for maybe a bit of comfort from her.

The rest of the town had begun to bustle, though there was a quietness to it. The store was closed, though he could see Tia inside, sat at a table and seeming a bit off. She just sort of stared at the wall, so lost in thought she didn't even see him through the windows.

Eying her for a moment through the glass, Leon stepped up to the door and knocked on it gently. He didn't care to startle her, especially if she was bothered.

Her eyes darted to him and then immediately softened. She opened the door for him and wrapped him in a warm, loving hug. Her hair was piled up on the back of her head in a bun, pulled away from her face and allowing her beautiful features to shine.

"Hey, baby." She smiled, her hand rubbing down along his chest. "Shitty day for you to show up, but I'm so glad you did."

Seeing her in such a poor mood softened his heart, and he gave her a strong hug, lifting her off the floor as his thick arms squeezed. Kissing her cheek, just beside her ear, he placed her back down. "Then I'm glad to be here," he replied in a low voice, smiling to her warmly. "Need someone for support? Or just to unload on?" he asked gently.

"Maybe we should go for a walk," she suggested, her tone quiet. She had been so soft spoken since he got there, and he wondered if she didn't want to be overheard. Her suggestion to go elsewhere surely spoke to that.

Shrugging his pack off his shoulders and laying it down beside the counter, he kissed her forehead. "Sure," he said. Stripping away his vest and trench coat, he put his arm around her and led her outside. "Faith alright?" he asked, concern for the woman high on his mind now.

"Naw." She shut the door behind them, sticking close by his side despite their difference in height. "She's still pretty broken up. I mean, they've been missing for a few weeks... since you were last in town, actually. Doctor said they must have been dead since then." Her shoulders quivered as though she were suppressing a sob.

"You feel bad when they run off and join the bandits, or you worry when they take off on their own, but for something like this to happen to two of our own... Everyone's taking it really hard."

"Since I was in town?" he muttered back in response. "The two new ones?" he asked. He'd pushed such worries out of his mind. What the hell could have happened? "They disappeared?" He was still very lost, unsure of what to make of this.

"Yea." She gave a soft, sympathetic smile. "I mean, they weren't around last time you were in. Faith had said she couldn't find Will that day. Said their house was locked up. After that, no one saw them again until one of our hunting parties stumbled across them." She shook her head. "You never even met them, but they were lovely kids."

They were only a couple years younger than Tia, hardly kids by any stretch of the imagination, but the fall did funny things to the concept of age and youth.

With his eyes wide, Leon could scarcely believe what he was hearing as he held Tia by his side, walking her away from her home. "They were found dead? Killed by bandits?" he asked, none of the alarm he felt showing in his voice, ever the rock on the outside despite his inner turmoil.

She frowned, shaking her head. "They don't know what happened, but they found the gun dropped between them. It..." She was struggling to fight back tears, but she forced herself to remain strong. "It looks like they took their own lives. Poor

Faith. She can't understand." She sucked in a breath, holding it against the sobs. "She's been beatin' herself up for days, thinking he ran off because she wouldn't... you know. Go through with it. But then we taught her and I really think she was excited..." She rambled a bit, obviously having a difficult time with it.

Stopping in his tracks, he put his two arms about Tia again, pulling her in against his chest and resting his head down atop hers. Holding her closely for her comfort on the outside, though inwardly he felt troubled himself. Unable to shake the feeling that this must have been at least partially to do with his incident with the woman. Though he couldn't imagine what would possess the two to react so dramatically.

"These are fucked up times," he finally said in his deep, soothingly strong voice.

She nodded sadly, looking up at Leon with tears in her eyes. "Leon"—she choked back a sob, trying to remain in control—"I don't know how I could lose you. I mean... the reason we wanted to practice a more inclusive style of society and relationships is so we'd always have someone there. Someone to comfort us even when we lose someone close to us.

"But with this happening, the more I think about it, the more I realize that if I lost you, no one could console me."

A foot taller than her, Leon bent down, almost crushing her in his arms at those words. He just couldn't help himself from hugging and holding her tightly. He had wanted to be with her for so long, most of the time since the Fall in fact. But they were both so stubborn.

"Oh Tia," he said huskily, his own voice finally betraying a bit of his emotion; tenderness, for her. "I worry about you constantly," he confessed.

Her arms dug in at his side as they stood on the outskirts of town, her face buried into his heavily muscled chest. "I've tried to steel myself against it. I know your job is dangerous, but every day..." Her throat closed off for a second before she could choke out the words. "Every single fucking day I'm thinking about you and hoping you're okay. That I'll see you again. I never know. It might be weeks or months before I could ever know. Faith was going crazy not knowing, but that's how it always is for me."

His heart broke at that. He tried not to think of her worrying about him when he was off. He just had to live a more interesting life than she wished here, more independent and in charge. So knowing that, he just tried his best not to think about the costs of it.

He didn't know what to say in response. As he'd never allowed himself to face this reality really. He squeezed her, let his hands run up and down her back, his fingers combing through her hair along the back of her head.

Her arms were so tight around his hard body. They were alive, now, and her response spoke to just how grateful she was to that fact, and how terrified she was that it would end. She was stuck between her love for him and her devotion to the town and her ideals, and it wasn't a decision she could make lightly.

Still, the events of the last few weeks had obviously struck her pretty hard, and her hands dug into his shirt. "And I was so fuckin' stupid and I really fucked up with you," she sobbed harder.

His mind was so embroiled in turmoil it took him a while to register her words. Stirring, he shifted, brushing his cheek against hers as he lowered himself to her level. "What do you mean, Tia?" he asked comfortingly, almost afraid of the answer and what it might do to him.

Her fingers swept away some wetness, trying to turn stoic and confident even though her face was swollen. "We weren't careful last time, Leon. I wasn't careful." Her lip trembled, threatening her once more. "And I'm late and I don't know, maybe it's just the stress of dealing with Faith but I'm worried." It wasn't like her to overreact to something like this, he knew.

It was exactly what he thought she meant, but was too terrified to dare dream it was.

Bending his knee, he descended down so that his face was at her level. The look he gave her wasn't one of fear or trouble though. He couldn't help but smile at her broadly. He feared she'd say this because he knew he couldn't be anything but ecstatic, and had no idea what impact it might have on him and his decision making ability. Then, what if it was a false alarm?

"Late?" he said, his face bright with excitement. Swallowing, he lunged in and kissed her hard, squeezing her again in his arms and never wanting to let go.

She whimpered against him, but she kissed him still with all of her pent up emotions of sorrow and confusion as they threatened to wreck her body. Her arms wrapped around his neck, but she was still too filled with sadness to really enjoy their salty kissing.

Breaking the moment at last, he slid his arms down from her back along her hips, brushing his thumbs over her stomach repeatedly as he gazed at her as if seeing her for the very first time. "Gods dammit, Tia... if it's true... if you're really..." He couldn't say it, because if he did, he worried, at the results, he couldn't control in himself. "This is nothing to be afraid of," he stated with absolute certainty.

"Leon, they keep dying." Her eyebrows furrowed. "It can be a death sentence for the mother, and..." She shook her head. "Even if I wanted to come back with you now, I couldn't be away from the Doctor," she whimpered.

She had been thinking of leaving for him?

It was all flashing through his mind so rapidly. "Maybe I could talk her into coming," he said. "She's getting older, I could offer her a secure retirement. With only a few people to care for... in a safe and relaxing environment." He swallowed, his throat running dry.

"Oh, Leon, but the people of the village need her too." She rested her forehead against his sweater, her hands stroking along his arms.

"I don't know. Maybe it's nothing," she sighed, but the slump in her shoulders didn't convince him. He'd not seen her so broken down, not in all the time he had known her.

He held her so firmly, yet so carefully. In his mind now, it was too late. She was going to have his child.

"Nothing matters but you and our child now," he stated with such authority, "nothing." Shutting his eyes, he brushed his lips to her neck, kissing her so softly, speaking soothingly. "It's safer at my place. It's a fortress," he stated. "Safer than here, but..." He paused. "It's okay. No need to rush. It's not even been a month. You'll have plenty of time to make the trip in safety... if we so choose."

She nodded against him, exhausted and spent as she wiped away her tears and tried to make herself look sensible. After a few moments, a strong smile was forced to her lips and she touched his chest. "Look, I'm just really glad you came. I missed you. I guess... you have things to trade?"

"Yeah," he said with a broad, toothy smile. "But fuck it for now. I just got the greatest potential news of my life," he stated firmly. "I've always wanted kids... and of all the women left in the world, you're the one I wanted to have them for me the most, Tia." Still touching her stomach, he brought the other hand up, cupping her cheek as he gazed at her so lovingly.

She was still struggling against her emotions, and couldn't meet his eyes, but she nodded regardless as she took a step back. "I don't know if Faith wants to see you or not. She won't speak to me, not really. Sometimes before she goes to sleep, but she's been having a hard go of it. I don't know how she'll react."

Nodding slowly, he squeezed his hand upon her

cheek gently. "Maybe she could use a fresh face to go to though," he offered. "I should at least say 'hi' and see, you think?" he asked gently.

"Yea," she agreed, taking in a breath. "Just give her space if she needs it." She began leading the way back to her store, but she looked so tired. She wasn't the same Tia he had left; she seemed older.

With his arm around her the entire way back, he managed to temper his enthusiasm with a dose of reality. But getting back to Tia's place, he kissed her lovingly. "I'll be careful, don't worry," he said softly. Looking to her stomach, he asked quietly, "Does anyone else know?"

"Of course not," she said, a little aghast. "Everyone's been worried about Will and Fiona. There's no need for me to add more to it. I can handle this," she said assertively, her moment of weakness past as she opened the door to the store. She was in control again.

Parting from Tia, albeit a little reluctantly, he headed on up.

# CHAPTER 22

Approaching Faith's room, he made no effort to hide his heavy, distinctive footsteps, though he gave a gentle knock to her door. "Hey babe," he called to her in a velvety tone, "been missin' ya."

It took her a minute before he saw the doorknob turn and a very unkempt Faith appeared. She was in her pajamas, her hair mussed up in a ponytail, looking as though she hadn't left her room in days. She couldn't have made it to a funeral, not like this.

She pushed open the door to let him in but quickly moved back to her bed, snuggling under the covers, a stuffed animal clutched to her breasts. "I'm not feelin' well."

Shutting the door behind him, he moved over, seating himself on the edge of her bed with a groan from the bed. Reaching over, he rested a hand lightly atop her ankle. "Still lookin' pretty even when you're sick," he remarked lightly. "How'd you manage that?" His suave voice delivering the joke in a carefully soothing manner.

She snorted, her blanket brought up to her chin, hiding everything but the pinkened olive skin and her dark lashes, soaked with tears.

"This fuckin' sucks," she cursed, her body wracked with tears streaming down her face. It didn't seem like she could even control it, the way her body contorted with pain.

With a sympathetic smile, he rubbed her ankle and calf over top of her blanket. "Yeah," he intoned. "This world fuckin' sucks," he stated poetically, "you and Tia are about the only parts of it I truly enjoy fully anymore."

She nodded against the pillow, messing up her hair further. "Why'd he fuckin' have to do that, huh, Leon? I mean, even if for the reason that now we don't even have our two best hunters. They were young but they were really good! He was really good! Now we ain't got them and no one knows how winter's gonna go."

With a dismissive wave of his free hand, he stated definitively, "You and Tia need never worry about that. Never. You two can always count on me to support you, no matter how bad things get." He locked eyes with her. "No matter what, I'll come riding in to see you and Tia make it through the winter warm and well fed. Got it?" He would, too.

She nodded, her wet lashes so thick over her eyes. "It's just scary."

She shifted, taking the blanket with her in an uncomfortable manner so she could lean against him, still wrapped in the thick material.

Taking his hand off her ankle, he draped it about her and her blankets, holding her lightly, his hard fingers stroking over her hair now, gently rearranging her mussed-up curls. "Be scared for others, but not for you, Faith, I'll protect you." Smiling faintly to her, he continued his gentle caresses.

She didn't speak much, but she seemed to enjoy his comforting presence. She stayed curled up against him for a long time before he realized that her breathing had become steady and deep, and that she must have finally been able to fall asleep. The way she was behaving, it wasn't likely she had been getting much of that since he last left.

Bending over, he gently placed a kiss to her forehead and temple after having cleared her hair back. He got up, easing his weight off the bed before he made his way back down to find Tia again.

She was sat back at the table, though she was staring at a book and quickly put it down to watch him descend the stairs. She took in a deep breath as she moved over to him, her breath held. "How is she?"

"Asleep," he said with a reassuring smile, putting his arms around her. "Not quite as glad for my company as you, but I think I did some good," he stated, kissing Tia's forehead. "How are you feeling?"

"A bit better," she admitted, though her mood still seemed a bit foreign to him. "How long do you think you're staying for?" she enquired.

Pondering it a moment, he said, "If it'll help I can stay a couple nights. Though I do have some business to get back to." He gave an apologetic smile. "I wouldn't have committed to anything had I known you could use me so."

She shook her head, leaning up and kissing his jawline. "Leon, you know how happy I am to see you, and how much I love you. But this time... maybe a short visit is best. Come back soon but... just give us some time to get back to normal." She stared up at him. It sounded harsh, but he knew that wasn't the intention. She had always needed her space.

Soaking that in, he nodded. "I'll leave in the morning," he stated then smiled to her warmly. "We've got a lot to think about, and best we do so with a clear head anyhow."

Before she could say more on it, he peered around. "The new guy has his own place now I assume? Where can I find him? Got a few surprises for him," he stated.

"Yea, he's staying with Marcia and Luke. She needs a bit of help now, but she's out of hot water, anyways. Just needs bed rest, and Christian volunteered."

Nodding slowly, he said, "Ahhh, so he has a use other than lookin' pretty after all?" He gave her a joking grin.

"He able to pull his weight around here, you think?" he asked with genuine curiosity. "I know helpin' out like that is kind of an 'anyone can do' task."

"Yea, I think so. He said he was pretty good with

a few things. He was going to school for art and accounting when the fall happened, and he's really good at keeping everyone's spirits up. But he said that when the bandits had him, he used to spy for them."

That last bit was somewhat disconcerting, but he nodded casually. "I see. Well"—smiling to her warmly—"I guess I'll give you a bit of space and handle that."

Kissing her forehead, he turned and took his pack up, taking out the things he'd brought to trade with her. "Here's what I brought with me. Some of the usual." Seeing the romance novel he brought for Fiona, he paused, then offered it up, too. "Maybe Faith'll enjoy this as gift," he offered.

"I trust you'll gimme somethin' fair for the rest, bit of food."

# CHAPTER 23

She started sorting things out as he left, walking into the crisp air. He had traded with Luke and Marcia in the past and easily made his way to their small cabin. They had lost their baby just a month or so before, but the place looked well cared for. A new garden had been planted out front, though no flowers yet sprang from it, and the curtains were parted to let the sunlight into the bungalow.

It was only a moment after he knocked that a lovely man opened the door, Christian's face brightening at the sight of Leon.

"Well, well!" His lips parted with his smile. "Aren't you a sight for sore eyes."

With a hearty chuckle, he hefted the bundle he carried. "Santa's come early this year," he stated. "Got a moment?"

"Oh, sure." He shifted aside to allow the large man in through the door. "The loving couple has gone out for a walk so we have the place to ourselves. I was just tidying up some." The place looked fairly clean as was, and the thin, feminine man looked amazing even in the oversized shirt and the ill-fitted shorts. His feet were bare as he padded into the kitchen. "Did you want some tea?"

Pleased with the warm welcome, he smiled down at Christian pleasantly. "Sure, why not? I'd enjoy a bit of relaxation." Looking around the home as he made his way in casually, he continued, "Not been the best welcome I've ever received here, after all. Dark times and all."

"Yea," he agreed with a small shrug of his slender shoulders. "Everyone's pretty beaten up over it. It's hard when they're so young and healthy, a real blow to the community." He spoke as he gathered the materials together, setting the pan over a fire in the living room and returning to the kitchen. "Shouldn't take but a few minutes." He smiled as he sat down at the table. "Listen, I really... I feel like I made a fool of myself last time, so I really wanted to apologize. I hadn't eaten anything in a long time and was a bit... not myself."

Sitting himself down with the package rested on his lap, he waved his hand dismissively. "Don't be crazy," he said. "You've got nothin' to apologize for, I swear." He gave the man a pleasant smile. Despite the ill mood, after all, he was rather optimistic.

"Besides, I got you some nice stuff while I was away. Been dyin' to give it to you," he said, lifting the parcel and offering it over to him.

Christian's eyes widened excitedly as he stood to open it, pulling out the slick, smooth button-down shirts and plain trousers. They were of a lovely, high-quality material and felt delectable. A leather jacket and a pair of plain black shoes were in bottom, and he walked over to Leon, his face amazed.

"I had no idea anyone could get anything like this anymore."

Grinning wryly—just a bit!—he waved his hand dismissively again. "Nothin' for me, lad," he stated firmly. "I told you, I'm the best damn scavver in the land. There's no place I don't go to get what I want." Looking down over him, he asked, "If you care to try 'em on while we wait for the tea, I'm eager to know if they fit alright."

"They look right," he said as he moved back to them, lifting a deep-purple shirt and unbuttoning it before taking off his rather ratty T-shirt. His chest had filled out a bit more after his arrival, and he looked so much healthier. Even his skin looked to be in better condition, and he all too soon covered it with the long button-down shirt.

It was a perfect fit, clinging to his body just a little too tightly with his weight gain, though it only made it look better. He looked up at Leon a bit nervously for a second. "They're alright with nudity, but where you're from away...?"

His wry grin only grew at the man. "Why you think I come here?" he said in good humour.

He laughed as he unbuttoned his shorts, his blonde hair bobbing against his sculptured face as he nodded. "True enough." He pushed down the garments, revealing his plain, black boxers. He tilted his head as he stepped out of them, looking back in the box and noticing the other undergarments and considering them.

"Probably try those on after a bath," he decided with some finality before drawing up the black trousers over his strong legs.

"What do you think?"

Leon took his time, rising up and walking around the man, sizing him up in the new clothes. They were in excellent condition, or as good as anything could be in this age, and he smiled approvingly, reaching out and hooking a thick dark finger in one of the belt loops and tugging it, testing how well they fit to him. "Lookin' damn good," he stated. "Gonna be the talk of all the ladies in the village... more so," he added.

Christian rolled his eyes, though he couldn't help but smile at the compliment or, perhaps, at the closeness of the other man. "Well, they need something to perk them up these days," he replied coyly. He was only up to the chest of the other man, his features so androgynous and attractive.

Taking his time looking the man over, Leon peered behind him toward the living room. "Water's boiled," he stated. "Always good to see my judgement pay off."

Christian gasped, his thick lips parting before he moved away from the taller man, returning a few minutes later with the pot. Pouring them up two cups, Leon could swear there was a bit more of a saunter to his motions. There was something so appealing with the way those slender, male hips moved.

Seated back down, Leon made no move to hide his casual observation of the man. "So how you findin' things here, Christian?" he asked, thick biceps rested on the armrests of the chair, his sweater's sleeves rolled back to show the thick muscles of his arms.

"Different," he admitted, sliding Leon's mug across the table before sitting himself down comfortably. "Everyone's a lot different than the bandit camp, but I mean... I'd be really pissed off if that weren't true. If everyone was as sleazy as them."

With a hearty chuckle, he took the mug and smiled. "Thanks," he said, blowing on it then taking a sip. "How you findin' the work? This sort of thing up your alley?" he enquired, looking about the home. "Place is lookin' lovely anyhow. Outside especially."

"Better than before," he admitted, though there wasn't a lot of passion there. "I mean, I do what I can to help out, but nothing I really had a lot of interest in during... well, before, is much help now. No one needs a photography or an art critic," he admitted shyly.

With a wry grin he took another sip of his drink. "Though Tia said accounting." A brow quirked as he eyed the man again.

He nodded with a smile. "Yea, that was my parent's idea. They said I could take all the Arts bullshit I wanted, pardon my French, so long as I did something practical as well. So, accounting. I figured I could maybe freelance and do photography full-time, maybe grow it into a studio and then handle all the accounting side to it as well. Was almost about to graduate when, you know..."

It was obviously hard for him to talk about the fall. Things couldn't have been easy for such a gentle-looking individual.

Nodding slowly after hearing the man's story, he took his time mulling it all over. "Yeah, sorry to say I don't have an art gallery I can offer you a position in. Yet," he remarked with a smirk, lingering his dark gaze upon the slender man. "Never got around to the acquiring-art portion of my fortress building. Unless you count movies. Some posters."

He looked a bit weak to that, licked over his lips. "What type do you like best?"

"Movies?" he asked, shrugging his heavyset shoulders and looking down into his mug. "I like a lot, really. Action, drama... well, got a weakness for cheesy horror too, especially if it makes whoever's beside me squirm," he said with some amusement, looking back across at the man.

He laughed, shaking his head. "I only squirm when the horror isn't cheesy. The stuff from the seventies is beyond compare in that regard. It's just so raw." He leaned back, looking at Leon quite affectionately. "I think you and I are a little bit opposites. I'm barely alive out here, doing menial housework to try to earn my keep, and you're out there just... being badass."

Leon gave a hearty chuckle at that, finding it greatly amusing. "I tend to like things that way"—he sipped his tea—"not being badass, though I like that too. But contrasts. Opposites attract, they used to say, well... it's true for me at least," he said in his strong, low voice, always so calm and in control.

"Well, that's good to hear because I have to tell you, ya give me a bit of a complex." He grinned. He sipped his tea and placed it down on the table, leaning forward a bit. "Look, I still don't know what I can do for you to make it up to you about the clothes, but if you wanted me to spruce up your place or whatever..." He paused, his eyes growing a bit dark. "I used to have to work for the bandits, to hunt out their enemies, watch them, report back. Mostly on the Tribal front but they also had big issues with a few of the Government bosses. I... don't know if you'd need anything like that, but I'd be willing to do it again for you. No one sees me. I could follow someone for days."

He took a moment mulling over the man's words then shook his head. "You're a pretty man, you get along well with others, right?" he asked, looking to him. "I mean, you're good at convincing people to accept a good deal for you? Or getting people to see a certain side of things?"

"Absolutely. I mean, I had to handle some negotiations and whatever, and in school I learned how to get some kick-ass deals on a bunch of equipment. I mean, you just have to know what people need. Which, unfortunately, I'm at a loss with you." He flattered the other man with the way he said it.

With another hearty chuckle he looked the other

man over again, lowering his mug down. "I don't want to build you up falsely here or anythin'. But I am getting some things going." He paused, tracing his fingers along the armrest. "I'm a pretty picky person though with who I trust, I'll confess."

He nodded, paying rapt attention to the other man. "Well, you can always count on me. I mean, I like the people here and all and am very grateful for all they've done, but it's not really... me. Here, I mean. There's nothing for me to do."

Scratching his chin, he thought it over. "I'll be having a few people with me soon, it seems. A regular little camp of my own," he explained. "Women, really. But I won't be around all the time. And I could use someone good at keepin' the peace when I'm not there. Acting on my behalf. It'll be a tough spot to be in, because I'll need to know they're thinkin' with that in mind all the time. Of course, in return they'll know they can always count on me to look out for them. Keep them happy and well cared for."

He sat back in his chair, staring at the other man for a while. It had obviously taken him aback and he let out a low breath. "Wow." He shook his head, gold hair gleaming in the light from the window. "That is something. You're actually working on building a harem. And you're actually doing it." He laughed. "Well, you won't have any trouble trusting me around them, anyways." His lip quirked a tad.

The man's words only seemed to amuse Leon, and his dark eyes narrowed a little, his smirk widening. "I don't, do I?" he asked with genuine curiosity.

"No," he affirmed, holding his gaze for a long while before finally dropping them to his lap. "I mean, it's not like I'd want a harem of all women, even if, you know. I'm just not like that."

He nodded slowly. "I like you, Christian. And, you know, more ways than one." He finished off the last of his tea in a single pull, "Not gonna rush into anything long term. Sadly I'll only be in town here for the night, I'm afraid. But I'd like to get to know you better. Personally, I mean."

"Sure. I mean, I understand why you'd want to make sure before you invited me back as your harem moderator." He smirked. "I'm up for that. It sounds a lot more interesting than what I can offer out here."

With a hearty chuckle, he licked his lips. "Maybe I'll even pick up some art for you now and then, if you come along, some supplies for painting," he remarked. "Start a little art gallery of your own amidst the wastes of civilization."

Christian looked as though he would melt, just completely taken aback by the man's offer. He was taking it at face value, having already been proven the depths of his abilities with the new clothing he wore.

"Well... if there's anything I can do to convince you I'm your man, just say the words."

Leon thought it over. "Maybe a nice dinner sometime. Aside from the nudity," he said with a grin, "the best part of coming here is a nice meal. And nice company while eating it. You and me. Make me somethin' grand. Be warned, I eat a ton."

He smiled, looking pleased. "Alright. I can handle that. When's the next time you're in? I'll plan ahead and make it a feast to remember."

Scratching his chin again, he gave it some consideration. "Don't usually do things that set in stone," he stated. "But let's say two weeks from today, how's that sound, Christian?" He smiled to the man. "Plenty of time to prepare for a date, huh?"

"And at least now I have an outfit or two so I won't look so out of place at your side." He grinned, moving to collect the mugs. "Any requests?"

"Sweets and meat," he stated firmly. "They top the list."

Casually, the large man reached over, touching his large, dark hand to the other's pale digits as he picks up the mugs. It was a very deliberate move, feeling out Christian's smooth, pale skin.

He stilled, looking over at the other man a bit apologetically. "They'll be back soon." He shifted closer to Leon, though, and not away.

Meeting Christian's eyes, he nodded. "I know." His index finger rubbed up across the man's wrist, in under the cuff of his new shirt. "Just taking a moment, did you mind?" he asked in his low voice.

His lips quirked upwards and he shook his head, eyes fluttering shut. "Not at all."

Leon gave the slightest of half smiles back, always looking so supremely confident.

After a moment he rose up, slipping his hand back. "Well, I guess I'll leave you to your work then." Running a hand back through his dreaded hair, he said, "I guess I'll see you in two weeks. Oh"—he paused mid turn—"any special requests of your own?"

"This one will be all about you." He smiled, finally grasping the mugs and bringing them into the kitchen, setting them down gently. "And you'll love it. I promise."

With a hearty chuckle, Leon headed toward the door. "Later Chris," he called out firmly. "Be lookin' forward to the next time we meet."

# CHAPTER 24

Walking toward Doctor Benson's makeshift office, he saw the door was left open to allow the breeze in. She was sat atop her couch, glasses perched on her nose as she struggled to find the appropriate distance to read from her magazine. Her silver hair was cropped just above her jaw and styled very nicely, framing her face in a professional yet attractive manner. She was probably in her fifties, but she looked fabulous. The world was so young now that it was a rarity to see someone older than forty around.

With a light rap on the side of her door, Leon approached her as delicately as he could, his low, appealing voice carrying inside to her softly. "Doc, got a moment for a chat?"

"Hm?" She put down the magazine on the table, letting her glasses fall down around her chest. "Oh!

Leon! What can I do for you? I got the medication you brought last time. It did well." She smiled a bit sadly. "It's so hard to find pills that aren't expired anymore."

Stepping inside, his sleeves still rolled up, he gave the woman a sympathetic smile. "Always glad to help you, doc. Though this time I've got something of a proposal for you," he said, gesturing toward the free chair next to her couch. "Mind?"

"Go ahead," she allowed, settling herself into her couch. "Is something the matter?"

Seating himself down near her, he leaned forward onto his knees. Bent toward her, he began to speak in a low, suave tone. "How'd you like to run off with me?" The slowly forming grin on his face betrayed the casual humour of it.

She looked a little confused, then laughed, shaking her head as she caught on. "Oh Leon," she sighed. "You're really getting desperate in your old age." He chuckled back in good humour. "And you're only gettin' lovelier," he countered with a toothy grin. "I doubt you know, but I've got a nice, big place of my own. Well secured. Hidden, fortified. Safe. A good spot for a small band of survivors," he stated.

"We have a good spot for a small band of survivors here," she reminded him, leaning forward a bit. "What are you getting at, Leon? I really am not going to run off with you and leave the village to fend for itself."

"What if I told you I was bringing a few of these people with me who need you the most?" he asked. "And once there, I'd guarantee you a nice, luxurious life. Some of the comforts of the old world. Movie night each week. Lots of books to read." A mischievous glint entered his eyes. "A handsome leader who's most appreciative of you."

She leaned back in the couch, her eyes rolling over his face. "You're really serious, aren't you," she mused, amazement in her tone.

Getting up from his seat, he moved to the couch, seating himself beside her, one arm up on the back of it, the other on his knee as he looked to her. With his dark muscled arms out, and his handsome, broad face alight with his most charming smile, he was looking his best as he spoke. "I am. And I want you," he said, the husky words sounding so...

She stared at him, mulling over his proposal. She even looked thoughtful before she shook her head. "There's three dozen people here, Leon, all counting on me. If I left them, it'd be sentencing them to death."

Reaching over with one hand, he very carefully rested it upon her knee. "In the comfort of a nice, secure fort, you'd have the luxury to care for a few better. Maybe get a better idea of how to look out for the women and their problem giving birth." He gave a hopeful smile. "You could be doing more for future generations."

She shook her head. "I'll think about it, Leon, but really, unless we find someone else to care for these people, I don't know how I could live with myself."

His large hand resting upon her knee, he gave her a light squeeze, his velvety, rich voice insistent. "You've been training someone else, I bet, haven't you? And you deserve some comfort. The whole damn world has ended, and I'd like to see your beautiful self safe and secure, behind thick, concrete walls, Samantha."

Her brows furrowed and she gave him a slight nod. "I'll see," she promised him, her grey eyes intent upon his. "I can't just up and leave. There are preparations."

He squeezed her knee and brushed his thumb against her thigh a little, grinning widely. "Dammit, that's so what I want to hear, I could kiss you," he declared. "But I ain't even taken you out for dinner yet, so it feels unfair," he said with a cheeky, suave grin.

She laughed, but it was a bit dry and humourless, feeling him touch along the edge of her skirt. "Look, you better let me think of this before I need to patch you up a bit." She took his hand, placing it in his lap.

Shot down. "Aw, damn," he remarked with a following chuckle.

Nodding, he rose up. "All the same, doc, you are a fine-looking woman. Consider that offer too," he said cheerfully, meaning every word of it. He'd marry the woman right now.

"I'm sure I'd be in good company," she quipped, lifting her magazine once more. "All the best, Leon. Don't be a stranger."

With a good-natured chuckle he departed in high spirits, heading back to Tia and Faith for the night.

They were just serving up dinner—or rather, Tia was serving up both bowls of stew, just about to head up to Faith's room when he reappeared. He could see, through the window of the door, the visible relief in her body at his return, and she placed them back on the table to let him in.

"Hey, Leon, how'd everything go?"

"Great," he remarked, sweeping her into an embrace so easily. Leaning down, he whispered into her ear softly, "I had a talk with the doctor." Then pulled back to smile at her.

"Leon," she sighed out, her head tilted to the side, her arm on his bicep. "Don't drag her into this."

"I never told her anything," he said, pointedly looking to her stomach. "But I had a talk about my plans, and how she could fit into them. She's considering it," he declared proudly, rubbing Tia's sides.

"Fuck, Leon, even I'm only considering it." She slumped down away from him into the kitchen chair. "It's not something that's going to happen overnight."

He bent down onto one knee, resting a hand on her thigh. "I know, Tia. I ain't rushin'," he insisted in his soothing tone, "but these things take time to plan. And I ain't gonna sit back without planning. If this is... the wonderful thing that it is, I'm gonna make sure everything is perfect for you, Tia. I'm gonna be the best damn father and husband you could imagine."

"Look, bring this up to Faith for me? I'll serve you up some so don't linger long but if she needs you, that's all we can do, alright?"

He nodded adamantly, the smile engraved on his face. "You bet'cha," he declared, standing up and taking the bowl. "And where you go, she goes. You're my gals," he declared, heading up the stairs.

# CHAPTER 25

Faith answered the door more quickly this time, though she still looked haggard and tired. "I could hear you on those stairs," she murmured as she crawled back into bed. "I'm not really hungry though."

Walking on in, he shut the door and laid the bowl aside, moving to sit beside her. "I didn't wake you, did I? I'm so sorry, babe, just so excited to be back with you two that I'm bein' inappropriate," he said with a sigh, looking to her, concerned. "How are you feeling?"

"Like my boyfriend just got killed," she admitted, resting on her back and staring up at the ceiling. "I keep thinking about it. Like... their bodies, just lying there outside for weeks. Animals poking at them. I figured maybe they ran off on their own again, just didn't like the life. Or maybe he didn't like me. But now they don't get to smile any more, or laugh, or go to Celia's stupid meetings. Nothing."

Frowning a bit, he took a moment then leaned over her, kissing her forehead in a fatherly fashion. He wasn't good at showing sadness, so instead he mustered a melancholy, "What are you talking about? I thought I was your boyfriend now."

She let out a dry, hard laugh. "Why, because of what we did?"

"No," he stated, tucking the blankets about her meticulously. "Because I love you and you love me back, and I wanna whisk you away to my castle in a far off land," he declared softly, unable to hide the bit of cheer creeping back into his voice.

She rolled her eyes before closing them, her chest rising under the blankets. "Tia says I can have as many boyfriends as I want. Or girlfriends. But I don't know."

"You could. Or you could be my co-conspirator, and together get Tia to follow our plans, and I'll be your boyfriend, from now till forever," he murmured in a cheerfully conspiratorial tone, amusement rich in his words again. Part humour, all truth.

"I want you and Tia to be together and happy," she admitted, taking in a deep breath and letting it out. "But I want a boyfriend of my own. Who'd spend time with me and who I wouldn't have to share with someone else."

He frowned a little at that. That'd be a complication for his plans, to say the least.

Though he brushed it away in good humour.

"You sayin' Leon's not man enough to keep you satisfied?" His brows rose in a challenging look.

Her lip quirked slightly, her eyes slowly opening again. "Thanks for the food, Leon."

He leaned over her and kissed her forehead again, lingering a bit this time before pressing his nose and face to her hair. "I wanna make you so happy and safe, and protect you from ever hurting again, Faith. I really do."

"No one can do that, Leon. Not even you," she mourned, rolling onto her side so that her back was facing him.

Taking a moment, he shifted beside her, wrapping his arm about her and spooning to her back comfortingly. He waited before muttering softly, "Did you want me to give you some time and space? Because if you let me I'll spoon-feed you myself," unable to resist the bit of humour, of course.

"I just need some time alone," she agreed, taking in a deep breath. She was past the point of crying, almost gone numb inside, and her body language said as much. She was almost cool to the man she adored and taunted and teased so provocatively. Whom she had shared something with that was undeniably special.

Kissing her just behind the ear, he gave her a squeeze in his arm. "Okay, Faith. Tia thinks it best if I leave in the morning, but until then... if you need or want anything, I'm all yours. Understand?" He slipped back off the bed as carefully as he could, not wanting to disturb her.

He could hear her shift before the door clicked

closed, and Tia was waiting for him at the bottom of the stairs. "She's still bad, huh?"

With a bit of his enthusiasm deflated, he nodded to her. "Yeah. She'll be okay in time though," he said, smiling encouragingly to her. "How are you?"

Her arms wrapped around him, her lips finding his for a moment. "Exhausted. And so, so happy you're back. Dinner's served, if you're interested."

"Yeah, starved," he said, squeezing her in his arms then moving to go eat. The emotional turmoil of the visit was more exhausting than the trip there.

It was a delicious meal eaten mostly in silence as the two exhausted partners tried to deal with their own issues. When they finally had everything finished and cleared away, she tugged his hand, leading them to her room. "Assuming you have everything else done today?"

Surprised by the tug, he said, "Yeah." He followed her on to her room, "Are you okay with this? I can sleep elsewhere tonight if you're troubled," he offered.

"I really just need to be near you," she whispered at the top of the stairs, looking up at him. She seemed so fragile and not like herself. "If you have troubles, though, you can stay in the spare room?" she offered, quite genuinely. She wasn't the type of person who would hold it against him.

Leaning over and kissing her cheek, he didn't say anything more, just went with her to her room in silence, holding her hand firmly.

She stripped without fanfare, her entire movement speaking to the sore muscles and heavy burden she was carrying. Her body looked no different, but then, it was still only a month or so. It wasn't even certain yet. She slid in between the sheets, the candle placed on the nightstand.

Leon did his best to do so in the same manner, stripping down casually to nothing but his chiselled, black skin, though he couldn't help a twitch of physical response to Tia's nude form before slipping in beside her. Putting those powerful arms around her, he pulled her into his chest and held her, cradled her really, nestling his head against hers. "It'll all be okay," he promised.

She clung to him so tightly, her warm body so delightful even through these difficult times. He had consoled her before over the death of someone in the commune, but the way it had affected Faith and the added possibility of her pregnancy hung thick in the room. It was a difficult night for the both of them, but fitfully sleep found them, wrapped in one another's arms, their bodies pressed tightly together as if trying to become one.

# CHAPTER 26

The rhythm of sleep was heavy with Leon now, and he awoke before dawn, quietly rising to get his things ready and head out to meet with Celia. He tried not to wake the two women; it would do no good to have a tearful or sad good-bye.

Before taking off, he left her a note, explaining what he meant to address with Tia the night before. That Celia felt everyone hated and blamed her, and wanted a new life, so he was escorting her safely away. He apologized for not talking about it with her in person, but he had cut his trip short and events had made him put it aside.

The village still slumbered as the sun rose, the birds beginning to sing in the trees. It was a lovely day, not a cloud in the sky. It was a day so out of synch with everyday life after the fall.

Celia's door was unlocked, as was her bedroom, and she sat upon her bed, a bag packed next to her bed. She was dressed in pants and a sweater, obviously intent upon traveling, her long, black hair pulled into a sleek ponytail.

"'Bout time."

Leon was about ready to go himself, though his helmet was off and in his backpack at the moment, which he laid aside. Inspecting the dark-haired woman, he nodded approvingly. "Thought you might try wearing that skirt for the journey, and I'd have to rip it off you," he stated firmly.

She laughed, slipping on her backpack and bounding toward the door. She obviously didn't have much in the way of possessions, but the bag did bulge a bit. "I'm not stupid," she insisted.

Pushing his palm to the door and blocking her passage, he looked down at her. With a hard look, his early-morning voice, all gravelly and hard, rolled out, "Then why do you think you're leaving without servicing my needs first? It's a long damn trip, and I don't intend on doin' it with my nuts full, y'hear?"

She looked up at him, her entire body stilling. Her face turned up toward his, her body so much more petite than his, and her full lips parted in shock.

Taking in a deep breath, she murmured an apology, letting down the bag gently onto the floor next to the door.

Looking down at her grimly awhile he finally gave a nod of some limited approval at her obedience. Sliding his hand off the door, he stroked his hand along her hair before taking hold of the ponytail she'd tied, and pushed her down. "Can't hammer your cunt like I should though," he said, his voice so dark and almost ominous. "You need to be able to walk a long ways."

So with his hand on her ponytail hard, he reached down, undoing the zipper in his thick pants, "Reach in and get it," he commanded.

There was no hesitation, her tiny hands reaching within his dark trousers, through his boxers to grab at his thick cock. She was staring at it, delight twinkling behind her eyes. Her sweater didn't flatter her figure, more for utility than pleasure, and it made her look even smaller than she naturally was.

As those dainty fingers took hold of his thickening, black cock, he couldn't help but give a wry, almost malicious smirk as he watched those digits rest beside throbbing, dark veins almost as thick.

He wasn't fully erect when she pulled his cock out, but he was getting there fast, swelling forward, its heft rising up of its own accord. "I'll blow in your cunt still," he assured, hand tightening on her ponytail, "so undo those pants and be ready." Then without further ceremony forced the thick meat into her mouth with a hard jab.

She looked as if she had been about to say something, immediately silenced by the overlarge member. It stretched her pink lips and made her eyes water, but immediately her tongue started working around his shaft. The tip of her tongue found a vein and pressed in upon it, trailing along the length and teasing it. She was quite good, especially considering his unprecedented size.

Leon didn't mess around, with a tight grip on her by her ponytail, he began to pump his thick dark shaft into those tautly stretched pink lips fast. He watched the lewd scene below him, the mass of black cock disappearing into those Asian lips as he began to grunt. It'd be a rough night without any relief, and as he struck the back of the woman's throat with his wide crown he was determined to make up for it.

Her hands dropped to her own button as she then unzipped the pants, pushing them and her panties down carelessly, leaving her half exposed underneath the large sweater. Her hands then clasped his thighs, keeping herself balanced as she worked him so skillfully.

His thighs were rock solid beneath her grasp, a perfect support for her. Reaching down with his free hand, Leon unleashed his heavy balls after, along with his cock, the heavy pair slapping against her chin as he forced himself down into her throat further with each successful pump of his hips.

He was grunting and groaning loudly before long, the veins along his shaft swelling with each throb of the organ as his release approached. "Fuck," he cursed, yanking his length out then purposely slapping the hard brown member against her pretty, pink face. "Up against the wall, pussy in the air," he directed harshly.

Up on her feet, she coughed and sputtered for breath, thick saliva coating her throat as she tried to swallow it down. She was soaking for him, and since her black panties had not a stain on them, it must have been recent. His act, his cruel taking of what he wanted was obviously doing it for her.

Stepping in behind her, he pressed her palms to the wall flatly for her, then took hold of her hips. Rudely, he jammed that massive dick into her sodden cunt and began to pump his hips quickly. Despite his promise not to fuck her so hard as to ruin the trip, he hammered her a while before his balls tightened.

When finally he was finished, it was with a loud, noisy roar that seemed to shake the cabin she lived in as he unloaded the thick, creamy, white seed of his loins deep inside her.

She hadn't finished, but the denial of it seemed to please her, even as she whimpered and ground against his cock. The feel of her tiny hands under his, the power she was affording him was pleasurable in its own way, and knowing she loved every moment of it was a delight.

She took in several deep breaths, her voice sounding strange and almost shy. "Thank you."

With a heavy sigh, he patted her ass in such a heavy manner it was more like a slap. "That's better," he said, unclear whether he referred to her meek "thank you" or his relief at having released his cum inside her. Likely both.

Without more fanfare, he bent down, took hold of her pants and panties, then in one swift move pulled them up and pulled his dick from her cunt, leaving his seed to drool out of her onto her previously clean clothes.

Doing up his pants, he said firmly, "Let's go."

# CHAPTER 27

She didn't seem to mind how dirty he made her and, in fact, there was more of a bounce to her steps. Strapping on her backpack again, she headed toward the door and shouted, "See ya!" at no one and nothing in particular. She slammed the door behind them and then let him lead the way.

Grinning wryly at her little farewell display, he moved on out with Celia prancing along. He set a brisk pace, moving on directly out of town without any intention of stopping until they were a couple hours out of the town.

Even then he kept on, but speaking to her he said, "Few things you should know," in a rough voice.

She had been able to keep up, even as the brush bit at her legs and the bugs swirled around in front of them. She didn't even complain.

"Yea?"

"Spoke to the doctor," he said, continuing on briskly. He wasn't terribly surprised Celia was able to keep up. She was fit and athletic, judging by her nude form, after all. There weren't many who went soft anymore these days. "Pretty sure I'll soon have us our own doctor to tend to childbirths and such."

Her eyes widened a bit, though she kept step with him. "What? What are you, a mind reader?"

With a smug grin, he turned to look at her just slightly. "You're mine now," he said, and the tone and manner in which he said it just reeked of possessiveness, as if the very act of him saying it was like a choke chain tightening about one's throat. "I look out for what's mine."

Her little smile was just barely noticeable as her face dropped to the ground, as though she had been reprimanded.

"What else should I know?"

He gave her a moment to wonder before he spoke again. "You'll not be alone like I thought. I found someone to tend to you while I'm away."

Her face darted up to his, looking suddenly a little frightened, her brows knitting. "What?"

Noting the shock he gives her a moment, "Someone you know," he said. He dragged it out, like a bit of torture. "I found you so appealing I went and tracked down another like you. Remember an Adrianna?" he asked curiously, at last revealing the information to her.

"What?!" she hissed, and it wasn't certain

whether it was shock or disgust in her voice. "When? Where?" She hurried to catch up to him, no longer submissively following along.

"Just before I left to get you," he said calmly, showing no sign that her outburst had fazed him. "Somethin' the matter?" he asked in his grim tone, looking down at her.

She cursed a bit, her eyes downcast as she struggled to process it before looking back up at him. "She's gonna fuckin' kill me, man."

Arching a brow down at her, he asked, "Why?" hard and simple.

"'Cause I was supposed to do somethin' and haven't," she responded back, though the lack of fear in her voice indicated it was less life threatening and more an expression. "Fucking village," she cursed.

Noting the tone, he carried on without pause, though he demanded, "Do what?" quite clearly, the tone indicating he wasn't up for anything but full disclosure.

"She wanted me to try to turn more people, and I couldn't even get one fucking follower," she cursed, looking up at Leon. "Best I did was with you and that's complicated."

After some consideration, he said, "Don't worry. You'll make more followers. Just in a different way than she intended," pointedly referring to their plans.

With a pause, he licked his lips and said, "So your sister was a Cultist? She doesn't hang with them anymore, if so."

"Oh?" She perked up a bit, muttering quietly, "Maybe the plans changed, then. How did you find her?"

Putting his hand at the back of her neck as they walked together, he remarked harshly, "Don't ask me questions when you haven't answered mine to my satisfaction yet." He shot her a brief look to show he meant it.

She jumped a bit, and he could feel her pulse quicken in her neck. "She used to be! Yes! Once we were chosen, she and I sought to convert people, but the group grew stagnant and it became harder to find followers, so she sent me off to convince people!"

His hand gripping the back of her neck gave a rough sort of massaging motion briefly in reward. "Tell me about your sister. What's she like. Everything." That last word punctuated with authority.

"I don't know, she's always been bossy. She's good at leading people. She believes, unequivocally, in the righteousness of the gods." She thought a few more moments before she continued. "I don't know. I'm glad she's alright, I guess," she admitted.

Thinking this over he said, "She's a very... persuasive woman... isn't she?" He still didn't know what had happened with Adrianna to make him such a buffoon, but he was determined not to return to that same simpering behaviour. Especially not with Celia about to see it.

"She's been blessed," she agreed, looking up at him a bit skeptically. "Is that why you came to get me? Because of her?"

Immediately he gave a derisive, "No. I had planned to take you long before I even met her," he stated definitively, hand still on her neck and shoulders.

Softening at her worry, he asked, "You're troubled that she'll be there, aren't you?"

"Of course I am." She frowned, her head dropping a bit. "Fuck, I don't mind being treated like dirt, but I hate being treated like dirt because everyone's too busy falling over her. There's a difference."

His hard, dark hand rubbed at her neck in a more relieving fashion. "Good," he stated, clarifying afterwards. "Your sister's good stock," he said in a roundabout compliment to Celia herself, "but I don't want her thinking she can run the show, understand?"

He looked down to the woman as they walked, studying her for her reaction.

She nodded, but continued to seem troubled. "It's just... she's been blessed. You know?" She looked up at him, searching his eyes. "She can make you do things you don't want to really do. Or even if you do want to..." She trailed off, shaking her head. "She's been blessed."

His brow furrowed at this and he wetted his lips. Some of the pieces falling into place. "Celia, I chose you first," he stated firmly. "You should be above Adrianna in my harem by rights, as long as you can give more and better children." He was playing with something strange here, he could feel, but he wanted to probe the woman for information to help. "With your help, maybe I can undo that advantage of hers, huh?"

He looked down to her, hoping she'd be of some use here. If her sister really did have some strange "blessing," it could destroy everything he worked for. Ruin all his plans with Tia. Because he knew he wouldn't be able to abandon Adrianna. Even now, so far away, he couldn't think of it.

"How do you undo something done by the gods?" she posed, her eyes falling downwards. It was only now that he realized just how fragile her faith was, yet she stayed by his side, her feet a bit heavier against the underbrush.

"She can't make you do something you'd never, ever do," she said in earnest, taking in a deep breath, "but everything else is fair game. As long as she has her talisman, and there's no way to get it." He'd never noticed a talisman, even when he had undressed her.

His heart seemed to stop, and he paused, pulling Celia aside behind an outcropping of rocks and brush. Sitting himself down, he pulled the woman into his lap, his thick arms about her. He held her tightly, too tightly really, though he knew she'd appreciate that more than gentleness. "The gods reward those of strength, Celia." His voice gravelly and rough, determined. "What they gave your sister, they'll gladly let slip away if we prove stronger." He looked to her, his dark gaze so piercing.

Her lips quirked, and he could tell she was smitten.

"I can help you," she purred, her entire body and her backpack pressing against him. "I've looked into it. There's a spell that can show you invisible things. I was able to try it out a couple months ago."

His own full lips spread into a wide grin at the woman, eating up her mischievous delight. Raising a hand up to her face, he rubbed her cheek and chin roughly, raising a thumb to fondle her lower lip hard, husking out his words with such harsh authority. "Do this with me, and I'll make you the pride of my harem, Celia."

Leaning in, his nose touching her face, he muttered roughly, "I'll give you such opportunities to taste vengeance on your sister... nothing to ruin her potential as a breeder, but oh... you'll get such privileges."

She met him and took a breath. "But there's a problem," she murmured, seeming a bit sad about having to tell him that.

He pulled back a bit at that and asked gruffly, "What? It can still be done, can't it?"

"It can, it's just kind of going to be a bitch," she sighed, her head pressing against his. "You know how she is. It's hard to resist her. Impossible to lie to her. She doesn't know about the spell, but we'll have to act fast so that she won't get suspicious. She'll know you brought me, even if you lie, and after that we'll both be under her thrall," she sneered. "So we'll have to be certain."

Pausing, he gave a nod, "She already knows you're coming. I told her." He narrowed his eyes in irritation. "You know how it is." Mulling it over, he said, "We need a plan. Do you know where she keeps this talisman? Or would she have any reason to be concerned you'd try to do this to her?"

"She has no idea I even know she has it, but she

has ways of finding out. Hence... we have to act fast. I think she usually keeps it around her wrist, but it's hard to tell. It kind of... exists in the same plane as the gods, so it's there but not really. I found a way to call it back into our world temporarily and then it can be claimed or destroyed. Ah, takes a special fire to destroy it, but we can deal with that after."

Nodding, he looked to her with narrowed eyes. "Don't try to claim it for yourself," he warned. "You're my favourite now, but if you take it and try to use it against me... well, it'll only be a matter of time before the tables turn again and your sister takes it back and you won't be able to look to me for help. Got it?" He leaned in, gritting his teeth as if angry. "You're mine," he asserted, nearly crushing her petite body in his grasp.

"Why would I want that power over you?" She whimpered through his grasp, the thought obviously never having occurred to her. The way her face contorted was absolutely adorable, a mixture of confusion and lust.

He couldn't help but smile at that sincerity. This woman lived to be his, he realized. He gave her a harsh kiss and rubbed his dark thumb back against her cheek roughly. "I trust you," he said.

Back to business, he asked in rapid succession, "How fast can you cast this spell? How long will it last? I could feel your sister's influence still over me a long ways away, Celia."

"It takes about a minute to cast, but I'll have to be near her. Like, pretty close, so it's going to be hard. You'll have to distract her. Hopefully she'll be concentrating so hard on you it won't be so hard. I know she doesn't act like it, but it takes a lot of power for her to do what she does.

"Can you feel it now?"

He shook his head, "No," he stated firmly. "It wore down by the time I was at the thick of the forest near my place. Just a faint tickling of a sensation by that point," he said. "So it'd need to last at least an hour," he stated.

She nodded, looking a bit thoughtful. "And how long was she able to do this?"

"Most of a day and into the night," he confessed with some irritation. Looking down to her, he stated, "You have to be able to do this, Celia. Prove you're the stronger sister for me. That I made the right choice by picking you." He stroked his hand roughly back over her cheek and hair repeatedly.

She inhaled and then nodded, a smile creeping to her lips. "If this doesn't work, well, we'll just have to look at other options." She nuzzled into him, whispering softly, "She's blessed by the old ones, but so are we."

He kissed the top of her head and squeezed her harder. "When we've done this, I'll tie your sister down and let you rub her face in our superiority, Celia. You'll get to see the look on her face as she learns who is the more blessed of you two."

She laughed, sounding gleeful. "Mmm. I was made to belong to you, wasn't I, Leon," she purred, her voice still low. "How far are we?"

He stood up, lifting the woman with ease and putting her feet to the ground. "A few more hours," he stated, "but I wanted you to know everything first, so we could come up with a plan." He began to walk again, arm still around Celia's back. "I'll warn you when we have to cast the spell. So be ready," he commanded.

She seemed stronger to him now, as though she had been inflated and made larger, just by virtue of his belief in her. Strangely enough, she began singing softly under her breath, something so similar to her sister, though it had no effect on him other than the beautiful melancholy the foreign tune held.

That thought made him smile, and he rubbed her neck and shoulder again in that harsh but reassuring manner.

Since the fall he'd come to accept a lot of bizarre things about reality, though even a few days ago he'd not have bought into a sorceress working some magic on him. Now? He knew it to be true, and had already plotted how to fight it.

# CHAPTER 28

They walked mostly in silence as their shadows shifted and shortened underneath the forest leaves. Celia remained close to him, her hand and arm brushing against his lightly as she trekked, not at all complaining about the distance nor what she was about to do.

She was a small woman, but she claimed to contain power beyond reason of this world, and her determination was visible in the set of her jaw and the focus of her eyes.

Leon had spent the rest of the walk quietly preparing himself mentally. The world had changed, and he felt he had a grasp on it. These new developments, however, shook that belief.

Coming to a stop near the edge of the forest, he turned and rested his large palms upon Celia's shoulders. He had to bend a knee to meet her gaze a little. "It's time," he said. "I'm entrusting you with a lot here." His hands gripped her so firmly, almost painfully so, it might've been a threat to any other woman. "Don't let me down," he ended firmly.

She glowed at his compliment, her shoulders squaring slightly as she hummed a few chords, singing a short song that sounded to be a lullaby. When it ended, it felt as if she'd sung the whole thing, but only a few moments had passed. The bird flying above them had only managed to head a few yards south, and her hand stroked his cheek lightly.

"A good luck token," she murmured, beginning to walk once more.

He could feel a strange tingling in his body, almost as though it were coated with something, but it was hard to determine.

Something had changed, he knew it, but he couldn't see what just yet. Though one thing he did understand was his growing fondness for the strange little woman. If she pulled this off, he'd owe her, and more than that he was just coming to like her even.

Moving on, he kept ahead of her, asking one final question. "Your sister has no reason to suspect anything like this of you, does she? She wouldn't bend you to her will magically because she'd have no need to, I'd imagine it'd be a waste of her power." He looked down to her, hopeful about the answer.

"We have a strange relationship," she agreed. "She sent me out to do her bidding. I've failed. I don't know how that will impact things." She spoke so confidently, however, and glanced at him one final time. "Don't worry."

He nodded to her and squeezed her shoulder again. "I'm not. I just need all the information," he asserted. "Let's hurry on, I'm eager to get this over with." That wasn't the whole truth. He was eager to see Adrianna again, he realized. The feeling only growing now.

The closer they moved, the faster his footfalls became until they were nearly sprinting. An unfamiliar smile was on Celia's face, and their bags struck noisily off their backs and hips as they approached the hidden entrance.

The feeling was the same, for him. That desire, that burning need to be with her, his headache only growing the closer he got to her as though it were forcing him on.

He cleared the way to the passage, and only a deep seated concern for Adrianna let him take the time to conceal the entrance way properly again after entering. He grasped the back of Celia's neck, not wanting her to leave, though logically he knew she wouldn't. But this was his gift for Adrianna! What she wanted returned to her. He had to deliver her promptly, he thought as he headed up that final basement tunnel before coming to his grand home.

Adrianna's face softened with a smile upon the sight of the two of them, and she seemed to him a goddess, all light and radiance. Her black hair was in her customary ponytail, and she had been distracting herself with a deck of playing cards. Her see-through blouse and tight black skirt had been washed and they looked brand new against her slender, perfect form.

"You've returned," she mused happily, moving over to Celia and embracing the younger woman. Celia's arms wrapped around her sister's body as if she had missed her terribly, more than words could possibly say, especially as she began to sob for joy.

Leon dropped his backpack full of supplies to the ground and watched Adrianna with such reverence. "I did exactly as you wished," he stated, his husky voice awed by the sight of her. She was so exquisite! "I hope you're pleased." And he did. He really did.

Adrianna's hand stroked along Celia's ponytail as the younger woman sobbed, her wide eyes up and glossy at her sister. "They wouldn't listen to me. They deny the old ones their rights." She shook her head. "I'm so sorry."

"Shhh, shhh," Adrianna murmured, forcing Celia's face to remain up toward her. "There's no need of that. It was my failure. I shouldn't have expected you to be able to handle such a simple task," she cooed. Her tone was not condescending, only sympathetic.

Celia blinked her eyes, her lower lip trembling. "I thought I had something with Leon but then you got him better."

Leon couldn't help but nod and affirm. "You did, Adrianna. You're so much more... convincing," he said, his dark eyes alight with adoration for the stunning woman. How he wanted to please her.

He began to shed his outside things, taking off his trench coat and vest. "I've brought fresh food for you," he said. "I hope you didn't tire of the things I had here."

"Not at all." She wrapped her arm around Celia's slender shoulders, guiding the girl back to Leon, both of them watching as he silently worshipped the elder sister.

"You see, Celia, this is where my talent lies. We just need to find where yours lies," she purred.

His outdoor things shed, he stood before the two in just his pants, boots and sweater, still smiling dreamily at the elder sister. "She's very good and dedicated to breeding you more followers," he stated in pure honesty and eagerness to please.

Celia inhaled, just slightly, staring at Leon through her glassy eyes. A half smile approached her lips as nodded to Adrianna. "It is not much, but it's true. If only I'd been a male I could be more efficient," she mused.

Adrianna pet her sister as though she were a cat. "How interesting," she agreed, her hand slipping from the shoulders as she moved forward to Leon. "You're dismissed." She looked over her shoulder at Celia, her eyes growing cruel. "Head somewhere else and get lost. This place is big enough for it."

The girl shuddered, but did as instructed, her eyes scanning over the large place as she made her way south, disappearing from their sights.

"I'm glad you did as I instructed," Adrianna purred.

Her mild little compliment made his face beam. He never appeared happier than to hear her approve of him. "Thank you, Adrianna," he husked. "I never wanted anything more than I do to make you happy," he confessed, looking as if he wanted to touch her badly, but wouldn't dare without her approval. "And I can make you happy, I swear it." His eyes full and round as he watched this perfect woman.

"You must be very tired," she murmured, and suddenly he felt exhausted. "We should take you to bed." She took his hand, already leading him toward their "shared" room, her boots clicking on the cement flooring and echoing off the walls.

His whole body felt like leaden weight, and it took all he had to follow her so obediently. But he did, of course he did. He would expel the last of his energy to tread in her trail, to admire her slender, beautiful form as he did her bidding.

She was quite comfortable in his home now, though she had changed almost nothing about it. There were no new decorations, and aside from the cards, it seemed almost entirely untouched, except for the bedroom. There, candles burned brightly, the blankets strewn in a strange manner, ridged around the edges so that the centre was free of the comforters. It looked almost like a bird's nest, and she bid him to undress before her once more.

The room smelled strange, like burnt oils, but he couldn't see the source.

Pulling his sweater up over his head was so difficult, the man, for all his ripped, bulging muscles carved in ebon flesh, could barely lift them so far. As his belt came undone and he disrobed as ordered, he said wearily, "I'm sorry Adrianna, I feel so exhausted... I wanted to be able to serve you better." The disappointment at his own failing thick on his voice as he peeled away his pants, standing before in all his nude glory. Oh, his shoulders slumped a little from weariness, but he was as masculinely gorgeous as ever, so strong and powerful, his extremely large organ so thick and veiny, full and rigid at the sight of her, of course. No amount of exhaustion could change that, he realized.

She nodded, her hands taking his and moving them to her blouse. "Undress me and you may sleep for a day." She smiled, the words sounding like the best reward he could have been offered.

"Thank you," he said, sounding so tired but genuine, his large hands, so dark in comparison to her pale flesh. The fine buttons of her blouse such tiny, delicate things, hard for him to grasp as he deftly undid the garment, fumbling only due to his exhaustion as he peeled it away, revealing those perky, perfect breasts of hers beneath. He wanted to cup and hold them so badly, but didn't dare. He merely laid her top aside, then undid the zipper of her skirt, tugging it down and off, lifting her legs one at a time so gingerly to strip her down to nothing but her exquisite nudity.

She undid her own holster, laying it aside before she turned to him.

"Get into bed," she ordered, her voice so stern, "and lay back." She began to hum, foreign words slowly adding to the beautiful song, in bits and pieces before it became fully lyrical. He felt so tired, the same, hazy state he had slept in during the last time she was here. It felt slightly different, though. He couldn't move, as before, but this time he couldn't see as well. He could feel, though, her hands wandering around him. Trailing over his body, and the fact that he couldn't see her only made the sensations feel more erotic.

It was so tantalizing, and he tried to move, finding himself remaining still despite his efforts. Just as he felt her hand touch his throbbing phallus, though, it stopped. It was then he realized he could no longer hear, but he could sense something was wrong. So very wrong. Something had happened.

It felt like hours that he lay there, unable to move or see or hear, just feeling the harsh blankets wrapped around his form. They didn't feel like his regular sheets, they were too scratchy and... cold? He wanted to shiver, but even that he couldn't do, his mouth frozen in place until suddenly it was over.

The sensations left him, the heaviness holding him down, the chill... It all disappeared as his senses returned to him, and the first thing he noticed was that Adrianna was lying on the floor, her forehead bloody. Celia stood over her, panting and gasping as she clutched some invisible thing in her hand, and he was reminded of their plan.

The forced servitude all melted away, and he could only see his former grovelling as disgusting and weak. With a grimace, he rose up, looking to the two women. Realization swept over him, and his eyes went wide. "You did it?!" he asked abruptly, a bit of shock at seeing the elder sister bloodied and unconscious. "You held nothin' back, did you?" he remarked as he pushed his feet over the edge of the bed.

A moment's worry entered his mind, seeing the younger sister standing there, undoubtedly holding the object that was the source of his imprisonment.

"Of course I did it." She smiled triumphantly, though her eyes remained down at her sister's bloodied skull. "She'll be fine," she murmured as she dropped to her knees, pushing the bangs from her sister's face. "She's always fine." Adrianna's rib cage still rose and fell, giving credit to Celia's words, though she seemed a bit off. There was a lot of awe and respect in her motions, and her nails dug into the palm of her flesh as she squeezed that invisible pendant tighter as she stood. "Maybe that'll teach her a few lessons." She looked to Leon. "Tie her up. I'm assuming you'd have handcuffs?"

He did, he'd raided a police department early into the crisis, and handcuffs were just the thing that would have multiple uses for him. Rising up, he shook his hand through his dreads, rotated his shoulders, and generally just did every little thing he could to try and shake off the dirty feeling of being someone else's tool.

"Yeah," he said, stepping over to her and petting Celia's hair. "Here," he said firmly, holding out his hand. "I'll store it safely for now." Nude as he was, he towered over her, looking as commanding as ever, though inwardly he was afraid the temptation might be too much, even for this young woman that lived to be dominated.

"You can't even see it," she scoffed, smiling up at him. "If I wanted to use it on you, you wouldn't be asking that right now. By the way. Besides, you don't know the destruction spells and, fuck, I don't even know if you could feel it. It exists outside of our reality." She opened her palm, showing it to be empty to his eyes.

"The spell I used on you only prevented her from reading your mind during sex." She smiled.

Furrowing his brow, he said, "We had sex?" With a shake of his head, he said, "That doesn't matter. I'll store it if I can feel it, so that she can't get to it before we're able to destroy it. You can come with me to put it in the safe, if we must, but someone should really watch her in case she wakes up before we return." Fair enough, he thought. He felt he could trust Celia, but still, she couldn't just carry it around until they were able to destroy it. Adrianna could steal it back.

"Just please get the cuffs, Leon. Really. We'll handle one thing at a time." She moved toward him, lightly closing her hands and pressing her nose against his chest. "Once she's secured, we can deal with the spell."

He bent down and kissed the top of her head, not liking the sound of that but silently acquiescing. He wasn't gone long before he returned from one of his supply cabinets, wrist and ankle cuffs in one hand, a sturdy chair in the other to attach them—and her—to.

"Here we go," he announced. "This'll be her comfy new home for a bit," he declared.

# CHAPTER 29

She was still dressed in her sweater and pants, no longer clutching an invisible thing in her hands. "We need to do it outside of this room. As far from here as possible while still being in the building," she commanded, though he didn't feel a magical compulsion to obey. "This place is set up to be her strong point. Really, I'm kind of amazed I could take her on in here."

Leon inspected the room again after those words, the odd arrangement of things surprising him. "Maybe she was busy trying to solve the mystery of my unreadable mind," he said, grasping at straws to understand all this nonsense he'd thought fantasy before now.

Adrianna's nude, unconscious form was no trouble for him to lift and arrange upon the chair. One thing of note, he had to confess, was that her beauty really wasn't an effect of any spell. She was stunning, and it did take a bit of conscious effort to ignore it as he shackled her to the heavy chair.

"Let's go," he said to Celia. "I know the place." He put a hand on the smaller woman's shoulder and led her on. It was cool in the building, but he didn't bother to put on clothes. He had to get this done immediately. He led the younger sister down the ramps and across the great halls of the building toward one of the former entryways. The real entrance was blocked off by wooden walls, forming one of his "rubble rooms," but the area surrounding it was empty but for reinforcement.

"Here," he stated.

She took in a deep breath, shrugging off her backpack and opening it up. There were numerous items that she spilled out, strange jars of herbs and bugs that he had never seen before, and a large tome that he recognized as the one she was reading when he barged into her room last time. She had been planning this for longer than he knew, and as she lit the strange-scented candles, he felt like he was being pulled in two different directions.

Atop a gold plate, she lay, well, nothing to his eyes but he sensed it was the object. A few subtle signs from her hand, and there was a strange background noise that started out so low. What was it? His ears strained, but he couldn't make sense of the reverberating sounds.

"I need you to be my anchor," she murmured, her eyes lidding as she sang a soft hymn like tune, and suddenly he could see something else in the air. It was almost as if he was seeing the space between, and his body felt a bit queasy. Her voice started to ring out, echoing off the walls of the room even though the small area seemed hardly large enough to echo her words. They filled him, though, and he felt the urge to hold on to her hand, squeezing it tightly as her voice crescendo.

He could see the object now, a tiny, teal gem, no bigger than Celia's pinky, pointed and see-through, swirling with dark particles. It didn't seem to follow the normal rules of geometry and seemed, to his engineering-trained eyes, to be unfeasible. Somehow it was staying together, but it looked as though it shouldn't.

Celia gasped as her head went up to the ceiling, and as his eyes followed, they could both see something swirling and growing larger in the darkness of the room. It was equal parts light and shadow, bright and dark, and its shape changed so quickly it wasn't easy to get a good idea of what it was.

Her words, though, seemed to make it shy away, a loud, shrill noise reverberating through both of them before it swirled into the object, devouring it and dispersing into the air. It was all around them, the strange amalgamation of impossible matter, and Celia closed her mouth and held her breath.

When finally the air settled and the shade retreated, she sucked in a deep breath, her body falling back toward the hard floor. Leon, however, swept in, scooping up her slender body in his thick arms, lifting and cradling her with ease.

He had no idea what he just witnessed, it was some glimmer of the horror they had all witnessed with the fall of civilization. He'd hoped not to see that sort of thing ever again, and it chilled him to his core to see her conjure it up. Nevertheless, he lifted Celia against his chest and took her from the room, wanting to get away from the source of it.

Taking her to one of the other rooms, not wanting to use the sullied chamber Adrianna had tainted, he laid her out atop the bed tenderly. "You did good by me," he husked approvingly.

She was barely conscious, her eyes fluttering between opened and closed as her lips part. "We're not done," she whimpered. "We need to dismantle her room, and you can't risk what traps she has in there. Just give me a minute and move her out of the room. Somewhere far away."

Seeing her so weakened, he didn't care for that idea, but he nodded. "Okay, it has to be done," he affirmed. He lifted Celia up again, sparing her the energy of making the trip on her own. Gingerly, he put her down on her feet, steadying her and giving her dark-haired head a kiss before moving to the elder sister. He lifted her, chair and all, with ease. "You'll be alright?" he asked Celia to affirm.

She nodded, her hand resting against the door frame in order to steady herself. "Yea," she murmured, her eyes working their way around the room, over the strange decorations and candles, the odd bed. Her eyes were still adapted from the spell, and she could see the layers between reality, and took a few steps in toward the dresser containing all of the candles and herbs, slowly signing above them. Her voice began to hum and reverberate, and he could hear it all the way through the building as he moved Adrianna's limp form.

On the way across the great building, he stopped at one of the hidden caches. He fished out a first-aid box then continued on. He brought the limp, shackled woman to one of the smaller unused bedrooms, barely able to fit one of the king-size mattresses he'd used. Setting her down in the corner, he opened the kit and knelt before her, cleaning away the blood from her beautiful head, preparing to bandage or treat the wound. Even after what she'd done, he didn't care to see her injured, and certainly not dead!

She was very slowly coming to, a mere mortal once more, and her eyes went to his face with disdain. Inhaling deep and tasting the blood in her mouth, she scowled. "I knew I should have killed her," she lamented. "She's manipulated you away from me!"

Seeing the blood trickle along her lips as she spoke so bitterly, he reached to the first-aid kit and took out some of the clean water there, pouring up a small cup of it. "Kill your own sister?" he remarked casually but curiously in his deep tone, lifting the cup to her lips. "I'm glad you don't seem seriously hurt, Adrianna."

"You have no idea what you've just helped her do," she warned, her tone icy. "I was trying to get her back so that she couldn't go ahead with her little plan, but you've only helped her along!"

# CHAPTER 30

His broad, handsome face, framed by thick dreads didn't show his worry, but he stroked her cheek softly. "Here. Take a sip to clean the blood from your mouth and then tell me," he said, the subservience gone from his voice, but still rich with concern and a bit of adoration. She was still quite stunningly beautiful, after all.

She did as instructed, running her tongue over her lips and spitting out the water and blood onto the floor. "She's just using you to get what she wants!" she moaned, but her words lacked conviction. Adrianna sounded desperate and needy, and he wondered briefly if the amulet had been the cause of her confidence and easy mannerisms. Even though her beauty hadn't faded, she had lost a spark.

Leon didn't buy it, but he also didn't care to

make this entrapment rougher than necessary. The woman knew where his home was, was bitter and vengeful, and he wanted to soften that.

Knelt before her, he still had to bend a bit when he leaned in to kiss her forehead tenderly. "It's okay," he assured her. "I'll take care of you still," he asserted confidently.

His tenderness seemed to strip everything away, and she sobbed. She'd lost so much; her power, her control were all taken from her and by someone she loved, no less. She looked to be such a broken shell of an individual and she shook her head sadly.

"I need to be alone," she begged.

That was no problem for him, for though he showed her compassion, he was still angry with her himself. With a final stroke of her cheek and back over her hair, making sure he'd treated the wound right, he left and returned to Celia.

The room had been almost entirely dismantled, the strange items heaped in a corner as Celia stared down at the bed, looking quite thoughtful. She was moving from one corner to the other, her hands signing above it as she sang, but she was troubled.

Not wanting to disturb her, he watched her actions awhile, waiting to hear her verdict. He went to his clothes, and before he started to put them on, he hesitated. Was this somehow corrupted too, now, he had to wonder.

She didn't even notice his entry, so engulfed was she in the task at hand. When finally her hands circled widely and her voice cracked, the bed turned suddenly cold, icicles visible on the sheets for a brief moment before they melted away, leaving no puddles in their path. She smiled broadly at her success before looking to Leon, finally noticing his presence.

"They're fine," she assured him. "The spell threads have all been sent to their own realm."

Smiling at that reassurance, he dropped his things again anyhow, despite their safety. Moving to her, the six-and-a-half-foot-tall man dropped to one knee and put his arms about her, squeezing her roughly to his chest. "You did excellent," he commended, kissing her neck hard. "How long was I out anyhow?" he murmured.

She winced a little, seeming to not want to say as she licked over her lips.

"Two days," she murmured, her hand stroking along his bicep. "I tried a couple times to get close, but she had some type of barrier up. I think she only dropped it to try to break you. But she didn't."

The idea of losing two whole days troubled him, and he grimaced a little.

Pulling back enough to look Celia over, he gave a warm smile. "You did well. You proved you're the better, stronger sister," he stated firmly, his strong hands rubbing her shoulders, then moving down over her chest to her hips. "More worthy," he said, the words so profoundly stated.

Her pulse quickened, and he could tell from the flush in her cheeks. Her eyes dropped from his face, down over his chest.

"I don't want this to change things. Anything. It's done now, and unless I have to do something like that again, I just want to go back to how things were between us. Whatever that was."

He gave a hearty chuckle at that, both surprised, and not by her desire to return to normal. She had such power in her hands and she cast it off to be his. "I never dreamt of having it any other way," he stated resolutely, his thick digits groping at her body rather openly, feeling her through her sweater and pants.

"It's been days," he stated in a husky, authoritative tone. "I need some relief and some food." He started undoing the buckle of her pants. "You'll provide one, then the other," he instructed, offering no reprieve for the weary woman.

# CHAPTER 31

Her hands reached to the bottom of her sweater, pulling it up over her head. Her ponytail was a bit staticky from the motions, but as her familiar top followed, exposing her bare breasts to the air, her sleepiness seemed to dissipate.

Instead, she was all warm desire and passion, moving to fill the distance between the two of them so eagerly as he dropped her pants and her black panties to the ground, allowing her to kick off the shoes and socks, leaving her just as bare as he.

He had no doubt she'd provide, she was a pleasingly submissive woman like that, and he felt his hard hands out over her bare form, squeezing, rubbing, and handling her roughly. He crushed her breasts to his hard abs, the stirring of his cock rising, brushing against her legs.

Her arms wrapped around his neck, hoisting herself up against him. She wanted him, and every motion of her body, every sigh that passed her lips spoke of her desire and need for the large, muscular man. They had only met so recently, yet they had forged something strong in the ruins of their world.

With her upon him so, he wrapped his arms about her and pushed her back to the bed, climbing atop her. After so long out of consciousness, he had a deep-seated hunger that was about more than food. And his gratefulness to this petite woman was immense, but ultimately, serving her was all about helping himself.

He abruptly pushed her thighs apart, his heavy, dark dick prodding down against her sex immediately. There was no time wasting with them, and he began to feed that thick shaft into her cunt by force.

She hadn't had much time to revel in his arousal for her, and she felt only slightly damp against his prying tip, but the more he pushed, the louder she moaned, her body adapting. As her legs lifted to wrap atop his pelvis, her cunt drew him in, the thick, black member piercing into her tight, pink labia.

She writhed beneath him, but there was nothing she wanted more.

Groaning, he pulled back from her for a moment to marvel at the way her tight folds so lewdly stretched to swallow his dark, veiny girth. It was such a sight, the pale flesh looking nearly at the breaking point as he fed more and more of that thick length into her twat.

The sight of it only made him hornier, and he arched his back and bent down, biting her neck hard as he buried himself in fully. The rough imprints of his teeth marred her slender stalk.

No longer was she bossy. She apparently trusted him to understand her needs and desires, and the more he proved her right, the louder her moans and pants became. She was enthralled by the thick man, and she wriggled against him, trying to help him sink deeper and deeper into her depths.

There wasn't the slightest of pauses after he bottomed out his cock inside her when he began to tug back, the tacky, tight walls of her cunt snugly pulling at him as he began to pump his meat into that sleeve. With a loud, husky groan, he continued, his pace growing, becoming harder, more merciless as he took her faster.

That broad chest of his heaved as he looked down, diving in to kiss and nip at her hard as his one free hand gropes her tits like an angry, needy young man would upon his first time.

Her body sang of his pleasures, her nerves tingling as her form arched and yielded to his more powerful muscles. The longer he fucked her, the wetter she became, urging his rough pace to continue unhindered by the fear of harming her delicate slit.

The rapid pistoning of his manhood was spreading that slick honey across that tight cock sheath of hers. Leon was rocking back and forth, his whole body rife with deliciously taut and bulging black muscles as he rutted into her.

There was no reservation in his actions, he was

riding her hard and fast, no attempt to satisfy her as he would most women. For he knew she got her satisfaction from being used. From being dumped in and told what to do.

"Squeeze me tighter," he demanded, "milk it out of me," his voice a dark husk as his dick throbbed within her.

She obediently squeezed her lower muscles, her jaw tightening as she focused upon the task, holding her breath and putting every ounce of energy into squeezing his cock. Her legs loosened against his back to allow him greater range of motions, and her eyes stared up at him so lovingly.

There was no return look of tenderness or longing to greet her back though, just his hard, chiselled face contorted in growing pleasure as he pounded into that tight cunt of hers. The strikes were jarringly hard now, rocking her whole form despite the resistance of her milking sleeve. He was breathing huskily, his dark balls slapping against her less noisily as they began to tighten.

She was already so tight to his large size, the extra squeeze was excessive. In no time he was bucking wildly into her, his mouth open as he grunted and groaned in a lewd, harsh tone as the eruption of his seed flooded into her in a creamy white stream.

Her eyes stayed glued to him as he found his pleasure in her, a smile parting her lips that was bordering on triumphant. She squeezed him harder as though in thanks, finally sucking in a long, hard breath and exhaling a low moan.

Relief crossed his face as he finished unloading into her fertile depths, and his whole broad form relaxed a little, muscles losing their tension. Shifting to the side, he appeared like a mountain about to topple over, but his thick arm took her with him and he pulled her on top of him, still joined at their loins.

"Don't worry," he stated heavily, his breathing still elevated as he kissed her hair, "you'll always be mine. All mine. With only the worries of an owned woman from now on." And he squeezed her tighter, crushing her to him.

With his words, she clutched his spent cock harder, her hands seeking out his arms and shoulders.

Perhaps it had been her difficult life, always being forced by her sister to be more aggressive and in control. Maybe it was just who she was, and everything else was just an attempt to be someone else.

But when it came down to it, she was his. As their naked bodies pressed together, he could tell that everything in her sang to be his; to have him control and breed her. To keep her here in his makeshift home, in the wastes of civilization, and to be the first in his harem.

Dreams do come true.

# NOTE FROM THE AUTHORS

Thank you so much for reading and purchasing our story. We hope it made you squirm, and that once you recover, you'll take a look for more of our works available on http://www.jmkeep.com.

Did you enjoy yourself? Take a quick second to leave your opinion on Amazon and Goodreads!

**Connect with us:**
Website: http://www.jmkeep.com
Twitter: http://www.twitter.com/jmkeep
Facebook: http://www.facebook.com/jmkeep

Get Pussy Cat Club – a dark, contemporary erotica with a sexy stripper and her bouncer lover – for FREE by joining our Newsletter!

# RECOMMENDED FOR YOU

## VILE WASTELAND

### J.E. & M. KEEP

When a sheltered 'bunker babe' enters the wastes of society, she realizes that the world is far harsher than she could have ever anticipated.

Trading, bartering and kicking ass on her way to security, she works to save her people from starvation in the bunker. Yet she faces a ticking clock, and there's something not right about anything she finds.

Filled with lust, flings, and a determined young heroine, Vile Wasteland seamlessly combines action, adventure, and sex.

Welcome to the vile wasteland.

# MORE BY J.E. & M. KEEP

**Erotic Novels:**
The Mistress – Erotic Thriller
The Warlord's Concubine – Dark Fantasy Romance
Vile Wasteland – Post Apocalyptic Erotic Romance
Wheel and Deal – Dark Fantasy

**Collections:**
The Ultimate Erotic Horror Collection – Contains Her Master's Madness, Bad Wolf, Be Good and Led Into Temptation
Teenage Slut #1–10 – Contains Books 1–10
Amy's Innocence – Contains the entire series
Anjasa Between Dungeons – Contains Cutting a Deal, Demon's Den and Dragon's Lair.

Sweet, Spicy and Seductive – Contains A Night of the Arts, Teenage Slut #1 – Schoolgirl's Detention and Pussy Cat Club

**Erotic Novellas:**

Brutal Passions – For D&D fans that want some more erotica in their campaigns
Led Into Temptation – Tentacles meet a Catholic School Girl
Outcast – Dark Fantasy / Taboo
A Son's Devotion – Mother/Son Incest
Brought the Stars to You – Sci-fi Romance
Bound as the World Burns – Post apocalyptic BDSM Erotic Romance

*A Dark Fairy Tale – Novella Length*
Bad Wolf, Be Good – Werewolf Horror Erotica
Her Master's Madness – Epic Fantasy BDSM Horror Erotica

**Series Shorts:**

*A Dark Fairy Tale – Short Length*
Bred by the Monster in the Forest – Monster Breeding Horror Erotica
Bred by the Monster in the Forest 2 – Monster Breeding Horror Erotica
May Beauty Eternal Lie – Fantasy Fairy Tale Monster Erotica

*In Search of Innocence – High Fantasy Action Adventure Erotic Soap Opera*
Part 1
Part 2
Part 3
Part 4
Part 5

*Amy's Innocence*
Part 1 (Purity) – Deflowering
Part 2 (First Love) – Coming of Age
Part 3 (Family) – Pregnancy

*Anjasa Between Dungeons*
Cutting a Deal – Fantasy ménage erotica
Demon's Den – Demon/elf rough sex
Dragon's Lair – Dragon/elf cock worship

*Enslaved*
Finding Her – Mind Control Romance
Taking Her – Mind Control Gangbang

*Teenage Slut #1-10*
Schoolgirl's Detention – School girl / barely legal
Teacher's Slave – May December Domination
Punished by Daddy – Reluctant Daddy/Daughter Incest
Spanked and Bred by Daddy – Daddy/Daughter Breeding
Fucked by Daddy and Brother – Forced Sleep Sex
Blackmailed by Brother – Brother/Sister Taboo
Sister's Surprise Gangbang – Barely Legal Gangbang

Tagteamed by the Mechanics – Barely Legal Menage
His Daughter's Virgin Ass – Barely Legal Bimbo Transformation
Fucked by the Big Black Stranger – Sleezy Interracial Creampie

*The Lost Lagoon – M/F Twincest Romance*
Part 1
Part 2
Part 3

**Standalone Shorts:**
Bred by the Monster in the Woods – Reluctant Virgin Monster Breeding
Doctor Dom – Mind Control
Daddy's Spoiled Princess – Daddy/Daughter Incest
Blessing of Fertility – Divine Monster Breeding Gangbang
Serving the Dark Demi – God – Demon Cock worship
Blackmailing the Secretary – Blackmail
Pussy Cat Club – Rough Sex
A Night of the Arts – Exhibitionism/Pussy Worship
Hot Desert Daze – Gay M/M Submission
Don't Lie to Me – Infidelity/Cuckolding Fantasy
Wedding Present – Contemporary Interracial Infidelity

**Coming Soon:**
Novel: Corrupted Hearts

# BIOGRAPHY

J.E. & M. Keep love to combine fantasy, scifi, horror, romance and mystery into exciting and titillating novels.

They are long term, loving partners in a very happy relationship and because of this, they love to torture their characters. Dark romance touches all of their stories in one way or another, from elicit trysts to forbidden love.

Some of their work contains dubious consent and erotic pain, so it's not for the faint of heart. Their stories are often called twisted and arousing—at the same time.

All work is 18+, trigger warnings available on the second page of every book. If you want to hear about new releases, sign up for the newsletter!

Website: http://jmkeep.com
Newsletter: http://jmkeep.com/newsletter
Facebook: http://www.facebook.com/jmkeep
Twitter: http://twitter.com/jmkeep |
http://twitter.com/jekeep

Made in the USA
Charleston, SC
16 January 2017